Adventures in Time Bundle

The de Vargas family series
Books 1 and 2

by
Annie Seaton

ISBN 978-0-6485563-6-7

Dedication

To my mother, Daphne May, for instilling in me a lifelong love of words. I just wish you were here to read them. She walked the beach with me when I was a small child showing me the bridal veil of foam on the sand. My mother sang to me and she read to me, and I discovered books and music. But most of all she taught me love, as I watched her love my father and her heart broke when he passed. She has gone to sing in heaven.

Book 1

Cornwall and the Amazon
Winter of the Passion Flower

Chapter 1

'Twas a shame.

An opportunity for a brief, but she was sure, satisfying sexual interlude had not been taken up. The courier who had delivered the missive from London was a young man with a very pleasing physique and Indigo de Vargas y Irausquínno had been tempted to indulge for a fleeting moment.

But not to be. Her desire was destined to remain unfulfilled.

The young man had insisted on setting off on the return trip in his small dirigible after partaking of a quick refreshment, despite the howling winds and driving snow. His gaze darted nervously around the salon and even a suggestive fingertip run down his chest did not persuade him to stay for more than a quick cup of mulled wine. However, thoughts of a sexual diversion quickly disappeared as Indigo broke the seal and read the document from London.

"Absolutely impossible," she said emphatically as she read the document before her. Gripping the document tightly, she strode across the sitting room to the warmth of the blazing fire as she continued reading in disbelief.

The Great Exhibition of the Works of Industry of all Nations to be held in London three months hence, and now Henry Cole, representative of Prince Albert, asked…nay, demanded, the exhibition prototype be finalized within a month. Reading aloud, Indigo refused to believe that Henry Cole gave credence to her dastardly neighbour's trivial complaints. She knew Duke Lorca constantly sent erroneous information about her and her business to London. One consolation—

She was well aware she remained a thorn in Lorca's side and would continue to do so while ever her enterprise was successful. He was just a snivelling jealous little man without a shred of intelligence.

"Grrr." Indigo grunted in frustration and continued reading.

"I am of the advice that your product will not be manufactured in the timeframe required for display at the Crystal Palace. I urge you, Madame, to respond to my letter forthwith and provide evidence that your prototype will be forthcoming within the period of one month. Duke Leopold Lorca is willing and able to exhibit a selection of steamed farming machinery in the space and will be allotted the aforementioned space if a timely and satisfactory response is not forthcoming from yourself. Yours sincerely, Sir Henry Cole, Representative of Prince Albert, Patron of Society for the Encouragement of Arts, Manufactures, and Commerce."

Indigo threw the parchment to the floor in disgust. "Over my dead body. That snivelling coward Lorca will not get his manipulative hands on my exhibition space."

The wind whistled through the door as Mrs. Grimoult, her housekeeper, locked the cogs behind the departing courier but Indigo paid scant attention. Bending to retrieve the parchment from the floor, she tore it in half and threw it on the flames, muttering as it curled and disappeared up the chimney.

"Round one to you, Lorca, but not for long."

It had been a long and frustrating day with a procession of bad news coming to her door. And the latest shipment of blooms from South America was late; Indigo had passed much of the day in the viewing room, alternately pacing the floor and peering through the large telescope mounted on the high platform, awaiting the arrival of her submarine, the *Artemis*.

Now, sitting at the bay window in her salon, she fumed over the missive. The dismal weather matched her mood. The large trees facing the sea bore the brunt of the strong wind gusting fiercely off the Atlantic Ocean. An old oak tree bent with the weight of the fallen snow, creaked ominously as the huge boughs pushed against the walls of her manor house. She plucked at the velvet tassels of the scarlet cover on the window seat as her temper worsened.

A loud knocking on the entry door interrupted her brooding and she waited impatiently for Mrs. Grimoult to announce the unexpected visitor. The knocking became louder and Indigo rose, sweeping through the foyer, heels clicking on the wooden floor.

"I don't know why I bother keeping staff," she muttered crossly to herself as she unlocked the series of cogs securing the heavy oak door. She held the door firmly against the wind and flurries of snow swept through the opening.

"Gothewhar daa." A mellifluous voice came from beneath the silken folds of a hooded cloak, which concealed the face of the speaker. Indigo leaned forward, intrigued to hear the Cornish dialect. The stranger with the deep voice stood hidden in the deep shadows of the porch, where the candles flickered from the wind gusting from the ocean.

"Good evening, sir. May I ask what brings you out on this miserable night?" she asked curiously.

"I need an audience with Madame de Vargas as a matter of urgency. Is she in residence?"

"Who shall I say is calling, sir?" Indigo wanted to know the business of the tall, broad-shouldered stranger with the deep voice before revealing her identity.

"I would prefer to introduce myself to Madame de Vargas, if I may," he replied.

She stood back, carefully scrutinising the dark stranger before replying. Well-spoken and expensively dressed, he was obviously a man of standing. "I am Madame de Vargas. Come in from this foul night and state your business." She ushered him in as the heavy door pushed against her hands.

The stranger stepped through the wide doorway and dipped

into a sweeping bow. "I am here to offer my services as captain of your vessel. I believe you have urgent need for a captain to master your next expedition, Madame?" The silk-edged cloak of black wool slipped from his shoulders as the stranger stepped forward and pooled sinuously upon the wet floor. Indigo choked back a startled gasp before it could escape her lips. She looked up slowly, and her gaze locked with eyes the colour of midnight. For a long moment, she held his gaze and his lips tipped upward in a slight smile. Indigo looked away disconcerted by the confidence of this man.

She pursed her lips; it was most unusual for a man to challenge her. Her gaze dropped to his chest as she tried to think who he may be; but he was unknown to her.

The removal of his cloak had revealed a muscled forearm dusted with a sprinkling of dark hair. At the edge of his wrist, the tattooed petals of a blue passionflower contrasted with tanned skin, and her eyes narrowed as she saw the intricate green tendrils snaking their way to his elbow.

Very interesting…and very strange.

"Who are you?" Indigo demanded, regaining her equilibrium.

"Captain Dogooder, at your service, Madame."

She regarded him for a long moment and his gaze held hers. Flakes of snow blowing through the open doorway melted, making small puddles on the wooden floor.

"You had better come in to my salon, sir, and tell me why I need a new captain. And especially one with such an…interesting name. I am intrigued." Ushering him in from the foyer, Indigo caught sight of her reflection in the mirrored wall opposite the main door and was satisfied with her appearance, considering she had such a handsome, albeit, mysterious guest.

She had dressed that morning in a revealing ruby red bustier and black silk skirt. The intricate folds of her long skirt moulded to her derriere. Luxuriant black curls surrounded her face, and her lips were painted ruby red and her eyes outlined with black kohl. She stood straight and drew a deep breath. She was well used to her occasional gentleman visitors using words such as bewitching loveliness, statuesque beauty, and not to mention her commanding cleavage as she took them to her bed. This visitor was of a different nature, she suspected.

Following Indigo into the salon, the captain strolled to the fire, removed his leather gloves and spread his fingers in front of the leaping flames. He reached into a deep pocket of his breeches and Indigo's gaze dropped to the muscled thighs outlined by the tight leather as he removed a brass chronometer and checked the time before casually returning the timepiece to his pocket.

"Are you expected elsewhere on this fierce evening, Captain?" The peculiarity of the situation was beginning to grate on her.

"No, Madame," he replied quietly.

She indicated for him to sit in a deep-winged chair in front of the fire as she pulled a brass lever on the wall, requesting the housekeeper's services. Mulled wine would warm them both while he provided her with an explanation for his visit. A sharp bell sounded down the corridor but there was no response. Indigo went to pull the lever again and the housekeeper bustled into the room.

"Madame, oh Madame …" Wringing her hands, Mrs. Grimoult trailed off, eyes widening as she realized her mistress had company. The captain rose from the chair and hurried across to the doorway, gently taking the little housekeeper's hands between his.

"'Tis all right, Madame. You can speak."

Indigo looked from one to the other, as the housekeeper pulled away from her visitor before lifting her apron and dabbing at her eyes. She stepped away from him and spoke to her mistress.

"Oh, Madame, the *Artemis* has returned."

A huge sense of relief filled Indigo until Mrs. Grimoult

began to weep noisily into her apron. Indigo looked across at her, worry quickly replacing her relief. Her housekeeper was generally an unexcitable creature and it was unusual to see her showing so much emotion.

"The crew is gone. There is only my man returned." She lifted her apron, wiping more tears away.

"Where is Mr. Grimoult?" Indigo stood with her hands on her hips, concern filling her chest.

"Upstairs, Madame." The housekeeper's voice was muffled by the apron covering her face.

Indigo turned to the captain, who leaned against the doorway. His shoulders were bent forward, and he dipped his head dipped to avoid touching the lintel. She strode over, pushing him back, putting her face close up to his. Reaching down, she pulled an embossed brass knife from her long boot and held it at his throat, the finely-honed edge pressing against the tanned skin. Mrs. Grimoult lowered her apron and gasped, her eyes wide with surprise.

"Tell me what you know, man? Why are you on my doorstep the night my vessel strikes trouble?" Indigo kept her voice low.

The captain pushed the knife aside with little trouble, holding her hand tightly as the knife dropped silently to the Turkish carpet. Bending to retrieve it, he wound the fingers of his free hand tightly through hers as he examined the embossed handle. Holding the knife out to her, he spoke quietly but firmly. "Take me to your viewing room."

Indigo tried to pull away from him as she took the weapon and slid it back into the side of her boot. His fingers tightened on her arm as he steered her toward the door, his other hand hard against her back. She twisted but was unable to escape his vice-like hold.

"Let go of me," she snapped. "If you wish entry to my

viewing room, you must release my arm." Keen to get upstairs to see Mr. Grimoult, it was apparent she was going to have to take the risk and allow this stranger entry to her sanctum upstairs.

The captain released her arm and Indigo strode across to the side of the salon. Putting her hand behind a large trompe l'oeil of painted books, a gentle whirring noise sounded as an entire panel turned inward and a doorway appeared in the wall. Stepping into a dark corridor, she gestured impatiently for him to follow. Candles in brass sconces were placed at intervals on the embossed scarlet wallpaper lining the corridor and pierced the inky darkness.

"Follow me," she said tersely. He stepped in behind her and followed her into the shadows. Mrs. Grimoult hurried along behind them.

"How do you know of my viewing room?" she asked him looking back over her shoulder as she strode along the narrow corridor. To her knowledge, only her two loyal retainers, Mr. and Mrs. Grimoult, knew of the room upstairs and they alone were aware of the extent of her enterprise. The captain did not reply, and her mouth tightened as she held her temper and mulled over the dilemma in which she unexpectedly found herself.

It was common knowledge that she, Indigo de Vargas y Irausquínno, owned two hundred acres of exotic blooms surrounding an exclusive holiday retreat perched high on the wild cliffs of Cornwall. But the holiday biomes camouflaged her true business, and Indigo knew Duke Leopold Lorca, owner of the castle next to her property, envied the success of her enterprise and would do anything to put obstacles in her path. She also suspected Lorca knew of her pharmacological production and feared her plans for the Great Exhibition may now be at risk. The mysterious events surrounding the arrival of the *Artemis*, the disappearance of her crew and the appearance of this stranger on her doorstep within minutes of the submarine arriving home were too coincidental for her to remain unworried.

As Indigo and the captain reached the end of the corridor, she considered the complication of his mysterious arrival. The captain knew of the *Artemis* and her viewing room; he must have a connection with the Grimoults. People she would trust with her life. Either that or information had been leaked. Indigo's mind worked furiously as she pondered how much she could disclose to this man. The development of the prototype would fail unless the *Artemis* made one more voyage to the Amazon to collect the blooms. Without more passionflowers, there would not be enough pharmacologicals or cosmecuticals to display at the Great Exhibition.

All their preparation would have been for nought.

If the captain knew of her activities, someone close to her had felt a great need to share the information with him.

Why had it not been shared with her?

"Do you have a vessel?" Indigo reached across and spun the large brass cog mounted on the wall next to a pair of embossed scarlet drapes. A soft humming began as it turned, interspersed every couple of seconds with a loud grinding noise.

"I do." He spoke loudly to be heard over the increasing noise.

Indigo slipped her hand behind the drapes and pulled a hidden lever. The drapes opened, revealing a solid door made entirely of brass interlocking cogs whirring and clicking in constant movement, not unlike a clock mechanism.

"Watch your hands," she warned as the door opened out toward them, the cogs winding furiously as the humming became unbearably loud. Indigo and Mrs. Grimoult lifted headpieces with ear covers from a large brass hook and placed the contraptions over their heads. Indigo passed a third headpiece to the captain and he placed it over his head. The door closed and the movement of the cogs slowed. Warm air rushed past them as the small room ascended and Indigo watched the captain closely. His eyes were shut tightly, and he clutched at his stomach when the room lurched upward. Indigo was accustomed to the gravitational pull of the perambulator and the weightless effect on internal organs.

Her gaze travelled slowly down his body during the ascent. His broad shoulders and tautly muscled body were clad in expensive garments. The height and breadth of this mysterious man made her feel small and feminine, despite her being taller than most women. His straight black hair framed sharp cheekbones before falling untidily past a starched linen collar. The dark stubble covering his jaw barely concealed a small white scar near his lip. Yet, despite his dark, mysterious appearance, he had the bearing of a gentleman.

As the perambulator slowed, Indigo placed her hand on the control cog on the intricate lacing of wrought iron which continued to move horizontally. The captain's eyes opened slowly, and the pallor of his face contrasted with his dark stubble. He examined the small room with interest and his hand reached to touch the spinning cogs.

"Steam lift," Indigo spoke loudly above the humming. "Precision movement defined by the cogs. The perambulator ascends, descends and moves sideways if needed. You did well. Most people heave on their first trip in this directional perambulator. It was one of the first models invented last century."

Hanging the three headpieces back on the hook, she stepped back, allowing Mrs. Grimoult to exit the perambulator in front of them. Indigo turned to the captain, and she held his gaze as she gestured to the door. "Follow me."

The perambulator opened into a huge circular room surrounded with the darkness of the ink-black sky. Glass walls allowed a three-hundred-and-sixty-degree vista of the panorama surrounding the manor. The lights of an icebreaker, clearing the shipping channel, reflected off a black, stormy sea as huge wind gusts pushed snow flurries against the window.

A little old man sat at a square table inside an inner circle, his head in his hands. Scattered tufts of *grey* hair covered a balding pink scalp. Indigo knelt beside him, placing her hands on his slight shoulders. "Tell me what happened, Mr. Grimoult?"

The little man turned away from her, shaking his head. "They're all gone, Madame. The crew, the captain… and I regret to say…the shipment."

"What about the *Artemis*? Where is my vessel?" Dread overcame her as she considered the possibility of losing everything.

"It is intact. We loaded the cargo and started back. I went to the underskin for a quick nap," he replied. "I do not know how long I slept because all of the chronometers have stopped working. When I woke, I could not hear the pump jets working, nor feel the hydrodynamic drag. I ran up to the control room and they were all gone. Each and every man."

Reaching up, she gently removed his hand from his hair as his gnarled hands pulled at the few remaining tufts. "It was not of your doing, so do not distress yourself unduly."

"Madame, I know how critical this shipment is." He shook his head.

"That is true." Indigo stood and began to pace the room. "How did you get back to the pier with no crew to assist you with navigation?"

"That is the strange thing, Madame." A lock of hair fell across his forehead as his head moved slowly from side to side. "The *Artemis* was back at the pier and the escape hatch was open when I awoke. I disembarked and came straight back to the manor."

Indigo turned and looked at the captain, who had followed the exchange with interest. "And coincidentally, a new captain materializes on my doorstep this very evening," she said in a cynical tone.

Mr. Grimoult looked up. The distress left his face immediately and his mouth widened in a broad grin. Indigo watched with amazement when the little man jumped to his feet and caught the captain in a tight hug, reaching up and thumping the stranger's back.

"Zane! Zane Thoreau!"

The captain looked at Indigo as she stared at the tableau in front of her, her disbelief overwhelming her.

"What exactly is happening here?" she asked suspiciously. "Captain Dogooder?"

"Purely a nickname, Madame," the captain said with a smile.

"Right." Indigo stepped back and looked at the two men grinning at each other and decided it was time to take hold of this situation which was rapidly getting out of her control. "It is time for some serious talk." Standing next to the large table in the centre of the circle, she looked at Zane, pointing to a chair. "You, sit there." She turned to the housekeeper who had now recovered her equilibrium. "Mrs. Grimoult, some refreshments, please." The housekeeper lowered her eyes and stepped from the room.

"Mr. Grimoult, do you need some time to compose yourself or are you able to join us now?" Indigo continued in a tight voice.

"I am fully recovered, Madame."

"Good." Indigo frowned as she noticed the captain's interest in the traveling attire of the older man. Denim jeans covered his legs, the faded blue fabric topped with a soft uncollared shirt, the short sleeves barely covering his small biceps. Mr. Grimoult noticed her disapproval and his face *coloured*.

"I didn't think to change back, Madame. I returned with haste. I did not expect we would have company."

"Not quite company," Indigo said shortly. "No matter. We have more important things at hand." Indigo waved a dismissive hand as the perambulator door slid open once more. Mrs. Grimoult stepped out with a silver tray holding a plate of Turkish delight, a large jug of mulled wine and three goblets, and then walked across with her head lowered before placing the tray on the table.

Indigo stood quietly for a moment as the captain examined their surroundings. A considerable sum spent during a recent voyage to visit Sofia in Paris had equipped her sanctum with the most modern technological devices. In the center of the inner circle, two analytical engines with large black glass rectangles covered with brass knobs sat side by side. A tray with the letters of the alphabet inscribed in a peculiar mix of buttons sat on the table in front of each engine. A periscope head hung from each side and an ornate timepiece, comprised of coils of copper wire and brass screws, with a small light bulb on each side, sat next to each of the alphabet rectangles.

Indigo observed the captain as he moved around the room, examining the equipment. His fingers played with the alphabet tray and he took a hurried step backward when a picture of a submarine with a fish shaped prow appeared in a series of *coloured* lights on the black glass. She let him explore for a few moments, and then tapped her fingers on the table impatiently.

"Sit down, Captain, we don't have much time." Looking across at Mrs. Grimoult, a silent message passed between the two women. Mrs. Grimoult nodded and entered the perambulator; the door slid shut and the machine descended noisily. Indigo sat at the head of the table and then looked pointedly at the captain as Mr. Grimoult poured the wine into the elaborate goblets. "All right, Mr. Thoreau, Zane or Captain Dogooder or whoever you may be, you can start with your explanation. Why are you here and what do you want with me?"

She regretted her words as soon as they left her lips, unsure if it was his proximity or the level of her worry causing her heart to pound erratically. Her breathing quickened as she awaited his reply. Attempting to meet his eye, Indigo noted the captain's gaze fixed on the top of her bustier and folded her arms across her cleavage when he replied.

"I received an urgent missive from Edward, your captain. He advised you were in need of immediate assistance with your next shipment and that you required a master for the *Artemis*. I have no idea of your cargo, or your destination, however I would trust Edward with my life. I am available immediately, as my vessel is currently under repair."

Mr. Grimoult interrupted. "Madame, if I may speak? Zane is trustworthy. We were in the merchant navy together. His nickname is well deserved." He turned to the captain, smiling. "I would trust Captain Dogooder with my life."

"And I am here simply to offer my services," he said, but Indigo felt his smile was a little too innocent. She was slow to trust; the death of her father in the Amazon had left her wary of ever trusting readily again. She sat staring the captain as her mind worked furiously. All would be lost without one more voyage. It would be necessary to trust him, and Mr. Grimoult seemed certain of the man's worth.

Rising slowly from her chair, she moved around the table, turning her back to him. "Unlace me."

The captain sat without moving, his face expressionless.

"Go ahead, lad. Do as Madame says," said Mr. Grimoult.

Zane rose, pushing the chair aside. He paused, fingers brushing against the ribbon lacing at the back of her bustier. Indigo raised one shoulder, waiting for him to undo the ruby *coloured* lace at the edge of the garment.

"Hurry up." She encouraged him, but her tone was waspish "We don't have all night."

Shrugging his shoulders, he undid the top lace, loosening the rest of the ribbon in the brass eyelets. Strong, calloused fingers lingered on her skin and she struggled to keep her composure as warm hands brushed against her bare shoulders. Indigo reached around, pulling the garment down, exposing her back. She heard a quick intake of breath as her tattoo was revealed and the captain realized it was identical to his.

"Can you now see why I will trust my life and my livelihood with you on such a short acquaintance? We are connected," she said. "Now, lace me back up." His fingers trembled against her shoulder, pulling the laces tight, and finishing with a clumsy bow.

"That will do," she said quietly turning back to face him. "Now, sit back down. We have a long night ahead."

As Indigo saw the question in his eyes, her face broke into a sultry smile.

"Not the sort of night that you anticipate, sir." She leaned back in her chair. "That may come later if you are good and do as you are told."

In the early hours, Mr. Grimoult stifled a yawn and his head dropped until he snored quietly into his chest. The captain remained alert as Indigo described her biome tourist enterprise and the smuggling of exotic plants in her steam-powered submarine. Her wealthy clientele, escaping the bitter English winters, holidayed in warm luxurious environments in one of three huge biomes simulating a variety of temperate climates. The biomes were accessible from the longest pier in Cornwall via a steam-powered funicular railway that traversed the steep cliff. The entertainment biome catered to the wealthier members of society and a procession of clowns, minstrels and variety bands provided entertainment for the patrons and their children. A skating rink, miniature zoo and theatre completed the entertainment biome. A simulated beach enabled sea bathing holidays in the coldest months and provided a therapeutic option for the rich clientele in the beach biome. Water was pumped in from the ocean and warmed through a series of steam rooms.

Discussion turned to the voyage ahead, and planning a mission without her usual, experienced crew.

"The *Artemis* is fitted with a greenhouse and a steam generator pumps ocean water, which maintains the tropical temperature during the expeditions. It enables us to keep the plants alive. Mr. Grimoult has invented a light reproduction device," Indigo explained.

Seeing the disbelief on the captain's face, Indigo nudged Mr. Grimoult awake with her elbow.

"Mr. Grimoult…Mr. Grimoult? Would you please tell the captain about your light device?" The old man raised his head slowly and caught up with the conversation. He rubbed a hand over his weary, lined face.

"Yes, Captain. Madame speaks the truth. I use luminiferous aether, sprayed onto the back of brass tubing. When the submarine is submerged, the aether is released in small doses and keeps the plants alive."

"The plants are purely for the pleasure of the guests at the complex," Indigo emphasized. "The opportunity to exhibit at the Great Exhibition in May will source more financial backing and facilitate an expansion of our enterprise." Indigo paused, tapping her fingers angrily on the table. "I am sure Duke Lorca is behind the disappearance of my crew."

She explained that the duke, who lived in a towering castle overlooking the next cove, had offered her financial backing. "I am unsure of the reasoning behind the offer. I believe that he may have some knowledge of the plants that I have been cultivating." She looked down at the table, shuffling her papers, without meeting the captain's eye. He did not need to be privy to her whole business. "He believes a union between us will be an easy way to reverse the losses he has incurred recently. Lorca even tried wooing me and became most despondent when I rejected his proposal of marriage last week." She laughed at the memory of the duke stomping to his dirigible in high dudgeon, after she had not only rejected him but also thrown him out of her manor. Indigo expected to hear more from Leopold, as she doubted he would let a woman get the better of him. A ridiculous appearance camouflaged a cunning mind.

Gathering the maps together she said, "Captain, you are a man of few words."

The captain drained the last few drops from his goblet and looked across at her. "Madame, you are a woman of much confidence."

Reaching over, Indigo ran her fingers along the tattoo on his arm. The muscles tensed beneath her fingers as sudden warmth singed her skin and she snatched her hand back quickly. Taking a deep breath, she fought to regain her composure, looking into the dark eyes across the table.

"Zane, it is essential that I can trust you to take charge of the *Artemis*. We must complete one more voyage if we are to have enough botanicals for our quest. We have only until the end of the month to complete our prototype for the exhibition."

"Quest?" His brow wrinkled above those midnight eyes. "That is a peculiar term, Madame."

She stumbled over her reply. "I mean our quest to get the prototype ready in time. The Amazon voyage is essential."

"The Amazon? I am more than happy to pilot the *Artemis*, however a South American voyage will take seven weeks to complete. I believe you have a month until the prototype is due?"

Indigo allowed a secretive smile to spread across her face as she rested her chin in her hand. She turned to Mr. Grimoult, almost asleep in his chair. "Captain Dogooder is obviously not a mariner of your ilk, Mr. Grimoult. You will have to teach him a thing or two."

Mr. Grimoult nodded at Indigo.

"Madame, I beg to differ," the captain corrected her, his

voice polite. "I have completed a voyage to the Amazon. As an experienced mariner, I know the time a safe journey takes."

She reached over, stroking his arm soothingly. For some reason her skin craved contact with his. "Don't worry, Captain. I am in charge. All you have to do is navigate."

Indigo stood, reaching around to adjust her loose corset, revealing considerably more breast than before her laces were undone.

"We must rest. There is not much left of the night and there is still much to do. We shall discuss your remuneration tomorrow, Captain. Mrs. Grimoult has prepared a guest room. Follow me."

The captain stepped outside and paused before entering the directional perambulator. Crossing her arms, Indigo laughed as he hesitated.

"Nervous, Captain?" She offered her hand to him. "How can I possibly trust you under the Atlantic with my submarine?"

Ignoring her outstretched hand, the Captain entered the contraption. Indigo leaned against the wall observing him. Eyes met and held as the doors clanged shut and the perambulator dropped quickly. The unaccustomed butterflies in her stomach were caused by the sudden descent, not the attraction she felt for the brooding stranger.

That was all that was causing this heady feeling.

As the perambulator descended, his gaze left hers to travel slowly from her bare shoulders, over the laced corset and down to her high boots. The door opened as the perambulator reached the lower level of the manor. Indigo walked ahead of him down the corridor, deliberately swaying her hips. Pausing at the last door, she turned an ornate knob, entering through the back of a guest room, and ushered the captain past her.

"You should find all you need here. We will speak again in the morning."

Indigo turned to leave, but a warm hand descended on her

bare shoulder.

"Not so fast, my beauty," said the captain. He pushed her gently back against the velvet-lined wall and strands of her hair caught on the soft nap. Eyes narrowing, she stiffened as firm thighs pressed her legs back against the wall. Strong callused fingers slid down her bare arms and the captain trapped both of her hands in one of his, raising them high above her head. His moist lips trailed up her neck until his soft breath warmed her lips.

"I sense there is much that has been left unsaid tonight. We will explore that in due course. But first tell me the significance of our identical tattoos." He spoke against her mouth. The vibration of his words on her lips sent delicious shivers shooting downward to the juncture between her thighs. She leaned away from him, tossing her head and black curls surrounded him. Indigo freed her arms, linked her fingers behind his head and snared his legs in the folds of her skirt. His grip loosened as she moved her mouth back toward his. Their eyes locked, and she moistened her lips in a slow and sensuous movement. She moved in closer and the captain's eyes darkened with anticipation.

Indigo bit him sharply on the lip as she brought her knee up hard to his groin. Pushing him away, she spoke coldly. "You will learn your place in the scheme of things. Do not ever touch me without invitation. And do not ask questions about things best left unsaid."

Before the door slammed behind her, she watched as he rubbed at his mouth, wiping a small drop of blood off his lip.

* * * *

Indigo returned to the viewing room alone and sat staring into the darkness until the black sea lightened to a dull grey and the first rays of dawn light crept in from the east. She had not returned to the Amazon for thirteen years, and she pondered on all the Fates had thrown at her with the disappearance of her crew and the arrival of Captain Dogooder, a man to whom she was instantly attracted.

Her eyes filled with tears as she recalled her father's excitement when he left for the final leg of that fateful trip. The passionflower and its pharmaceutical properties and the moonflower and its potential for extending human life had formed the basis of a lifetime of research for him. He had left Indigo alone in Ilo and travelled not only into the Amazon, but two centuries into the future to find the source of the passionflower. He had found a wild plantation at the headwaters of the Amazon and had also discovered that the healing properties of his beloved passionflower had increased tenfold over the intervening two hundred years.

Upset at her father's refusal to take her on his trip to the future, Indigo had spent the day in a tattoo parlour, ensuring the importance of the passionflower to her would be inscribed permanently for her father to see on his return. She clearly recalled a young drunken sailor with a Cornish lilt to his slurred voice. He had lain beside her in the tattoo parlour on that last fateful trip. She had ignored him, and he had been so drunk, he had paid no attention to the young girl next to him.

Unfortunately, the Fates decreed her father never see the magnificent passionflower tattoo on his eldest daughter's shoulder. Bandits had waylaid the group as they returned from the expedition. Professor de Vargas had been buried in the Amazon jungle in 2008, one hundred and seventy years into the future, leaving Indigo, and her stepsister Sofia, fatherless.

"Madame?"

Indigo jumped when Mr. Grimoult appeared at her side. She hadn't heard the ascent of the perambulator.

"Have you had any sleep?"

"Just thinking," she replied. "I have been thinking of my father and how proud he would have been of our progress."

"It was most fortunate we retrieved his notes from that final expedition, Madame.”

Indigo reached over and squeezed the older man’s hand. “It was all thanks to you, Mr. Grimoult. You risked your life to retrieve his research papers and I am forever in your debt.”

She stood and spoke briskly. “Now, enough of this reminiscing. I need to be certain of one thing. Can I trust Captain Dogooder?”

Chapter 2

As the sun rose over the Cornish landscape, Duke Leopold of Lorca paced around the second mezzanine ring deck of his ancestral home, Castle Lorcathian. Accessible via a long suspension bridge, only a select few were privy to the knowledge of a steam door for underwater craft, which provided a less dangerous entry to the castle. The castle dominated the coastline, the huge moving cog on the eastern parapet used by mariners for navigation past the treacherous rocks.

Leopold did not notice the soft pink light creeping over the broad open fields to the east nor did he notice the small man shadowing his steps. Closely followed by Brixton, his faithful retainer, the duke stopped frequently, peering out across the ocean through a long glass monocular with a large brass handle. Muttering as he fiddled with the cogs on the device, the duke headed off for another circuit of the deck. He paid no attention to the automatic gas lamps dying as the morning sun touched the walls of the castle. Stopping suddenly, Leopold turned around and the little man scurrying along behind him tripped over the duke's feet.

"Get up, man." The duke cuffed the small man's head. "Tell me again, Brixton, you are sure you didn't see where her crew went?"

Brixton, whose little face complimented the sharp rat-like features of the duke, climbed back to his feet, clinging to the edge of the parapet. "No, your Grace." His voice trembled. "But it has been confirmed that neither does Madame de Vargas know."

"What about the cargo?" The duke raised his voice and Brixton flinched

"Gone also, your Grace."

Brixton's eyes widened as the duke threw the monocular

toward him in a fit of temper. He ducked and the large device whistled past his pointy ears. It bounced off the edge of the parapet before clattering down the side of the castle, pieces of brass landing on the rocks far below.

To his great disgust, the duke could see the de Vargas holiday complex from most points of his ancestral home castle, further fuelling his jealousy of Madame de Vargas' successful enterprise.

"It will all be mine soon," he muttered. "I will ensure that before the month is out." Madame de Vargas had foiled each of his previous schemes, including a marriage proposal. Clenching his jaw, Leopold recalled her cruel laughter as she coldly rejected his proposal.

"Is she attending my soiree this evening?" The duke looked down at the little man beside him.

"Madame de Vargas has accepted the invitation, your Grace. Her brother is accompanying her." Brixton replied.

"Her brother? What brother? I was unaware she had a brother," he asked crossly. "She has a sister. No matter, he may distract her from her task. What about Henry Cole? Have we heard back from him?"

"Confirmed, your Grace. The dirigible transporting Mr. Cole will arrive at eight o'clock."

The duke rubbed his hands together with a smirk, satisfied with the turn of events. If all went to plan, he would have the better of Madame de Vargas, sooner rather than later.

"In that case, please activate the carriage to ferry him across the bridge. But only Henry, Brixton. Madame de Vargas and her brother can walk. With any luck, she will fall from the bridge and then my troubles will be over." Leopold pinched the bridge of his nose. "Bring my snuffbox. I must keep my wits about me." Scurrying away, the little man's head bobbed in agreement.

Duke Lorca entertained frequently. Guests attending

functions at the castle crossed the suspension bridge in a steam-powered rail carriage if the duke was feeling sociable. Those out of favour walked across the swinging bridge. Feeling more satisfied by the moment, the duke chuckled as he awaited his snuff. "As the Prince Consort says, if you need steam, get Cole."

* * * *

Indigo sat in the breakfast room going over their plan, toying with the idea of entrusting Zane with the true reason for their Amazon voyage. Two hours passed as she waited for him to make an appearance, her temper growing as the clock struck noon. The lingering memory of that strong, muscular body pinning her to the wall had given her a sleepless night. It had been some months since her last sexual escapade, she reasoned to herself. That explained the way her body responded to him. Although she found Captain Dogooder most intriguing, he was only another man.

Nothing special.

But he did not seem intimidated by her, as most gentlemen in her acquaintance were. Traveling to South America in the *Artemis* provided occasional contact with men of a different time, who were receptive of her confidence. The captain appeared not at all perturbed, and a thoughtful smile curved her lips as Indigo recalled his interest. However, she would forget all thoughts of a dalliance until after the voyage. Having come to a decision, she returned to the matter in hand.

Indigo rang the breakfast bell impatiently. "Mrs. Grimoult, is there any sign of the captain rising from his bed? Would you go and wake him please?"

The housekeeper came from the kitchen, carefully placing a fresh pot of tea in front of her mistress. "I believe Captain Dogooder has gone back to the Skip Shaft Inn in Tin Town to collect his kit. He did not know what welcome you would give him, so he did not come prepared to spend a night. You do have a fearsome reputation, my dear."

29

"Good." That perception pleased Indigo greatly. "Does the captain have evening attire for the soiree at Castle Lorcathian this evening?"

"I believe so." Mrs. Grimoult looked down, smoothing her apron, not meeting the eyes of her mistress. "Have you told him about the—"

"Enough." Indigo held up an imperious hand. "I will tell him when the time is right."

"Very well, Madame." Mrs. Grimoult bustled from the room.

Indigo laughed at the disapproving look on her housekeeper's face. Moving across the chilly room to the chair beside the window she sat, chin in hand, looking out at the Atlantic Ocean, wondering for the umpteenth time why her crew had disappeared and where they were.

* * * *

Zane sauntered into the salon as the last blood red rays of the setting sun shot from the horizon. Tight lipped, Indigo looked at him from head to foot. Dressed beautifully in golden breeches tucked into high, buckled boots, the outfit was topped with a gold embossed smoking jacket, and the captain looked the epitome of elegance. A large, brass, cogged timepiece hung from a golden chain around his neck, matching the brass goggles on top of his head.

"It is a pleasure to finally have your company, Captain." Indigo welcomed him, keeping her face expressionless and her hand across her bare neck, concealing the fast beating pulse in her throat.

"No, Madame, the pleasure is mine," he drawled. "May I say how fetching you look this evening?"

Indigo burst out laughing, appreciating his blatant admiration of her attire. Dressing with deliberation, she had planned to upset the equilibrium of Duke Lorca this evening. A prudish stickler for convention, it was rumoured the sight of a piano leg would offend him. Servants draped shawls over the offending furniture in the castle. The sight of her, scandalously attired in an incestuous clinch with her supposed brother would distress the priggish duke, distracting him from the attention of Mr. Henry Cole.

"Come, dear brother, it is time to leave and seek out our information." Indigo flashed the captain an appreciative smile.

Wisps of mist puffed from their mouths in the icy air as they hurried to the streamlined scarab vehicle for the short journey to the castle. Mr. Grimoult hovered around the vehicle, flipping back the glass roof of the sleek three-wheeled contraption with a brass hook. Zane proffered a hand to assist Indigo and a frisson of warmth shot up her arm as his strong fingers brushed hers, distracting her from the task in hand.

"I will drive," she announced crossly. Zane smiled and deferred to her, moving across to the passenger side, pulling the brass goggles over his eyes. Sitting with him in the confined space of the vehicle sent sharp thrills coursing through her body and she attempted to ignore the effect his proximity appeared to have on her traitorous limbs. Pulling out the brass stops on the ornate dashboard with shaking fingers, she laughed loudly as loud shots of steam hissed from the large pipes coiled on each side of the vehicle. Zane jumped in surprise, grabbing the support bar in front of the sloping glass screen as the vehicle shot forward at great speed. Roaring down the cobbled road to Castle Lorcathian, Indigo glanced across the road to the ocean. The wind was still gusting strongly, and the water was decked with white-capped waves. She smiled when she saw there was no steam carriage waiting at the end of the road for the guests. The duke obviously expected them to walk across the suspension bridge in the wintry winds which swirled in off the ocean. Putting the scarab into overdrive, the wheels folded up underneath the chassis as the airlift engaged. The vehicle flew over several well-dressed guests who clung bravely to the sides of the swaying rope bridge, hundreds of feet above the angry waves crashing on the rocks below.

"You certainly enjoy living dangerously, Madame," the captain commented.

Glancing across at him, she smothered a laugh. His posture was stiff, white knuckles still gripping the bar even as their speed slowed. Perspiration trickled past his collar despite the cold. The poor man had experienced a wealth of new technology in her manor house over the past day and Indigo smiled at the thought of the voyage ahead of him later tonight.

The scarab stopped outside the entry to the Grand Hall with a final hiss of steam. Waving the duke's valet away with a dismissive hand, she reminded Zane of his role. "Just follow my lead as we planned. You should enjoy the evening. If our plan works, we should get what we want from Mr. Cole in a timely fashion. The Grimoults are preparing the *Artemis* for departure now and we shall depart for the Amazon as soon as we return from here."

Indigo and Zane entered the Grand Entrance Hall of Castle Lorcathian, arms entwined. Several demurely clad matrons sitting on cloth-shrouded furniture gaped at Indigo's attire. Shocked gasps were heard across the hall as she strutted over to join the duke, her voluptuous body the center of attention. Leopold stood with a tall man in a far corner hidden by large ferns. Wearing a morning suit with a top hat, holding a monocle against one eye, the man had the appearance of an important dignitary. Indigo broke away from Zane and tapped Leopold on the shoulder. As the duke turned, Indigo reached over, took his heavily bejewelled hand and placed it firmly against her breast. Bending down, she leaned into him, placing her open mouth on his slimy lips, hiding the revulsion that coursed through her veins. She thought of inserting her tongue; however, she decided she would rather lose her entire enterprise than sink to those depths.

"Leopold, *dahling*," she drawled, keeping her voice bored. "What a wonderful occasion. Thank you so much for our invitation."

The duke pulled back from her grip with a surprised gasp, his face reddening as her breasts wobbled under his chin. Her ruby red corset fit her like a glove, and when Indigo leaned forward the tips of her dusky pink nipples were just visible. The steel bars pushed her bosom upward, further enhancing her cleavage. She watched with delight as Leopold's gaze travelled down to the sheer lace skirt brushing her mid-thigh, exposing bare legs clad in high black boots. Her satisfaction grew as his ruddy complexion deepened and his bulbous nose turned purple as he struggled for words. The duke truly was an ugly little man, both inside and out.

"Are you going to introduce me to your friend?" Indigo flicked Leopold's cheek with a finger bared by fingerless lace gloves. The duke bowed rigidly, turning to the tall man beside him. "Mr. Henry Cole, may I present to you Madame de Vargas y Irausquínno."

"A pleasure, Mr. Cole. I believe we have some business to discuss." Turning her back on Leopold, she took the arm of the speechless Mr. Cole, before walking him across to the long windows on the far side of the room. Delighted to hear more gasps of displeasure from the Victorian matrons, Indigo engaged Mr. Cole in an immediate discussion of the forthcoming Great Exhibition.

She remained aware of the intense interest the duke was displaying in their conversation. Keeping Leopold in her sight as he stared intently from the other side of the large room, she noticed when he summoned Brixton with a snap of his fingers. The duke hissed instructions into the little man's ear, not taking his eyes off Indigo and Mr. Cole, who remained deep in conversation. Brixton moved across the room, sidling across to stand behind Indigo, his pointy ears twitching. Zane came up behind the little servant, winking at Indigo as he gripped the little man's arm.

"Brixton, I believe?" Zane held the little arm in an iron grip. "Come, my man, I would like an introduction to the duke, as my dear sister is otherwise occupied. I am Captain Zane de Vargas y Irausquínno." He dragged the small man back across the room to the duke.

As the little man squeaked over the introduction, Henry Cole laughed heartily, and Leopold glared across the room. Mr. Cole reached down, took Indigo's hand, and placed it against his lips.

"I wish you all the best with your enterprise, Madame," Mr. Cole's imposing voice boomed across the room.

Indigo winked at him and walked back to the small group of interested onlookers surrounding the duke, her hips moving in an exaggerated sexy sway. She smiled at the captain willing him to keep a straight face. With a bored look at Leopold, Indigo leaned against Zane, running her fingers down the front of his tight breeches. "Come, brother, the entertainment is sadly lacking here tonight. Take me home. Together we will make our own pleasure." Reaching up, she placed her hands on each side of Zane's face, placing her lips on his, smiling as Leopold spluttered next to her.

"Disgraceful, incestuous behaviour, Madame!" His face coloured as red as Indigo's corset, knotty veins appearing above his frilled collar. "Be gone. You are not welcome in my abode, any longer." The duke threw them one last disgusted look and grunted rudely, before stalking over to re-join Mr. Cole.

Walking through the Grand Entrance Hall, Indigo waggled her fingertips as she bid farewell to the speechless guests.

Looking down at her with admiration as they passed through the castle entrance, the captain appeared most impressed. "By God, Madame, you should be on the stage."

She nodded at him briefly, her heart still pounding from

their kiss. His taste lingered on her lips and Indigo's nipples tightened as his eyes locked with hers. It was too soon, much too soon.

There was no time for dalliance. Not yet.

Her flirtatious demeanour disappeared, and she responded impatiently as they entered the scarab.

"You can drive." She sat back, waiting impatiently for the vehicle to move. Pulling out three brass stops on the dashboard before the vehicle rose, the vehicle flipped on its side and teetered over the edge as it roared across the suspension bridge.

"Jesus, man," Indigo yelled above the roar of the steam, "Are you trying to kill us?"

"I'm a submariner, not a landlubber." The captain laughed, fiddling with the brass speed stops. The vehicle left the bridge and rose, gaining height, and flew above the road at a great speed. Approaching the manor, Indigo reached over and pulled a lever under the dashboard. A camouflaged door rose vertically in front of them and Zane steered the scarab through the entry with a whisker to spare on either side.

* * * *

Indigo's expectation that the Grimoults would be ready to leave on their return received a setback as she followed Zane from the vehicle storage room. Mr. and Mrs. Grimoult sat in a small salon at the end of the corridor, drinking tea. When she strode across to the table, Zane caught her arm, pulling her back.

"Now, don't go off half-cocked before I explain to you what is happening," he said.

Indigo glared at him, shaking his hands away angrily. Her anger grew as the Grimoults smiled at each other.

"Before *you* explain?" Her voice was ominously quiet.

"Yes, there are things that must be said before we embark on this voyage. If you want the expedition to succeed, sit down and pour yourself a cup of tea while I explain," said the captain.

Mrs. Grimoult hurriedly picked up the teapot, pouring a cup of fragrant tea for her mistress. Zane pulled out a chair, placed his hands on Indigo's shoulders and pushed her down onto the chair, none too gently.

"Stop the mouthing. I know that the visit to the castle gave you the information you were seeking. Now it's time to share everything, both ways"

"Just who are you?" Indigo spat the words at him as her bottom hit the chair.

"I am Captain Zane Thoreau. That is my real name. I am an excise man, working for the government seeking illegal traders. The Comptroller General has information about the flowers in your complex. You are under investigation for illegal importation."

"Get out." Indigo screamed at him and rose from the chair, lunging at him, her fists balled.

"Madame," Mr. Grimoult interjected. "Please listen to the captain."

She paused, turning to her two faithful retainers with a look of dismay. "Please don't tell me you already knew this?"

"Would you please listen to me?" Zane ran his hand through his hair. "I will explain and then you can decide if you want me to leave or navigate your vessel. It is to your advantage I pilot your vessel. It does not affect me one way or the other."

Indigo sat back in her chair and reached for her teacup, her hand shaking with rage. Her eyes locked onto his, all thoughts of passion gone in an instant.

"You have five minutes, captain. Be warned, I do not like deceit."

The captain spoke quietly. Indigo calmed and her confidence returned, her heart resuming a normal beat. Sitting back, she sipped her tea and listened intently as the captain explained why he had come to her door last evening.

After leaving the merchant navy, Captain Zane Thoreau

joined the government as an excise man. Most excise men traditionally came from the constabulary, this being the policy of the Comptroller General of the coast guard.

"My retired friends in the mariner community use their local knowledge for smuggling. My ideas on keeping rural order have changed. I have become indispensable and I feed them much information to keep them safe. I hate the thought of Duke Lorca and other upper-class leeches making even more money from their workhouses to the ill of the society. Mass production, elitism, social climbing. Pah!" He thumped the table with his fist and the fine porcelain teacups rattled in their saucers. "That soiree tonight is a perfect example of the wasted wealth that occurs in the upper echelons of our society."

Indigo smiled, regarding Zane with a new respect. It appeared he shared her social philosophy. "And what exactly do you know of the *Artemis* and my expeditions?" she asked.

"You are importing the plants in your biomes from South America. Duke Lorca has been keeping the government informed and becoming more vociferous each day. I have been sent down here to conduct an immediate investigation."

Indigo opened her mouth to protest but Zane raised his hand.

"Wait, hear me out. There is no evidence. It was commonly believed that your pier is for the transport of your tourists, and the existence of your vessel was unknown."

"What do you mean…was?" She narrowed her eyes.

"I was on the pier yesterday afternoon when the *Artemis* surfaced. I recognized your emblem on her side. I have now instigated a plan to close the investigation once and for all. It will show Duke Lorca to be nothing but a jealous fool, who has become malicious since your refusal to combine your enterprises by his proposal of marriage."

Pushing his chair aside, the captain moved around the table

to Indigo. Placing his hands on her shoulders, he reassured her. "We have transferred the botanicals to a safe house."

Indigo frowned at Mr. Grimoult, even as the warmth from Zane's hands moved from her shoulders down to the pit of her stomach.

"We? You were involved in this, Mr. Grimoult?"

The old man hung his head. "I thought to have only a quick nap. However, this all ensued whilst I slept in the underskin bunk."

"Mr. Grimoult awoke whilst the crew was moving the cargo. Luckily, he left before the excise men arrived," Zane explained. "We were not even aware he was on board. I did not board the *Artemis*. She looks to be a fine vessel. After your captain advised me of the removal of your cargo, I called in my excise men to search the vessel. They are satisfied there is no smuggling. The rest of your crew are in the lock up in Tin Town." Lifting the golden chain holding his timepiece, he smiled. "No, by this time, your crew should be drinking ale at The Rattling Cat."

"Ah, The Rattling Cat." Mr. Grimoult laughed. "Legend has it that the bones of excise men were tied to the collars of the cats and when a stranger came to town the rattling of the bones would alert the smugglers."

"Enough." Indigo slammed her hand on the table. "This is all well and good, however, we still have another voyage ahead of us. We do not yet have enough of the blooms to complete our quota for the Great Exhibition." She turned to the captain. "I am appreciative of your work protecting my enterprise and I thank you. It is obvious that we cannot take the crew on an immediate voyage, as they will be under surveillance." Indigo stared at him for a long time before continuing. "You have shown me that you are trustworthy. Now, I will tell you of my venture." Mr. and Mrs. Grimoult both nodded their little heads enthusiastically.

"Whilst I have a highly successful enterprise where the wealthier members of society indulge themselves in the winter, it also provides a lot of employment, as well as pleasure, for the local people and improves their living standards. I do not profit from the activity at all. It all goes back into the pockets of those who help me."

The captain's face lit up with a smile. "I am pleased to hear we are of a similar philosophy, Madame."

"However," she continued. "You are obviously are not aware of my main business."

"Your main business? The biomes?" Zane looked at her, a surprised frown on his face.

"No, the real industry I have developed, despite government regulation. The scientific community is highly possessive of their laboratories and the development of pharmacologicals is slow. There are ridiculous levels of regulation. I have a laboratory, hidden from prying eyes, which produces pharmacologically, cosmecuticals and hallucinogenics. That is the purpose of our voyages. We collect more specimens from the Amazon. The holiday biomes provide a cover for my scientific activities. It is commonly believed the propagation of blooms in my conservatories is only for the pleasure of the guests." Indigo paused, taking a deep breath. "That is nowhere near the truth. We must hurry as time is of the essence. I am unveiling my true enterprise at the Great Exhibition in May. Tonight, Mr. Henry Cole has provided me with more time. He has agreed that I may create my actual display, without need for a prototype. Duke Lorca will not be given my exhibition space."

Zane reached down, taking both her hands between his. Dark, brooding eyes locked with hers and Indigo could not tear her gaze away from those black depths.

"That is excellent news, Madame and I pledge my unerring support to you. However, I have one more request. Before we embark on our voyage tonight, may I see your complex?"

* * * *

A strong wind buffeted the scarab on the short journey to the biomes. Drifts of snow covered the fields beneath them, the wind pushing the vehicle off course. The blade flicked across the glass as the snow iced up around the glass. Zane leaned forward to touch the other levers on the panel in front of him and Indigo pushed his hand away impatiently.

"You will have us upside down," she snapped as her heart raced from his proximity

Indigo parked the scarab in a low tunnel behind the complex, before leading Zane to a door at the back of the beach biome. They entered the huge dome through a series of doors, circled by cogs with levers on each side. The happy squealing of children muffled by the soft whoosh of waves greeted them as the final door slid closed noiselessly behind them, camouflaged behind a large sign. Stepping onto a wide esplanade, Indigo stood back with a satisfied smile, watching as Zane's eyes widened in disbelief. Children built sandcastles with buckets and spades on a beach bathed in sunshine. A panorama of seaside activities stretched along the esplanade. Donkeys, roundabouts and a Punch and Judy show added to the noise of gulls screeching overhead. Parents strolled with their children, eating fish and chips, fairy floss, and ice cream.

"Never in my wildest dreams did I imagine something like this could exist." Zane turned to Indigo, eyes still wide as he took in the vista before them.

"How is it daytime?" He pointed at the brilliant blue sky above them and brushed the rapidly melting snow from his shoulder. "Where does the sunshine come from? It is midnight and snowing outside."

"You have many questions. It is satisfying to see the wind taken out of Captain Dogooder's sails." His interest pleased her greatly and she smiled at the unintended pun. "I will quickly show you the other biomes. Then we must embark on our voyage. You have many more surprises in store this evening, Captain. Are you up to the challenge?" The desire in his expression as he held her gaze sent a shiver skittering down her spine and Indigo was the first to look away. They re-entered the scarab and made the short journey through the tunnel to the next biome.

Indigo turned to Zane and placed her hand on his arm. "There is one question you may have that I am unable to answer at this time…but the time will come."

Entering the biome through a similar sequence of sliding doors, the last metal door was overlaid in the familiar pattern of their tattoo. Indigo pushed the door open slowly, inhaling with pleasure as the sweet smell of exotic blooms hung in the air around them. She passed the captain a pair of dark glasses and donned a similar pair to protect their eyes from the intense blue of the sky. The humid warmth of the biome and the deafening screech of multi-coloured birds darting through the treetops surrounded them. Indigo led the way past rows of high benches, containing hundreds of blooms at various stages of growth.

"They are all the same?" asked Zane

Indigo spread her arms wide. "Captain, this is the reason for our next voyage. The blue passionflower."

Zane removed his jacket as the heat became unbearable. He rolled back the linen cuff of his shirt and held his arm in front of her, looking at the tattoo of the blue passionflower replicated in the thousands of plants around them.

"Madame, I know we are somehow connected through this tattoo, but the memory of it keeps slipping from my mind. It is elusive and I cannot hold it. Tell me."

She turned away from him. "First you must prove your loyalty to me. Now come, we have a voyage to make."

Chapter 3

Zane looked around the *Artemis* in amazement after following Indigo and the Grimoults down the metal ladder leading from the hatch to the boiler room. A massive boiler dominated the center of the room, flanked by two big fireboxes. A cylindrical water reservoir linked it to the side skin, each pipe covered with coiled rope. He reached out, carefully touching the rope.

"For insulation," advised Mr. Grimoult, walking to a series of analogue dials at the front of the room. "We have approximately twenty-five minutes left."

"It is more modern than my vessel, but I am sure my knowledge is easily transferable." Zane spoke with confidence.

"Your role is to navigate through the harbor once we get there. Come to the control room before we change our clothing."

Zane turned to Indigo, confused. "The harbor? What about the long journey across the Atlantic?"

She simply smiled and held out her hand out to guide him through the narrow gangway. Immediately Zane felt the usual hit of warmth from their close contact and stepped back to out some space between them.

A series of small spaces led to the control room at the front of the vessel. As they bent through each low space, Indigo outlined its purpose. "Sonar space, temporal storage, escape pod, greenhouse, bunk room."

"Where are the rest of the bunk rooms?" Zane scanned the room for another entry, confused by the lack of quarters.

"We only need one," she replied.

"Where is the food storage and preparation area?"

"There isn't one. We don't need it."

Her reply confused him further and an uneasy feeling settled in his stomach. Looking around the control room, the unfamiliar dials and the analytical engine increased his apprehension. This was the strangest vessel he had ever boarded. Both the control room and equipment were unlike any submarine he had ever seen. A huge semicircular screen followed the shape of the hull, covering the front half of the room. A single analytical engine sat in the center, flanked by two small leather chairs. The only pieces of familiar equipment were the brass periscope and rudder levers. Feeling a surge of panic, he doubted his ability to master this strange vessel.

Mrs. Grimoult bustled in, carrying some clothing, and handed a bundle to each of them. "Hurry up, fifteen minutes until temporal movement commences."

Zane narrowed his eyes suspiciously. "What is temporal movement?"

"You will see shortly, sir." Mrs. Grimoult hurried out, avoiding looking at him.

Indigo turned away from him and unlaced her corset. Peeling it off and throwing it aside, she stepped out of her skirt. Turning back to face him, she stood bare-breasted, clad only in a miniscule red undergarment. Never before had he seen such a magnificent and confident woman. Her statuesque beauty took his breath away.

"Breeches off, please, captain."

The blood drained from his head and immediately pumped to his nether regions. With shaking fingers, Zane undid the flaps on his breeches as instructed, stepping out of them. All thoughts of navigating this unfamiliar vessel disappeared in an instant. Indigo pulled on a pair of strange blue trousers, which hugged her long legs like a second skin. His linen undergarment strained against his rapidly growing erection and he turned away from her, but too late.

"Impressive, but not now." Her smile was wide, and her eyes glinted with amusement. "I hope those pants will fit you. I did not realize you were so big…your thighs, I mean, Captain."

The blood rushed back to his face and warmed his cheeks. At times the unpredictability of this woman made him as nervous as a young buck. He could not keep up with her. Leaning forward, she pulled her hair back and threaded a piece of circular stretching twine such as he had not seen before through her hair, confining her black curls into a high ponytail.

"What is that?" he asked.

"An elastic band," she replied. "It is made of rubber from the latex plantations in the south American rainforest. It hasn't been invented yet."

"I beg your pardon?" he said. "What do you mean it hasn't been invented?"

Indigo ignored his question. "Hurry up and get dressed, we will be underway shortly." Her voice was muffled as she pulled a tight, red shirt over her head. Zane followed her instructions and quickly pulled on the blue pants and the soft, tight shirt. When he held it up it was in the shape of a large T. The interlocking metal teeth that closed the opening at the front of his pants intrigued him and he stood there sliding it up and down for a moment, watching the teeth grip and open and close with each movement. When he glanced up, Indigo was watching him with a wide smile on her face. He hurriedly slid the metal teeth to the top and snapped the brass button at his waist. They were the most comfortable trousers he had worn.

"Ten minutes," yelled Mr. Grimoult.

Indigo moved across to the machine in the center of the room. A quick tap on the alphabet board in front of the rectangular glass lit the screen and an analogue clock appeared. "This is our origin time. Can you please check that your timepiece is synchronized?"

Glancing down at the chronometer on his arm, Zane replied. "Eight-fifteen."

"Eight-fifteen, morning, fourteenth February 1851," she

confirmed.

As she quickly tapped on the keyboard, Zane watched the detail on the screen change to a string of numbers. "Four dot fifteen, fourteen oh two, twenty eleven. Seventeen degrees, thirty-eight minutes, twenty-two seconds south. Seventy-one degrees, twenty minutes, fifteen seconds west."

"Two minutes," yelled Mr. Grimoult. "Prepare for temporal movement. Time engines half full. Set for one hundred and sixty years."

Disbelief filled his mind as a whoosh of steam sounded from the boiler room and a loud humming began in the control room. The Grimoults hurried in, dressed in similar clothing to his, the little housekeeper looking most peculiar in the tight blue pants. A flashing blue light rotated slowly across the top of the control room, and the humming continued as the submarine suddenly submerged. Zane clutched at his stomach as the light rotated rapidly and a soft blue haze suffused the entire room. Grabbing at the edge of the table as the room faded, he was unable to keep his balance. The faces of Indigo and the Grimoults stretched beyond recognition as he looked up at them from the floor. The roof of the control room spun around him and the light disappeared.

* * * *

"The captain did well for a first-timer," said Mrs. Grimoult leaning over Zane who lay on the floor rubbing his eyes.

Indigo leaned over him, her long fingers stroking his face. "Wake up, Captain. We have entered the harbor. We need you to steer the *Artemis* through the marina."

Mr. Grimoult assisted Zane to his feet, guiding him to the rudder controls. Pressing the fingertips of one hand to the bridge of his nose, Zane used the other hand to adjust the periscope with the brass knobs.

"Do you have a map of the harbor?" he asked, his voice shaking.

A pang of remorse shot through Indigo; perhaps it would have been kinder to prepare him for the temporal voyage. Zane's face was pale, his pupils dilated, and perspiration soaked the front of his T-shirt, it was clear to any onlooker his body was unaccustomed to the effects of time travel. Mr. and Mrs. Grimoult had acclimatized to the change of time travelling over the years and their many voyages, as she had.

Indigo touched the keyboard of the analytical engine and pulled up a screen of Ilo, the capital of Moquegua province in Peru. "We are a mile offshore at the beginning of a wide channel into the marina. Mr. Grimoult, would you please show the captain our usual mooring?"

Zane steered the *Artemis* successfully to the mooring as the older man pointed to the screen directing him between the hundreds of boats on the surface. He made no further comment, but his lips were tight and the pulse jumping in his check told Indigo he would have much to say once they were ashore.

* * * *

An hour after surfacing, Indigo and Zane climbed through the hatch, stepping onto the pier at the eastern end of the harbor. The Grimoults would stay on the *Artemis*, remaining submerged in the daylight hours.

"We will be back with the blooms in forty-eight hours. Be ready to meet us at the end of the pier at this time the day after tomorrow," she directed.

"Take care, Madame," said Mr. Grimoult. "And you too, sir." He slapped Zane on the back as he prepared to ascend the ladder

Giving them a quick wave, Indigo grabbed Zane's hand and ran along the pier, dragging him along behind her. He did not speak as he ran with her, tight lipped and his face expressionless. Reaching the end of the pier and crossing the deserted road, Indigo frowned at Zane, slightly surprised by his compliant behaviour.

"Are you all right? No side effects from your fall, Captain?"

Zane stopped, pulling her back toward him. Holding tightly onto her waist, he glared down at her. "What do you think, Madame? You ask me to pilot your submarine. You spend a whole night going through the preparations for the voyage. You pass me off as your brother to get the information you seek. You show me through your biomes. You even say you will trust me." He leaned down placing his face close to hers and a shiver ran through her as his voice deepened.

"However, you neglect one little detail. One piffling detail you obviously didn't think important. You forgot to tell me you have a vessel that travels not only through space. It travels through time as well. You neglected to tell me that not only are your plants in the Amazon, but they are in the bloody twenty-first century, and then you have the damned hide to ask me if I am all right!"

Indigo looked into his angry face and bit back a satisfied smile. Zane's anger pleased her. Compliant since they had first met; she wondered if he had any backbone. However, she was desperately in need of a captain for the water stage of their time journey, and she had gambled and cast her doubt aside.

Zane pushed her away and stepped back, running his fingers through his shaggy hair. Indigo reached up, grabbed his face with both hands, and gave him a swift, hard kiss on his tight lips. "That's an apology, Captain. Consider yourself honoured, because I do not do it often. Apologize, that is. Now come on."

The sounds of a town stirring to life in the early morning greeted them as they wound their way through the back streets behind the harbor. It appeared to be a seedy part of the town and they hurried though the rabbit warren of narrow streets.

"Do you know where you are going?" Zane's breath came in short pants as they ran down a narrow alley. Lights came on in a few of the houses they passed but there were no citizens on the road at this early hour.

"Of course, I do," she snapped. "We must be through town before the sun rises. We will meet Luis, our guide at the expedition lodge base. We have a long drive to the river, and then he will take us to the headwaters on a river barge. After that, we only have a short trek to the plantation through the jungle."

Indigo stressed the need to be alert. "I still don't trust the duke. There is still something causing me concern. I suspect he has bribed a member of the submarine crew. I suspect Leopold knows exactly where we are and what we are doing."

Their footsteps clattered down a narrow, cobbled lane. Indigo heard a quick intake of breath as Zane stopped behind her.

"Jesus, what now?" said Indigo with exasperation, following the direction of his stare to the faded board above the shop. Even though the paint was peeling, the sign advertising *Tatuajes por Juan* was legible.

"Tattoos by Juan," she read, and her heart started to pound. She was amazed to see the same little shop still in the same place. One hundred and seventy years had passed since she had last been there.

"I have been here before," Zane spoke slowly. "This is where I got my tattoo. I know that, but I don't remember it."

Indigo touched his arm gently. "I believe you. I also know we have been here together before. However, we will explore that later. Now, Captain, are you coming on this expedition with me or will I leave you here?"

* * * *

Luis drove the vehicle confidently through the mountainous terrain appearing unfazed by the steep hills and deep ravines and did not converse for most of the journey. As the vehicle bounced over potholes and corrugated washouts, Zane hung on tightly, occasionally looking over the edge of the escarpment, certain he would not survive the journey. He had survived a temporal voyage; however, this leg of their quest was filled with more danger.

Finally, Luis swung the wheel a final time and the vehicle entered a fenced compound near the headwaters of the mighty Amazon River. The sound of flowing water filled his ears and Zane pushed the door handle quickly when the Land Rover came to a sudden stop and he slid to the muddy ground. Looking up, he caught Indigo stifling a grin. Leaning out the window, she laughed.

"I think you handled traveling across two centuries with more aplomb than the last four hours, Captain."

Zane glared at her, his hasty exit from the vehicle leaving him a little embarrassed.

"Now, don't forget to watch out for jaguars, cougars… and oh…there are anacondas here too. And don't put your hands or feet in the water because there are electric eels and piranha in the river." Indigo said the grin spreading across her face

She burst into peals of laughter and he ignored her.

"We shall discuss my remuneration in greater detail when we return from the voyage, Madame," he replied stiffly. Turning his back on her, he walked away to explore the compound, examining the old rusted vehicles and discarded equipment littering the small area. Vines and broad-leafed vegetation covered the buildings, the solid green curtain contrasting with the rusted machinery. Broken windows and doors hanging from corroded hinges gave the place an air of neglect and it appeared as if it was rarely used for the expedition base it was purported to be. Zane glanced and across at Luis who gestured for him to assist with the unloading of the vehicle.

After the vehicle was unpacked, Luis drove it behind the smaller building, immediately camouflaging the large machine with loose vines. He constantly scanned the perimeter of the compound as he worked, appearing uneasy. Speaking to Indigo in fast Spanish, she turned to Zane. "Luis says there has been more traffic on the road than usual today. He is rather concerned. We must take extra caution."

Indigo entered the building, beckoning Zane to follow. "This was a base for the copper miners at the end of the twentieth century. When the mining boom declined, copper mines were abandoned throughout the Amazon basin. This suits our needs, as no one usually comes up here. It provides a safe base for gathering our blooms. We will eat and rest before we embark on the next leg of our trip. It is impossible to travel through the jungle in the heat of the day. "

Luis handed her a set of small keys before disappearing outside once more. Moving across to the back of the abandoned building, Indigo unlocked a door camouflaged by a piece of ripped hessian before ushering Zane ahead of her into a large room. Tinned food lined the shelves on one wall and two bunk beds were secured to the opposite wall. Crates in a clear white transparent material were stacked along the back of the room.

Indigo heated a tin of meat stew on the stove and Zane moved around the small building. He was still enthralled by the thought of being in the future and wanted to retain as much in his memory as he could. Picking up unfamiliar objects, he examined each one closely; interested in the strange shapes and materials He removed the lid of a small white crate, jumping as it made a sharp snapping sound.

"It's called plastic," said Indigo. "It will be exhibited for the first time at the second Great Exhibition in 1862. The government of our day resists every move to share these wonderful inventions with the general populace. Prince Albert, our Consort, has been fighting for an Exhibition of All Nations for many months. It will be wonderful to see Henry Cole bring the consort's dream to fruition."

Zane smiled at the passion in her voice and the light in her eyes as she emphasized each point. His gaze locked on hers; he was almost bewitched by this woman and fought to control his response to her.

Now was not the time.

He grinned to himself, trying to figure out what 'now' really meant to him. Shaking his hand in wonder he looked up as Indigo continued speaking.

"We must confront conformity and complacency.' She held his gaze and her eyes were dark. "We can make the world a much better place. We must unite to overcome the resistance of our government. It is up to us, the common people, to move our society forward. Look at the things we see in this century. We must be ready for the Exhibition in May. I believe the duke is under pressure from the parliament to stop my display at any cost, so we must work even harder to have our product ready."

Zane thought her words sounded impressive but wondered at her sincerity.

"You are hardly a member of the common people, Madame Indigo de Vargas y Irausquínno. Your cliff top manor and the way you pander to the rich with your elegant holiday retreat speak otherwise to me. Your passion is admirable but what do you know of the people in the dark alleys and the lower-class hovels?"

Her eyes narrowed as she stared back at him.

"Don't take what you see at face value, Captain Dogooder. You may be in for a surprise or two." He watched as she turned back to the stove, lifting the pan and dropping it on the table with a loud crash.

"There is food here, if you are hungry," she said tersely.

He smiled to himself as she moved across to the bunks, kicking off her boots, before stretching out on the bottom bed. Her beauty intensified even as her temper flared.

"I would suggest you rest while you can, as we have a long night ahead. It will be a hot and uncomfortable trip. Luis is used to the humidity of the jungle. He will load the barge while we rest." She rolled over, turning her back to him.

Zane did not reply. He ignored the food congealing on the

stovetop and climbed to the top bunk mulling over the day's events and the enigma of Indigo de Vargas y Irausquínno.

* * * *

Zane appeared fascinated by the energy of the rainforest as Luis steered the barge along the side of the wide river. Indigo was well used to it and had too much on her mind to appreciate the beauty as she usually did. She loved the jungle, it appealed to her nature; it was much more liberating than the Cornish society where she had to maintain decorum…*most* of the time.

The heat and the expectation of danger around every corner made the jungle an exciting place to be. The water racing past the barge held her gaze as she lost herself in her thoughts and after a while, she glanced up to find Zane staring at the shoreline mesmerized by the scene in front of them. Festive parrots danced along the low hanging branches and black-capped capuchin monkeys chattered at them as they peered curiously through the leaves. Occasionally, a black-collared hawk with iridescent green wing feathers dove down from high above, pinning them with a steely gaze as he swooped past. The movement of the barge disturbed the river life as taricaya turtles popped their heads curiously above the surface to peer at them with sleepy eyes.

Contrasting with the natural beauty were occasional villages which Luis avoided, steering to the opposite side of the river, and the barge slipped by quietly, unnoticed by the occasional native on the shore. The electric motor propelled them through the water silently. Zane stared intently at the small villages as they slipped past.

"The twenty-first century and still the wealth of the elite has not been shared with all members of society," said Indigo.

As the sun disappeared behind the treetops, the jungle fell silent instantly and darkness was complete within minutes. Luis turned the barge into a small bay where the jungle thinned. After securing it by rope to a small pontoon, Luis walked along the bank, scanning the edge of the jungle and speaking quietly to himself. Indigo followed the light from his flashlight, moving along the mud on the riverbank.

"There has been a boat here today," Luis pointed to the riverbank. "See… there are marks in the mud and the broken vegetation?" His voice was concerned.

"They have gone now, but all the more reason for taking extra care," whispered Indigo. Fear clutched at her throat, but she tried to hide it. "There is something not right. Keep your ears and eyes open. We will work with one small light. Luis, we will take the back path to the plantation tonight, in case there is someone on the main track."

Luis nodded. *"Caminar en silencio"*

Indigo translated. "Luis agrees. We must walk silently."

After the small crates were loaded into three large hessian bags and water flasks were attached to their belts, Luis led them into the jungle and forged ahead. His flashlight provided a small pinprick of light for them to follow at a distance.

"Stay behind me and hold the back of my pack," Indigo whispered. Zane followed her closely, holding her pack as they pushed their way along the track for more than an hour. Rustling and scurrying in the trees edging the track kept them alert.

Indigo was about to call to Luis for a break when suddenly the light ahead disappeared. There was a short sharp cry, then silence. Indigo grabbed Zane, pulling him off the track. Dropping her backpack, she whispered urgently for him to follow her.

"Leave your bag here, be absolutely silent. Our lives depend on it. With a bit of luck, we may have been far enough away, and they think Luis was travelling alone."

Moving stealthily in the darkness, Indigo and Zane walked deep into the jungle. Using a small flashlight covered with a piece of hessian ripped from one of the bags, Zane held it low to light their way. Indigo bit back a scream as a snake with a circumference as thick as man's wrist slithered lazily across the path before them.

"God, this whole voyage is turning into a disaster," she muttered under her breath.

After another ten minutes, she pulled on Zane's arm. "We will take a brief rest. I only hope they weren't watching for us and didn't see the three of us on the boat. We will have to take the long climb to the plantation now. It is isolated, but I am sure no one can find it without following us." Her voice shook—she was concerned for Luis. He had been guiding her for the last few trips and although he was a private man, she knew he had a young family back in Ilo.

Zane reached out to her and pulled her into a close embrace and for a moment she leaned her head on his shoulder and accepted his concern. He rested his chin on top of her head and she closed her eyes; it was not often she allowed a man to offer her comfort.

"Come on." She pulled away impatient with her moment of weakness. "It is time to go or we will not have enough time to pick the blooms."

They set off again and climbed steadily for another hour in complete silence as Indigo led Zane along the familiar path. Occasionally, a glimmer of moonlight lit their way as the top of the rainforest canopy thinned.

"We are almost there," she said quietly. Stepping over a large log, the ground opened beneath her feet. Bouncing down the steep sides, Indigo screamed as she slid to the bottom of a deep pit. She lay winded on the soft leaves covering the base, groaning with frustration.

"Indigo, are you all right?" Zane's concerned voice came from above, his head silhouetted by the soft moonlight. "Damn it, answer me, woman. Can you hear me?"

"I'm all right," she called up to him. "I didn't realize we were so close to the plantation. This is one of our own traps."

Crawling around on her hands and knees, Indigo felt around for one of the ropes she knew was hidden in the pit. Seconds later, she choked back another scream. Her hands encountered a skull, sightless eyes staring up at her in the faint moonlight. Worms wound their way through the sunken eye sockets. Breathing slowly and deeply, she moved away from it and felt her way around the side of the pit, encountering more bones as she moved to the edge.

"You need to get me out of here quickly, Captain." she called, her voice shaking. "There should be ropes hidden in the log we stepped over just before I fell. Hurry."

The sound of his footsteps and muttered cursing drifted down to her and within minutes a rope snaked down the sides of the long drop. Tying the rope securely around her waist, she called up to him and Zane began to slowly pull her up. As she neared the edge of the pit, he took the full weight of her body, and it must have thrown him off balance. She began to slide back down as the rope slackened and she let loose with a string of profanities. The rope tightened as Zane took up the slack and she bounced against the side of the pit.

"Fuck!"

"Sorry." Zane adjusted the rope to her weight, and she grabbed for handholds on the side of the pit as he pulled her to the top. Soon her head and shoulders were above the edge of the pit and the muscles in her calves burned as she braced her legs against the sides and pushed with her toes as Zane pulled her up the last few feet.

As she clambered over the edge of the drop to the path, Zane tried to pull her close, but Indigo pushed him away. Backing away from the edge, she sat on the ground and pulled her legs up, lowering her head to her knees, trying to control the shaking of her limbs and fight the nausea rising in her throat

As she regained her composure, she looked up at Zane

who was hovering over her. "We are in danger, Captain. They have found their way to the plantation."

"Can you hear something? How do you know?"

"No, there are three bodies in the pit."

Chapter 4

Indigo and Zane sat silently on the log, each lost in their own thoughts, until the first fingers of sunlight touched the rainforest. Melodious birdsong contrasting with the rough barking of the spider monkeys surrounded them as the light filtered through the dense canopy above. Indigo moved across to the edge of the pit and looked down at the skeletons below.

"I am sure the bodies are evidence of a failed attempt to breach the plantation, but we must remain on guard," she warned. "We have dug pits around each of the entry points. Make sure you follow me closely when we go in."

Zane nodded. He'd barely said a word since they'd left the boat and she wondered what he was thinking about. His touch had been platonic as he'd checked her for injuries. She did not hurt anywhere and was confident she had suffered no ill effects from her fall. Indigo had sat quietly as his warm strong hands traversed her body, biting down on her cheek when her heartbeat picked up, warmth lingering where Zane touched her with gentle fingers. Her body trembled and she knew it had more to do with his touch than from the fall. The buzzing of mosquitoes interrupted her thoughts and she leaned over to pull the netting down on Zane's hat, covering his face and neck, before doing the same to her own.

"Jungle fever," she explained moving back from the edge of the pit. "We didn't have time to take the preventative pharmacological."

Within minutes the sun filtered through the treetops, lighting up the rainforest around them. Indigo moved to the perimeter of the trees and peered out through the dense foliage. All was still and the lack of movement reassured her intruders had not breached the plantation.

She reached for her water bottle, taking a large drink of the cold liquid.

"Ensure that you drink regularly as we work. The heat of the jungle will sap your energy and we must finish quickly. There is a waterfall on the other side of the plantation where we can replenish our bottles."

Zane's gaze held hers as he tipped the bottle to his mouth. Indigo looked steadily back at him, fascinated by the muscles in his strong throat working as he drank deeply.

"When we have picked the flowers, how will we carry them back? We left the bags at the beginning of the track." Zane's brow wrinkled in a frown.

Indigo looked away from him, wanting to touch him, yet angry at herself.

"We only need gather the stamens. We will have to forgo gathering the whole bloom this trip. The stamen will suffice but it is critical that we keep them in the light," she replied tersely. "Don't worry. I have it under control"

"I'm sure you do," he replied with a smile.

"It will be a long morning. We must risk harvesting in the heat so we can see what we are doing. We have to return to the *Artemis* before the time window closes." Indigo was worried and she stared off into the distance as she did the calculations. "If we miss the departure, it may be days before the window is available again. If only we could contact Mr. Grimoult, he could start working on another departure point."

Zane smiled at her, lifting his wrist as he tapped his chronometer. "I can contact Mr. Grimoult."

"What?" she asked not understanding what he said.

He nodded and repeated his words. "I can speak to Mr. Grimoult."

Indigo watched in disbelief as Zane flipped open the small cog on the side of the timepiece. A small rectangular platform rose from its center, doubling in size as it opened. A tiny brass handle joined a long shaft that ran the length of the rectangle, with a circular brass knob that made a clicking sound when depressed.

"Have you heard of Morse code?" Zane tapped the small contraption with the tip of his finger.

"Yes, it is a new navigational aid using a unique sequence of dots and dashes. But I thought it was done with light?" she questioned.

"That's correct. However, it also uses sound as a signal. When we were in the navy, Mr. Grimoult experimented with me and we managed to shrink the transmitters and insert them in our chronometers. We achieved a small measure of success and we were able to transmit and receive over long distances. I noticed Mr. Grimoult still wears his."

Indigo frowned. "But will there be interference from the technology of this time?"

"One way to find out. I will send a message to him now."

She watched him, her body tense, as he tapped a series of dots and dashes using the small platform. Zane sat silently, not taking his eyes from the chronometer, waiting for a return signal. Parrots screeched around them, swooping in and out of the treetops as the chronometer remained silent. After ten minutes, he shrugged.

"I hoped we would have success." He was obviously disappointed. "Come on, let's get started."

Indigo put her hand on his wrist. "It is a fascinating instrument. Thank you for trying."

There was a loud click and the small cogs on the side of the chronometer began to spin slowly, followed by a series of softer clicks. Zane put the timepiece close to his ear, listening intently. When the movement stopped, he grabbed Indigo, picked her up whirling her around.

"Are you out of your mind?" she said coldly. "I told you quite clearly not to touch me unless I invite you to." Her heart raced and she frowned at him.

"Sorry, Madame," Zane said, grinning at her. "It was my way of telling you that Mr. Grimoult has received our transmission. Full steam ahead, when you are ready, if you pardon the pun."

A quick circuit of the jungle perimeter around the plantation confirmed Indigo's certainty the plantation remained secure. Stepping from the shade of the jungle into the open plantation, the warm sunshine caressed them like the steam of a Turkish bathhouse. Indigo stopped, pointing at the cliffs ahead, covered with a mass of brilliant blue flowers in full bloom.

"The blue passionflower," she said proudly. "The plant is complex. It has five sepals and five petals similar in appearance, surrounded by the blue corona. Each plant has five yellow stamens and three purple stigmas. As I said before we will only be able to collect the stamens today." She walked to the base of the cliffs, before reaching up to pick a large bloom. "Unless by some miracle, Luis arrives with the containers."

Zane watched her as she gently held the stamen between her forefinger and thumb before removing it from the rest of the plant. He did not move or speak, standing silently with his arms crossed.

"Do you have a problem with that, Captain? It is a very simple process."

Zane kicked at the damp mulch beneath his feet, turning his back to her, arms still folded across his chest.

"Oh God, what now?" she asked crossly, moving around in front of him. She stared at him. "What on earth is the matter now?"

"Madame." Zane glared at her. "Your botanical knowledge is most impressive; however, I am struggling to understand why in God's name, we have travelled over two hundred years for the collection of this plant. I have seen it growing wild in our time, against sunny walls on the Cornish coast. Indeed, some of my voyages in the navy were to protect expeditions that brought back this same plant to the temperate gardens of Cornwall." He shook his head and his frustration was apparent.

"Place your trust in me, Captain. If you recall, you were commissioned solely, to pilot my submarine. It is necessary." Reaching to touch his arm, she smiled as Zane walked toward the vines. "Now we must commence work. And watch out for snakes."

The morning grew hotter and perspiration trickled down Indigo's back and her shirt stuck to her uncomfortably. Working their way through the plantation, she insisted Zane break regularly to drink plenty of water. Finally, they reached the plants at the base of the cliff and she waved to him, calling him to join her at the point where the vines snaked up the cliff face.

"Now, to answer one of your many questions, Captain." With a mischievous smile, Indigo continued. "Take off your shirt."

Zane did not move.

"Please," she added.

He pulled his shirt off over his head and Indigo fought for self-control as she gazed at the well-sculpted chest in front of her. Tearing her eyes away, she held her hands together, fighting the urge to run her fingers across the taut stomach where a V of dark hair snaked into his jeans. Smiling up at him, she knelt down, using her knife to slit his T-shirt open down one side, laying it flat on the ground. Gently lifting each stamen from the small pile gathered, Indigo placed them on the cotton fabric. "Now we only need a few more of the larger blooms that grow on the cliff face and we will have enough. Can you climb up there?"

Nodding, Zane climbed a couple of meters up the cliff face, gaining footholds in the twisted stems of the vine. Drinking the last of her water, Indigo watched as he carefully removed the stamens from the largest blooms that were tucked into a small crack and protected from the weather. He cradled them gently against his bare chest and he stretched out for those just beyond his reach. The muscles in his tanned back flexed when he reached for the highest passionflowers, and the now familiar warmth worked its way down to the juncture between her thighs.

Can I trust him?

He was certainly a fine physical specimen. The captain would make a pleasant addition to her enterprise and to her bed. Making a sudden decision, Indigo followed her instincts, calling up to him. "You have gathered enough, Captain. We must rest before we make our way back to the river before dark."

After carefully laying out the rest of the stamens on his T-shirt, where they would capture the full sunlight, she collected their water bottles and sauntered toward the cliff, beckoning Zane to follow her. She moved ahead of him and walked through the sheer cliff, slipping through the fissure in the rock face. His footsteps echoed behind her as he followed her through the opening in the cliff, which was wide enough for two people to walk abreast. Rainbows reflected off the sheer walls and the noise of flowing water surrounded them.

Stepping out onto a wide rock platform, Zane drew a deep breath as shafts of light from the afternoon sun turned the mighty river into a stream of molten gold below them. A magnificent vista of green jungle edged with the distant deep blue of the Pacific Ocean spread beyond the Amazon River. Steep rocky cliffs tumbled away beneath them and a fine mist rose from the surging water of the roaring waterfall cooling their overheated bodies. Indigo pointed eastward, where a high snow-capped mountain disappeared in the clouds.

"*Nevada Mismo*. The source of the Amazon." She smiled up at him." Now, I hope you are not prudish, sir, as I am in desperate need of a cooling shower." He couldn't take his eyes from her as she removed her boots, setting them aside in a dry corner. Her jeans, T-shirt and minuscule red undergarment quickly joined them before she strode across past him and stepped into the fine mist

She beckoned him with a tilt of her head. "You are more than welcome to join me." Stepping into the curtain of cascading water, she turned and smiled at him as he quickly placed his boots, clothes and chronometer on the ground before following her into the fine mist. The clear water cascaded over their bodies, icy cold from the snow that fed the waterfall.

Zane stepped toward her, his arms stiffly by his side. Holding her gaze, he sought permission. "Are you ready for my touch now, Indigo?"

She leaned over and kissed him hard, pushing her breasts into his bare chest and he gently turned her around. She arched back against him and he bent down to kiss the beauty spot on her shoulder.

"I have wanted to do that since I first saw you," he murmured.

Tangling her luxuriant hair in his hands, he pulled her head back, sliding his lips down her neck, and Indigo pressed herself against him.

"I need to touch you," she whispered softly. Turning, she wrapped her hands around the silken length of his manhood. A shudder rippled through him as she brushed him with fingers as light as a butterfly wing. He sighed and Indigo pushed him against the hard wall of the cave and lifted her legs, wrapping them high around him, opening to him.

"Now," she demanded her voice thick with lust. Zane followed her lead. He entered her and she trembled in his arms. Waves of pure pleasure washed over him when she shuddered, out of control as she reached the pinnacle of her pleasure. He continued to pleasure her and her breath mingled with his as he moved slowly until he could hold back no longer. A guttural cry left his lips as he climaxed and he closed his eyes, dropping his head on her shoulder and Indigo turned into him allowing his lips to slide down her neck. She loosened her hold on him as he bent, putting his arms under her knees. Zane picked her up, his strong arms easily carrying her across to the ferns growing beside the waterfall. He laid her gently in the soft greenery, using his tongue to master her mouth and body until Indigo begged for completion. Sated, he held her close and they dozed lightly for a short time.

Zane woke slowly, his muscles aching from the physical work in the plantation. Indigo turned to him and cupped his face in her hands before placing her lips gently on his.

"It is time to leave, Captain," she said, and he could hear the regret in her voice.

The cascading waters provided a cooling shower and quenched their thirst. They dressed quickly and made their way back to the plantation. Maracuja fruit picked from the vine at the base of the cliff satisfied their hunger. Crossing the plantation to the edge of the jungle, Zane sensed Indigo gradually withdraw from him as they prepared for the return journey. Carefully wrapping the stamens in his shirt, she reminded him of the need to keep them in the light.

"They must be opened and exposed to the sunlight at least once an hour. It is not long until sunset."

Sending a quick message to Mr. Grimoult letting him know of their success and imminent departure, Zane set the alarm cog on his chronometer to an hour hence. Setting off down the shorter path, he led the way ignoring the stinging of his skin when the thorny vices slashed his bare chest and arms. Indigo followed him quietly and did not speak. The trudged silently through the afternoon heat and descended the path more quickly than the trip up into the plantation.

Zane stopped suddenly, pulling Indigo off the track into the jungle as a loud buzzing intruded on their senses. She pushed him away with both hands flat on his scratched chest. He glared back at her, grabbed her shoulders and sat her on the trunk of a fallen tree.

"Stay there, Madame." He spoke quietly but firmly and passed her the shirt containing the stamens. "The hour is almost up. Make use of the time to give them some light." Indigo's mouth dropped open. He smiled when she obeyed him without argument.

Zane crept silently along the edge of the trail; he was satisfied that Indigo was safe on the log. He slowed, and the hairs on the back of his neck rose as a sweet smell drifted across his to him. He moved closer to the source of the noise. Carefully making a break in the foliage at the edge of the path, he peered out through the gap and gagged as the bile hit his throat.

A body lay sprawled across the track, the throat slit from ear to ear. Black congealed blood circled the gaping throat like a macabre necklace. Luis was almost unrecognizable; the intense heat of the jungle and the carrion feeding on the body had rendered it to a pulp. Huge black army ants marched through his eyes, mouth and nostrils. Zane turned back to the jungle, silently making his way back across the slippery ground. Indigo sat quietly, the stamens spread around her in the filtered sunlight, as she stared into the distance. Her beauty contrasted with the ugly scene further down the path. Zane's stomach tightened, and protective warmth surging through him. Pushing herself up from the log, Indigo turned to face him, her arms folded across her chest.

"Well?" she demanded but her face was pale.

Zane walked slowly toward her and sat on the log dropping his head to his hands. Indigo reached over, the warmth of her hand clutching at his bare shoulder, soothed him.

"Luis?"

"Yes." Zane closed his eyes, unable to block the horrific sight from his mind.

"Is it safe?"

"I think so. There is no sign of anyone, but we must take

great care." Zane pulled her close, burying his face in her hair.

Lifting her head, Indigo said, "I think it may be best if we go back the long way."

Zane nodded. "I think that would be best." He did not want her to see the putrefied remains of her guide.

* * * *

It took them three hours to complete the return trip. Arriving back at the small bay, hot and tired, they stood in the deep cover of the thick foliage and Indigo sagged with relief when she saw the barge was still tied to the pontoon.

"Thank God," she breathed.

The cacophony of the jungle disappeared as the sun slipped under the horizon. Indigo's limbs trembled with exhaustion, but Zane insisted on waiting until it was dark before they left the cover of the jungle. Indigo followed him quietly to the barge. Dropping silently onto the deck, he moved across to the motor.

"Damn. The motor has been sabotaged. They have ensured if Luis had company, no one could leave."

"You're the mariner," Indigo whispered in frustration. "What do we do now?" She disliked feeling helpless and being dependent on another, especially a man did not sit comfortably with her.

"Wait here." Zane disappeared up the muddy bank before she could stop him.

A few moments later, he scrambled down the bank carrying two long sticks.

"We'll pole down the river. The current will be with us on the way back." He passed one of the long sticks over. "I trust you have some strength left to help?"

"I will try," she replied shortly.

Zane pushed the barge away from the bank using the pole to steer out into middle of the river. The swift current swept them along and all was quiet in the villages they passed. The moon rose and the small bays and inlets were faintly visible to them, and it was with great relief that Indigo finally recognized the bay where their journey had begun.

She grabbed his arm and pointed before they swept passed it and Zane turned the barge into the short pier. Indigo slumped, exhausted, across the back of the barge, and carefully cradled the stamens as he secured the boat. He held out a gentle hand her to as she stepped onto the bank and she grasped on to him tightly as he led their way to the deserted building.

* * * *

Zane woke with a start when the morning orchestra of the jungle roused him from a deep sleep. Rolling over, he peered down to the lower bunk where Indigo was still fast asleep. After swinging down off the top bed, he gently shook her bare shoulder, running his fingers down the scratches on her arm. Indigo woke slowly, her face rosy with sleep. Smiling sweetly as she reached for him, she pulled him down for a most satisfying meeting of their lips.

"Thank you, Captain Dogooder, you worked hard yesterday." Her lips were soft against his and he pulled back reluctantly, aware they had to leave soon.

As Indigo used the radio in the building to contact the expedition base and advise them of Luis' fate, Zane carefully packed the stamens into two plastic crates from the storage area. He groaned softly when he reached into the back of the Land rover; his muscles sore from the exertion of the day before. Pulling on an old shirt he found in the back of the vehicle, Zane smiled at the look on Indigo's face as she came out of the building.

"At least it covers the scratches," he said.

She seemed very unsure of him since their tryst under the waterfall. Although she now accepted his decisions, he was still wary of her temper.

Unease settled in his chest when she climbed into the

driver's seat. "Are you able to drive one of these vehicles?"

"As you are unable to drive—" she snapped "—I will have to manage. Come on, we are running out of time."

The acceleration pushed Zane back in his seat when she pressed the pedal to the floor. He put both hands over his eyes as the Land Rover slewed toward a steep ravine. Indigo held tightly to the steering wheel, her knuckles white, as the vehicle slid sideways down the steeper hills. A couple of times, when it shuddered sideways through the corrugations on the road, Zane gripped the sides of the seat. Each time he cringed, Indigo threw her head back, laughing as she took great delight in his reaction.

"Keep your eyes on the track, woman," he growled. "We have come this far. I don't want to die in a vehicle that's not even steam-powered."

Her driving skills and the steep descent enabled them to complete their journey down the mountain road in a much shorter time than the outward journey.

"What time is it?" Indigo slowed the vehicle as the outskirts of the township appeared. "See if you can raise Mr. Grimoult for a revised departure time."

Zane did not move and looked across at her.

"Please," she added.

He flipped open the chronometer and a series of dots and dashes clicked away. The reply was instant.

"First window for departure is in twelve minutes—" he said as the clicks continued "—and the next is in forty-eight hours."

"Tell him to surface now. We can make it." She accelerated and shouted a warning at him. "Hang on to your hat, captain."

His head hit the back of the seat as the vehicle surged forward. "I'm not wearing a hat."

Their progress slowed as they approached the town center. It was market day in the portside town, with crowds of shoppers spilling onto the road. Colourful stalls lined the footpaths and animals wandered along with their herders, blocking the road. Children darted in and out of the stalls, forcing Indigo to slow the vehicle to a crawl.

"Jesus, Jesus, Jesus," Indigo muttered under her breath. Spotting a gap between two stalls, she swung the vehicle between them driving down a narrow alleyway. With barely an inch to spare between the vehicle and the walls of the building, she turned onto the main road toward the harbor.

"We will have to leave the vehicle at the marina. We don't have time to secure it." She planted the accelerator once more. "Climb over to the back and get the stamens,'' she ordered. "Please," she added with a quick glance at him.

She swung the vehicle into the car park of the marina, narrowly missing two men standing on each side of the entry. Stopping close to the water's edge, Indigo jumped out of the vehicle and Zane passed her one of the crates. Clutching them, they ran for the end of the pier. Suddenly, shouts and thudding footsteps came from behind them. A ray of light whistled past Indigo's head, bouncing off the post in front of her. It exploded in a white flash. She screamed at Zane.

"Run—run quickly, they have ray guns!"

A cloud of steam rose in front of them, and they ran into the fog, which hid them from their pursuers. The brass fin of the *Artemis* broke the water at the end of the pier and Indigo grabbed for Zane's hand and they jumped for their lives as a stream of rays flashed past their heads.

Chapter 5

Indigo stood quietly in the doorway of the guest room, looking across at the four-poster bed. The side curtains were open, and Zane's body was hidden beneath the covers. His soft breathing broke the silence as she moved across the room closer to the bed. Black hair and tanned skin contrasted with the virginal white of the feather pillows and the soft lace edgings of the covers were at odds with the angry scratches on the side of his face.

Indigo moved across to the side of the bed, and she watched him sleep.

I must take care. This man is dangerous to me in more ways than I could possibly have imagined.

Strength of character, integrity and a gentle nature. A dangerous combination.

Indigo enjoyed flouting acceptable social norms and was frequently criticized by members of high society. This afforded great amusement to her as those same people did not hesitate to make use of her elite holiday facilities. Now, she remained wary of the relationship forged with the captain over the past two days. Zane respected her opinions and challenged her, which was a new experience for her. Nevertheless, she was not going to pass up the opportunity of a handsome man in a bed in her guest room, particularly after experiencing such a pleasant interlude at the waterfall.

Pulling back the covers, Indigo climbed into the bed beside him. She sighed with pleasure when her legs encountered the roughness of warm, hair-covered limbs. Zane woke slowly as she pressed her breasts to his side, and Indigo looked up to meet dark eyes, still hazy with sleep. "Good morning, my captain. I trust you slept well?"

Her captain smiled down at her. "I did, Madame."

"I have a proposition I wish to discuss with you."

"Hmm," he murmured as his mouth moved toward hers. "And this discussion could not wait until we breakfasted?"

"Perhaps I have two propositions," she murmured against his lips. "I believe we can get one out of the way before we rise."

Before he could answer, Indigo climbed across and straddled him. Reaching up, she pulled the red lace nightgown over her head and threw it aside. He was instantly ready for her, cupping a full breast in each hand as she flung her head back, letting her tight, wet womanhood accept him. She arched to meet each possessive thrust and he delved deeper into her with each rhythmic movement. Urgent hands held her hips and she leaned down to him, gazing at dark, dark eyes, enjoying the feel of the smooth ripple of muscle beneath warm bare skin. Indigo moved against him, hot, wet and abandoned as her pleasure increased. She cried out with unabashed delight as she reached her final shattering release, sucking in gasps of air as spasms of delight rocked through her. Zane quickly followed, groaning long and low as his pulsing life flooded her. Lying side by side, their laboured breathing gradually returned to normal.

"May I ask what the second proposition is, Madame?" Exploring fingers trailed down her body and Indigo turned to him, aware of her breasts pushed against his hard, muscled chest.

"Unfortunately, dear captain, the second proposition is of a business nature. We must not dally any longer as we have much to do."

Indigo ran her fingers along the scratches on his arms. "And this is the first thing we must deal with. Before we do, I need to tell you a little more about our venture."

She sat up and leaned against the feather pillows as her fingers played idly with his hair.

"My father was a forward-thinking man for his time and spent his life experimenting with pharmacologicals. He had experimented with the healing properties of the passionflower and was killed just as he discovered the strength of the blooms from the future."

She paused and looked down at Zane.

"I have continued and expanded his research. Mr. Grimoult was on the navy ship that escorted the last expedition to the Amazon and was the only other person privy to the knowledge that my father had overcome the temporal barriers." She pushed the covers back, rose from the bed and walked across to the window. On the same level as the viewing room the magnificent vista overlooked the stormy sea.

"My younger sister, Sofia has vowed to continue his work with the moonflower once she leaves her school in Paris and I am determined to see his work with the passionflower come to fruition at the Great Exhibition." She held both hands out to him. "Are you now satisfied why we had to travel to the future to get the last of the blooms?"

Zane reached up to her with a lazy smile on his face

"I am very satisfied, Madam."

When she arose for the second time that morning, Indigo led Zane to a small room adjacent to the guest room to draw a hot bath. There were washrooms beside each bedroom in her manor, as she paid more attention to personal hygiene than was the social norm. Zane joined her for a most pleasurable bath in steaming hot water pumped from the intricate brass faucets. A steam device for warming the drying cloths interested the captain greatly.

"Designed by Mr. Grimoult," Indigo explained. "He has developed many devices since his retirement. I am most fortunate to have him in my employ."

Opening an ornate marbled cabinet, Indigo withdrew a small glass vial filled with a pale blue lotion. She inserted a wooden spatula, smearing it with the sweet-smelling lotion. "Hold out your arms," she requested. "You will be about to experience the healing properties of the blue passionflower.”

Mrs. Grimoult was laying the breakfast dishes onto the warming tray as the captain and Indigo entered the breakfast room together. Indigo glared as she saw her housekeeper wink at Mr. Grimoult and the little woman returned to her kitchen with a wide smile on her face.

“Mr. Grimoult, would you join us for breakfast? I would like you to advise me of the progress in the laboratory.”

“Certainly, Madame.” The little man took a seat at the table with them as Mrs. Grimoult bustled back in with a large coffee pot.

“The product we brought back last night has already been delivered to the laboratory. The first process has been completed overnight,” he advised.

“Good, we are not too far behind schedule if that is the case.” Indigo turned, inhaling with pleasure as the aroma of freshly brewed coffee filtered across the table. She frowned at Mrs. Grimoult, who scurried back to the scullery, a guilty look on her face.

“I often wonder who is in charge of our household and voyages? It appears your wife found time for a foray to the market at Ilo?”

Mr. Grimoult suddenly found the contents of his plate desiring his whole attention, squirming uncomfortably in the chair. “We took the utmost care, Madame. We were only on the surface long enough for Mrs. Grimoult to disembark.”

“No matter, all is well,” replied Indigo. She turned to Zane. “Captain, if you accept my proposition, one of the side benefits is the fine cuisine Mrs. Grimoult creates from the exotic ingredients she collects on our voyages.”

Indigo poured more coffee. “Captain, pull up your sleeves and show us your injuries.” Zane removed the chronometer, rolled back the cuffs of his fine linen shirt, eyes narrowing. Not a mark remained where the many scratches and cuts had covered his arms the previous day.

"The passionflower lotion?"

"Yes." Indigo smiled. "Now, my dear captain, I would like to thank you for your perseverance and loyalty on our recent adventure. It will not go unrewarded."

Zane looked at her for a long moment without speaking. He finally nodded at her, his face expressionless. "I do not seek reward, Madame, in any shape or form." His voice lingered on the word 'shape.' Mrs. Grimoult smothered another smile. Indigo glared at them all as Mr. Grimoult cleared his throat loudly, looking embarrassed.

Examining his clear skin, Zane continued. "However, I can see you are much further advanced than I thought. The comptroller general believes you are illegally importing flowers for your complex. They have no idea that you are involved in pharmacological production, but--"

She interrupted him, thumping her fist on the table. "No, Captain, it is not about flowers or pharmacologicals. My quest is to fight against despotic governance, and their oppression of any new pharmacologicals that can help our population improve their health, whether they be rich or poor. If you are willing, we can work together. That is my proposition, for you to join our cause and unite with me." Zane began to speak but Indigo held up her hand. "Before you decide, I will show you our laboratory. Come."

Zane clutched at his stomach when the perambulator dropped quickly. Cogs whirred loudly as the door slid open to reveal a large scientific laboratory. Several workers in red coats glanced up curiously and nodded at their mistress. She returned their acknowledgment with a brief lift of her hand and they continued working.

The laboratory ran the entire length of the manor. Not a bit clinical in appearance, its decor in keeping with the rest of the rooms; the walls were embellished with vivid colours and textures.

Small groups of workers conducted experiments in each corner of the laboratory. A high glass wall facing the east allowed the morning sunlight to stream in, reflecting from a huge mirror on the ceiling, bathing row upon row of glass terrariums with sunlight. Large glass tanks filled with a variety of plants lined the side walls, overhung with tubular glass containers filled with the familiar blue passionflower vines.

"As you can see, the tropical temperature is maintained by the steam pipes." Mr. Grimoult directed Zane's attention to the ceiling where an intricate arrangement of brass piping protruded from each corner.

"When the light is poor, we supplement it with luminiferous aether, the same principle we used on the *Artemis*."

Indigo walked across the room, beckoning Zane to follow. "Captain, look at this." In the far corner of the laboratory a botanist in a white coat worked with a series of glass paraphernalia filled with steaming liquid. "This is the main production area. Once the stamen is broken down it undergoes a process to extract the elixir, the main ingredient of our pharmacologicals."

The botanist ignored them and tipped a clear solution into a beaker. As it filled, he looked across at Mr. Grimoult. "Sir, I would ask that you speak to the captain of the submarine. The stamens were in poor condition. It looked as though they had been carried by hand."

"Ahem." Mr. Grimoult stuttered. "There was a slight difficulty experienced on the voyage. I will speak to the crew and ensure all future shipments are in top condition for you."

"Come, gentlemen, we shall return to our discussion." Indigo led them back to the perambulator. As she entered the breakfast room, Mrs. Grimoult handed Indigo two sealed parchments. "A messenger has delivered these for your attention, Madame."

Indigo opened the first way and groaned. "Oh no, it is

Sofia."

Mrs. Grimoult looked up with concern. "Is she all right?"

"Probably," replied Indigo. "I do not know why pay exorbitant fees to that school in Paris. They cannot keep track of their students. She has disappeared…again."

Mrs. Grimoult smiled, and Zane appeared to be following the exchange with interest. Indigo turned to him to explain.

"My half-sister has an interest in the *haute couture* and would prefer to be in a draper's shop rather than at school getting a fully rounded education."

Mrs. Grimoult interrupted. "To be fair to your sister, Madame, it is Gagelin and Opigez and she is with her friends."

Indigo snorted. "I would prefer her to be at school. Anyway, enough of my sister. If she does not return, I am sure they will send another letter." She held out her hand to Mrs. Grimoult. "The other missive please?" Indigo quickly broke the seal after Mrs. Grimoult handed her the thick parchment, reading the message. "Hmm. A summons from the comptroller general. There is a meeting where I am to present my plans for the Great Exhibition. He wishes to ensure the local borough is adequately represented."

"That is a positive move." Mr. Grimoult nodded.

"It is. However, the comptroller has neglected to give much notice for the meeting. It is to be held this evening at the Market House in Tin Town."

"Shall I prepare the scarab, Madame?"

"Please have it ready by four o'clock, Mr. Grimoult."

Mrs. Grimoult turned to Zane. "Oh, I am sorry, Captain, there was a message for you also."

Quickly scanning his message, Zane looked at Indigo. "I will also be out this evening." Indigo regarded him, curious as to the nature of his business.

"Do not fear, Madame. You can trust me. I am committed

to your cause and will do my utmost to support you in completing your project for the Great Exhibition."

* * * *

Indigo drove slowly down the coast, enjoying the time alone. She parked the vehicle on a grassy knoll overlooking one of the scenic coves edging the ocean and sat for a time, pondering the dilemma she faced with the captain. For a change, the water was calm and had a tinge of blue reflected from the clear sky. As usual she drew her strength from the water and a peaceful calm descended on her.

She had no doubts about the captain's support. He had proven himself repeatedly during their adventures in the jungle. Her strong attraction to the man caused her most concern but she would not let that interfere with her quest. There was still much to complete; a dalliance may interfere with her ambition. Usually, her sexual conquests were purely for the fulfillment of her physical needs. This emotional connection concerned her greatly. Indigo did not know how to proceed.

It will prove dangerous to my well-being. I will leave him be from now on.

A slight wind blew in form the water and a few small whitecaps began to appear on the glassy sea. Indigo sighed. For the first time since her father died, she felt a connection to another person and was unsure how to proceed. She forced the confusing thought away and pulled the bras starter and the scarab rose and sped swiftly above the road to Tin Town.

The blood red sun dipped behind the horizon sending fingers of deep red across the twilight sky just as she brought the vehicle to a halt in the High Street. Indigo shivered and hoped it was not a premonition of ill to come.

Throwing her brass goggles on the seat beside her, she gathered up her papers and strode out for the Market Hall under the light of gas lamps piercing the shadowy darkness of the street. The

77

town looked grim and dirty as always. She placed the scarab controller in her small dilly bag, feeling in the side pocket for her knife. Her fingers closed over it and the cold blade reassured her. Goose bumps prickled down her arms and the hair rose on the back of her neck and she turned swiftly. A cold wind blew from the west, pushing leaves along the ground, the dry rustling breaking the eerie quiet. A blast of steam from the warming pipes in the gutter sent mice scurrying for cover, and a couple of dollymops leaned against the wall on the corner behind The Rattling Cat, waiting for customers.

Indigo entered the front door and was surprised to find the hall empty with no furniture set up for a meeting. The back of her neck prickled again. More mice scurried into the dark corners as she made her way across the large room, her footsteps echoing on the wooden floorboards. She put her hand back into the small bag, clasping the handle of her knife.

Something did not feel right.

Looking around, a large mouse moved slowly toward her. She watched as it rose on its back legs, and its features took on the face of Mr. Brixton as the mouse got closer to her, devilish intent wrinkling his pointy face.

A shape shifter! Lorca, you will stoop to any level.

Spinning around, she saw two more mice rise to their back legs as the trap closed around her. She spun back, throwing her right leg out in a strong kick, hitting Mr. Brixton on the chin, knocking him to the ground. The little man squealed as he hit the floor hard, rolled over to the dark corner, bouncing off the brick wall. She ran for the door as one of the other men lunged at her, grabbing her around the waist with furry hands.

She bit. She slashed. She screamed. No holds barred, she fought dirty.

Her life depended on it. Using her fingernails, she grunted with satisfaction as skin ripped beneath them. Her adversary released her as she ran for the road, pulling the scarab controller from her bag.

Damnation. Her vehicle was gone.

Turning swiftly, she saw three men heading toward her. Brixton brought up the rear, limping. As she looked at him, the little man raised a small ray gun, pointing it at her head and she dropped her papers, pulling her knife from her boot as she jumped to the left. She ducked and weaved, running for her life, grateful for the sturdy boots under her loose, flowing skirt. She pounded down the street past the Rattling Cat, egged on by the screaming of the dollymops. Light rays from Mr. Brixton's gun bounced off the buildings around her and small clumps of brick rubble fell to the ground.

"Run, sweetheart. Run!" The high-pitched excited squeals followed her as she ran. A string of curses sounded behind her as the two women stepped in front of her pursuers.

"Fancy a bit of skirt, gentlemen?"

The men pushed them aside roughly, running after Indigo as the women cheered her on. The delay gave her enough time to get around the corner to the next street. She turned her head from side to side, searching for a hiding place. The top of a massive oak tree rose behind the houses in the laneway at the end of the street. Running to the end of the street, Indigo crouched behind the steam pump on the footpath, watching the men come around the corner. They looked up and down the street and exchanged a few words before they split up and began searching down the short alleyways. Waiting until the three men were all out of sight, Indigo sprinted for the corner, throwing the scarab controller over a garden fence as she ran past. Heart pounding and dry-mouthed, she swung up onto the lowest branch of the tree, quickly pulling herself up the branches, thanking her stars for her childhood tree climbing exploits with Sofia. She laid flat on the widest branch near the top, hidden amongst the foliage, tucking her loose skirt beneath her legs and the footsteps of her pursuers pounded on the macadam under the tree as they neared the end of the street. Brixton gave a triumphant cry as he spotted the scarab controller in the garden. Pushing open the front gate with a loud clanging noise, he pounded on the front door of the house, demanding entry in the name of Duke Lorca in his little squeaky voice.

"Bugger off, or I will send for the constabulary." A querulous old voice berated them. They argued loudly about which way to go before moving away and their words faded, but Indigo suspected one of them stayed close, lingering quietly in a garden at the end of the street, not far from the base of her hiding place.

She closed her eyes and stayed still and silent, the cold hard branch pressing against her back as she thought up horrific payback for Leopold Lorca. Minutes passed and their voices floated up to her as the three men headed back to the township. She smiled with grim satisfaction at the frustration she could hear.

"You can tell the duke we lost her, Brixton. I'm not going to"

"Where did she go?" Indigo recognized Brixton's voice.

"We'll tell him she's a witch," the other man replied. Indigo bit her lips to stop herself laughing aloud.

Fools. They were not the brightest of henchmen, shape shifters or not.

"The duke is going to be extremely displeased." Brixton's voice wavered and he sounded close to tears. Indigo smiled to herself, imaging Lorca's displeasure as their voices faded away. She lay back on the branch, looking at the stars in the cloudless sky above as she waited for rescue.

* * * *

At the same time as Indigo entered the Market Hall, the captain was on the suspension bridge to Duke Lorca's castle. Zane clung grimly to the rope as the bridge swayed precariously beneath him above the massive drop to the wild sea below. Duke Lorca watched him through the monocular device on the parapet and spoke to the man standing next to him as they laughed together, watching Captain Dogooder fight his way across the swaying bridge.

"If you didn't wish to speak to him urgently, I would take great pleasure in dropping the bridge and watching her brother fall onto the rocks."

"He is not her brother, you fool."

The duke's jaw dropped as he lowered the telescope, glaring at the comptroller general. "Don't you…how dare…" Leopold spluttered.

"Captain Dogooder is my man and I have summoned him to report on what he has found. Her crew is in the lockup and he has infiltrated her business. I suspect, knowing the captain and his reputation with the ladies, he may also have infiltrated Madame Vargas." He laughed loudly at his own joke. "However, I suspect there is more to Madame Vargas than we have seen. We shall see whether the Captain can be trusted or not. I have information from the laboratory, and we shall see if Captain Dogooder lives up to his name"

The duke spluttered and stammered as he searched for words.

"Enough, man. Captain Dogooder will be at the door in a moment. If you want her space at the Great Exhibition, you will do as I say." His steely gaze left the duke speechless. A peremptory knocking heralded the arrival of a manservant who bowed to the duke.

"Your Grace, a Captain Thoreau is here asking for an audience with you."

"He may enter," said the duke, pulling himself up straight and retrieving some of his dignity.

The captain sauntered through the door and stood looking at the two men awaiting him. His face was expressionless, and he bowed to the duke before nodding at his employer. "Your Grace. Sir."

"Good evening, Captain. I hope you have much to report?" asked the comptroller.

The duke led them to a large table covered with parchments. The comptroller pulled an ornate timepiece from his pocket to check the time. "Madame de Vargas will be with us shortly. Duke Lorca has kindly arranged her accommodation in his dungeon." He smiled in anticipation of her arrest looking across at the captain as if to gauge his reaction. "Now, please tell me what information you have gathered over the past two days."

"Madame de Vargas is importing flowers to develop in her conservatory. She is determined to replicate many tropical environments in her tourist biomes. Despite her outstanding looks and her hard demeanour, Madame is not very clever. The man known as Mr. Grimoult, who is her manservant, is the organizer of the enterprise. Madame de Vargas merely provides the wealth and the exotic persona."

The comptroller looked hard at him. "Captain, did you see any sign of a laboratory in the manor house or in the biomes?"

"No, sir. Madame Vargas took me on extensive tours of the whole complex over the past two days. There is no laboratory there. She would have been vain enough to brag about it. I only saw conservatories for propagation."

The comptroller looked across at the duke, nodding, and the beady eyes of Duke Lorca glistened. Zane looked up, with surprise on his face, as Lorca's face started to shrink and disappear. The large rat jumped onto Zane's arm, sinking his sharp incisors into the captain's wrist. The comptroller smiled at the duke as Zane slumped in the chair.

"Now, we will await the arrival of Madame Vargas. I shall get the truth. It is obvious this man has sold himself to that woman." said the comptroller general. "I shall enjoy this very much."

* * * *

Indigo was still lying on the hard branch at the top of the tree. The town had bedded down for the night, cottages gradually dimming their lights until eventually the whole town was in darkness. She had been entertained for a short time when one of the dollymops looked after the needs of a sailor with great enthusiasm and much giggling at the base of the tree. As midnight approached, her limbs had become unbearably stiff as the cold seeped through her clothing, but she did not move in case a mouse or man remained on watch below.

"Duke Lorca, you are a dead man," Indigo promised silently.

A carriage cruised slowly through the streets of the town. Looking down, she recognized one of the vehicles from her manor driving along the cobbled street. She carefully climbed down from the tree and waited for Mr. Grimoult to stop the vehicle beside her.

"Not a successful meeting, I presume, Madame?" he commented.

"No, Mr. Grimoult, and the curs have also taken my scarab." She climbed into the old-fashioned steam-powered carriage. "They shall pay for that as well."

Fog surrounded them as the vehicle slowly made its way above the country lanes toward the manor. Mrs. Grimoult met them in the foyer, wringing her hands before she locked each of the cogs on the massive door behind them.

"We have more bad news, Madame. The captain has not returned. As you instructed, I followed him, and he made his way to Castle Lorcathian. I also observed the conveyance of the comptroller general enter from the ocean into the castle earlier today."

Indigo pondered Mrs. Grimoult's news. "Do you think we need a second rescue for the night? Or have I trusted too well?"

83

"Madame, I believe Captain Dogooder is solid. I have no doubt he is a loyal servant. Your captain will not betray us," said Mr. Grimoult.

"All right then, Mr. Grimoult. I will change and we will embark on another rescue mission. Would you please prepare the air capsule?" She strode through the manor house, heading for her rooms.

Shortly after, Indigo emerged from her dressing room dressed in her aviator's suit, her black hair confined under a tight helmet, making her unrecognizable. Dials covered the sides of the helmet, with a small mouthpiece extending from a flap on the front chin piece. She carried a small ray gun, agreeing with Mr. Grimoult's assessment of the situation.

Rescue may prove difficult.

"Are you sure you are up to this, Madame?" Mrs. Grimoult held her hands together tightly.

"Molly." Indigo bent to the housekeeper to reassure her. "If you remember, I spent half my childhood up a tree with Sofia. It takes more than one night in a tree to give me the vapors."

She had told Mr. Grimoult of the shape shifting earlier that night, but she did not want to worry the little housekeeper any further.

"Time to leave." Indigo headed for the vehicle storage room on the lower level of the manor house. She stepped up the ramp to a compact air capsule with Mr. Grimoult close behind. He closed the door up as Indigo hit the keyboard of a small analytical engine mounted next to the controls. A small map of the duke's house appeared on the screen and she scanned each room with a click of the optical device. All was quiet, with no sign of activity.

"Are you certain the captain entered the castle, Mr. Grimoult?"

"Yes, Madame. Mrs. Grimoult followed him. The castle has been under observation since he arrived. He has not left, by road, air or sea. Your captain is still in there."

"There must be a room we do not have access to via the time viewer. Would you please position the ship in the air space on the western side of the castle?"

A loud hiss of steam sounded and pushed the ship upward vertically, and they exited the building through an opening in the large tower on the ocean side of them manor. The air capsule crossed the open fields between the manor and the castle. With another hiss it turned toward the ocean before hovering high above the western wall of Castle Lorcathian. Indigo entered their coordinates into the machine and grunted with satisfaction.

"Found him. He is in the dungeon, but it will be difficult to access him there. I need a diversion."

Anger filled her as the figures on the screen moved. The comptroller moved closer to Zane, who was strapped to a chair, straining at the leather that confined his arms and legs.

"Not much longer, my sweet." Indigo murmured. "Leave him alone, you cowards."

The duke appeared on the screen, advancing toward the captain with a large magnet in his hand. Lorca moved it in and out of Zane's vision.

"Fuck, what are they doing now?" Indigo cursed soundly as Zane's head slumped and his eyes closed. The comptroller walked across, speaking to him and she saw Zane's lips move in response. She understood and reacted instantly. Turning to Mr. Grimoult, she spoke urgently. "We must move quickly. Drop me onto the parapet and create a diversion on the lower level on the eastern side." As she spoke, Indigo looped a rappelling rope around her suit, tying a double figure eight fisherman's knot under her breasts. She attached the ray gun to her belt and Mr. Grimoult secured the other end of the rope to a large brass hook on the opening of the airship. Before Mr. Grimoult could acknowledge her request, Indigo jumped, landing on the parapet thirty feet below.

Holding the airship steady until the rope detached, Mr. Grimoult then steered it to the far side of the castle. Within seconds, Indigo heard a loud crash followed by the ominous braying of the fog horn on the air capsule as it sent a continuous beam of sound down into the castle. She smiled grimly, pulling herself through a narrow opening in the castle wall.

They had always worked well together. She would trust Mr. Grimoult with her life.

Removing the ray gun from her belt, she moved silently through the maze of corridors winding down to the dungeon. Footsteps pounded above her, confirming the majority of the inhabitants of the castle were making their way to the eastern parapet to find the source of the commotion Mr. Grimoult was creating with the air horn. Indigo flattened herself against the wall and peered around the corner as the duke stepped onto the parapet. Creeping along, she quietly closed the door behind him and drew the bolt.

Making her way down to the lower level, she paused and listened at each closed door. The captain's voice came from behind the second last door. She listened, smiling as the comptroller said angrily, "I don't care about a fucking tattoo, man. Now tell me, what is she producing? We know she has a laboratory in her manor. Why did you lie?"

She grinned as Zane muttered sleepily. "The tattoo, I get the tattoo."

A sharp slapping sound of skin on skin hastened her entry. Opening the door, Indigo held the ray gun in front of her, entering the room silently. Zane and the comptroller were alone. She flinched as he slapped Zane across the face once more, calling over his shoulder. "Leopold, where are your instruments of torture?"

Indigo slipped up behind him, placed the gun at the side of his neck, speaking quietly. "Will this do, sir?"

His knees buckled and the comptroller put up no resistance,

he was a man of words and administration, not of action and obviously a coward as well.

"Untie him." She pushed the gun onto his neck. "Now."

With shaking hands, the comptroller undid the shackles holding Zane to the chair.

"Now lift him out." Indigo pushed the gun harder into the soft skin, beneath his ear. A slight hesitation and she touched the trigger lightly. As the smell of his burning flesh wafted across the room, the comptroller cooperated instantly. After a moment, Zane stood beside her, looking at her with a silly grin on his face. In a low voice, she continued and pointed to the chair. "Now, sit yourself down, and bind your feet and one hand."

Finally satisfied the comptroller was secure, Indigo put the gun in her belt, quickly binding his other hand. A loud banging and cries of rage filtered through the narrow window from the parapet above and Indigo turned to Zane.

"They have discovered they are trapped outside."

The captain looked at her, his eyes unfocused "The tattoo."

Realizing the mesmerizer still had the captain enthralled, Indigo looked around for the magnet. Finding it on the table, she smiled at Zane, and passed it quickly from side to side in front of his eyes. He woke instantly, looking at her, the confusion fading almost immediately. Reaching across to him, Indigo kissed him swiftly on the mouth.

"The tattoo, Captain?" Laughing, she grabbed his hand. "Come quickly, follow me."

Winding their way down to the water level via a circular staircase, they discovered the exit door at the base was locked. Footsteps clattered down the stairs behind them and Zane gently pushed Indigo to the side of the stairway. Before she could blast the door open with her ray gun, he flicked open the chronometer, twirling the large cog in the centre. There was a loud click and it swung open.

"I want one of those." Indigo grinned up at him.

"I want an air suit like yours," Zane replied with a smile.

The comptroller's submersible floated in the entry bay. The door to the ocean was open, ready for the boat to depart. They jumped on board and Leopold appeared on the dock just as the craft roared through the opening out into the rough water. Indigo took great pleasure in taking shots at the duke with her ray gun before pulling the cover closed prior to submersing in the comptroller's ship.

"One for each hour I lay in on that hard branch, Leopold." She laughed with delight as the duke jumped and danced to avoid the rays zinging around his short legs. Zane hit the cog on the chronometer once more and the steam powered door slammed closed. Indigo watched the duke disappear from sight, his little legs still jumping and twitching.

Chapter 6

The efforts of the duke and his henchman to end Indigo's preparation for the Great Exhibition failed and they did not attempt to interfere with her enterprise again. A very satisfactory debrief after Indigo rescued the captain from Castle Lorcathian set the scene for a most productive relationship between Indigo and the captain, much to the delight of her manservant and housekeeper.

In the months leading up to the Great Exhibition of 1851, Mr. Grimoult designed and constructed an innovative contraption to float behind the dirigible. It consisted of a series of trays that transformed into a display case. Zane assisted the little man in loading the products, before they finally sealed the container ready for flight as they prepared for their departure to London.

"Are you sure you have packed all of the pharmacologicals?" Indigo paced up and down beside the dirigible, her long skirts swishing.

"Yes, Madame."

"The cosmecuticals?"

"Yes, Madame."

"The hallucinogenics?"

"Yes, Madame."

"What about—"

Zane interrupted her. "Indigo, for pity's sake, we have checked the cargo for you constantly for the past two days. Leave it to Mr. Grimoult and myself. It is all there. I will stake my life on it." He grinned as she stormed off.

By God, she was a feisty woman.

However, it had not all been preparation over the past few months. They had shared many, many hours of mutual pleasure.

Finally, they were ready to depart the manor for their

journey to Crystal Palace and the Great Exhibition. Nations from across the world prepared to display their works of all industry in the mammoth glass construction in Hyde Park. For Indigo, a culmination of many years of innovation and rebellion were about to be realized and her excitement was palpable. Cheeks flushed, temper short, she displayed as many nerves as a dollymop in a church.

The combined efforts of the comptroller general and the duke had failed to deter Indigo from her goal. The government sent a member of the Royal Society for the Encouragement of Arts, Manufactures and Commerce to visit the manor in one last attempt to convince Indigo that her display should not go ahead. The member received neither audience nor cooperation from the lady of the house, protesting as she showed him the door, most impolitely.

"The folly and absurdity of the Queen in allowing this trumpery must strike every sensible and well-thinking mind. Trust me, it will lead to rebellion of the masses," he spluttered, making a hasty exit. Indigo threw his hat and cane after him, slamming the door behind him with a satisfying crash.

The new dirigible, custom-built for the journey. was transporting them to London. Mr. and Mrs. Grimoult and the captain were dressed in regulation air suits with brass goggles, but Indigo stood apart as usual, refusing to conform.

Her signature red bustier topped an emerald green skirt embossed with the symbols of industry flowed around her ankles, neither garment satisfying air safety dress regulation for dirigible travel. In honour of the occasion her hair was wound high around her head in an elaborate confection, ruby studded ribbons threading through the high loops of curls. The captain handed her a set of goggles as she climbed the short ladder to the dirigible. Shaking her head, Indigo refused to take them.

"I prefer a clear view."

"Madame, you will need the goggles when we enter the air space of London," Mrs. Grimoult said.

Indigo ignored her faithful housekeeper and Mrs. Grimoult took a deep breath as she laboriously pulled her stout little body up the ladder. "Breathe the clean country air while you can, my dears, as we will be a long time in the grime of the city."

As the ship ascended, the entire staff of the enterprise lined the dirigible pad to bid them luck. The submariners and the scientists stood together and gave a rousing cheer as the dirigible ascended slowly in a smooth and fluid motion. Mr. Grimoult turned it toward London. As they passed over Castle Lorcathian, they looked down on the duke who stood on the parapet, gazing out over the ocean, decidedly miserable. Leopold ignored their passing, as did the small mouse sitting on his shoulder.

Mr. Grimoult turned from the rudder, his ruddy face alight with mischief. "I heard down at The Rattling Cat that the duke has refused to let Mr. Brixton morph back to his human body. Did you see him sitting on Leopold's shoulder?"

The captain stood behind Indigo, both arms wrapped loosely around her waist. He laughed. "What upset him the most was his failure to properly mesmerize me. But it did retrieve my memory of my tattoo and the pretty young lady I proposed to at the time." The captain patted Indigo's swelling stomach possessively.

"Little did I know that the woman who declined my proposal in Juan's tattoo parlour would one day be my wife."

Indigo turned, pushing him away crossly. "I have not agreed to be your wife, Captain."

As Zane had come out of his mesmeric trance in the castle, he had recalled a voyage to the Amazon as a youth in the merchant navy. A visit to the harborside parlour for a nautical tattoo befitting a sailor had gone awry, with much rum consumed at various waterfront establishments along the way. The following morning, Zane awoke with a pounding headache, a rum-soaked shirt and a flower on his forearm, to the great mirth of the sailors in his cabin. The most vivid memory of a young woman with lustrous black curls beside him, her head turned to the wall, having a delicate blue flower inked onto her beautiful back, stayed with him. His friends ordered one the same for him, much to their drunken delight and his sober dismay the following morning. The passionflower had remained a permanent souvenir of that trip and, Zane now realized, had been a portent of things to come.

As the dirigible neared the great metropolis, the air turned foggy and the atmosphere became dreary. A myriad of air ships of all shapes, sizes and colour dotted the sky and Mr. Grimoult employed precise navigation skills to avoid collision

"Madame, here are your goggles," insisted Mrs. Grimoult, holding them out to Indigo as she peered down through the transparent floor of the dirigible. Indigo glared at her as she observed Mrs. Grimoult roll her eyes at her husband.

"Madame, the putrid air will not be good for the baby's health," coaxed Mr. Grimoult sweetly. Indigo reached over and donned the goggles without a further word, taking great care not to disturb her magnificent hairstyle. As the airship drifted over the Crystal Palace, Zane grabbed the controls to avoid a collision with a smaller dirigible, and Mr. Grimoult gazed down at the amazing building. Architecturally adventurous, it was almost two thousand feet long, constructed entirely of glass on a cast iron frame. The myriad of fountains and cascades within, were visible from the air.

"It makes our biomes look Lilliputian, Madame," said Mr. Grimoult, his voice hushed.

"It gives me great inspiration for our next enterprise, Mr. Grimoult," replied Indigo.

Mr. Grimoult gently brought the dirigible to ground on the landing bay in Hyde Park. They disembarked and Indigo and Zane strolled through the park to the Exhibition Hall while the Grimoults sought assistance to unload their products.

On entering the Exhibition Hall, the displays already in place dazzled them. A rich variety of hues appealed to Indigo's love of bright colours.

"Magnificent." She breathed in the atmosphere. Forming the center to the building was a gigantic fountain in a forest of trees with lofty and overshadowing branches which provided a restful haven in the busy atmosphere. Delighted to find her allotted display space was on the edge of the forest, Indigo grabbed Zane's hand and dragged him around the other displays already in place.

"Oh, look at the colours," she exclaimed.

Opulent fabrics from every corner of the world, flax, silks and linens surrounded them. General hardware, brass and ironwork of many types, locks, grates. Innovative machines and implements, marine engines, hydraulic presses, steam machinery in motion— the array of products was amazing, even to Zane who had travelled to many exotic locations when he was in the navy.

Indigo paused in front of an Astrolaberors, a device for navigation through time. "It is a different mechanism to the one we use," Indigo explained. "It relies on star combinations and arrangements."

"I am quite content to remain in our current time, my dear," the captain replied drily. It has taken him a few weeks to get over the effects of his trip to the twenty first century. The passion flower lotion had healed his physical injury, but it had taken him a long time to reacclimatize to the time change.

It took the rest of the day to unpack the dirigible, transport, and set up the display to Indigo's satisfaction. A miniature version of the holiday biome sat next to a small glass conservatory filled with tropical plants. A stunning display of products with the blue passionflower as the centrepiece was surrounded by the full range of pharmacologicals and cosmecuticals produced by Indigo's venture, all in the shape of the flower petals.

Looking around at the three people who trusted in her

endeavours and had supported her over the past few months, Indigo blinked back tears and Zane was filled with a surge of pride and love for this woman.

"We have achieved great things," she said, spreading her arms wide. "We are but a small part of the spirit of creation and we will continue to come up with new ways to make the world a better place."

She turned, smiling up at him. "Will you marry me, sir?"

"Please?" she added.

Epilogue

Indigo and the captain did not return to the jungle, neither in their time, nor by time travel. They left that to their children and Sofia.

Zane gave up his vessel and supervised the biome enterprise and production of pharmaceuticals and cosmecuticals. Four little captains over the years kept them busy as each of the boys inherited their mother's feisty temperament, much to their father's dismay.

Mr. and Mrs. Grimoult became surrogate grandparents and aided and abetted the boys in the pursuit of rebellion…and of course, time travel.

Sofia followed in her sister's footsteps and became a well-known couturier in Vienna and established her own haute couture salon…and embarked on her own moonflower research, of course.

But that is another story…and it begins below…

Book 2

Vienna and Scotland

Summer of the Moon Flower

Chapter 1

Sofia de Vargas shivered and the hairs on her neck stood on end. The chill wind blew in from the Austrian Alps and the departure lounge of Wien Westbahnhof was icy in the pre-dawn darkness. She pushed her hands deep into the pockets of her dark cloak, gloved fingers curling round the cold steel of the small weapon and her gaze flicked around the deserted space. Quiet footsteps to her left confirmed her suspicion— she was not alone. She stood completely still, ignoring the pounding of her heart as she listened in the silence surrounding her.

No sound.

Nothing.

She knew she was unrecognizable; a close-fitting, dark helmet with a small brass mouthpiece attached, hid her silver blonde hair from any curious onlooker. She stood to the left of the portal, hidden by one of the statue-crowned columns in the elevated departure lounge and waited for the arrival of the dawn train from Paris. A sudden movement to her right caught her attention and she turned quickly scanning the deserted lounge.

No one.

Nothing.

Now only the scratching of mice and the rustling of leaves blowing in the cold wind filled the cavernous space. Stepping back into the shadow of the ornamental column, Sofia spoke softly into the mouthpiece of her helmet.

"There is somebody else in here."

Silence.

No response. The range of the transmitter was blocked by the solid brick walls surrounding her and didn't extend out to her carriage. She swore under her breath in a most unladylike fashion.

The hissing of steam broke the silence as the train appeared around the bend at the edge of the station, making it impossible for her to hear anything else. Craning forward from the protection of the column as far as she could without stepping into the light, Sofia looked down onto the arrival platform. The steam fog from the engine trailed ghostly fingers of mist into the dark corners but there was no one waiting in the shadows. The end of the platform remained blocked from her vision.

Her carefully selected vantage point at the edge of this level would have ensured she was able to see anyone else awaiting the train's arrival. Not being able to step out to the edge of the balcony impeded her view and afforded her no end of frustration.

More worrying were the sinister noises around her and the certainty she was not alone. Sofia had not expected anyone else to be up here and her hand shook as she removed the tiny ray gun from her pocket. The muted voices of passengers alighting from the train below drifted up and she cursed again, fighting the urge to step out from the safety of the column to see if her mysterious passenger had alighted.

No. It was more important she not be seen. She twirled, the dark cloak billowing around her when footsteps sounded quietly behind her

She placed her hand on the cold marble of the circular post, before creeping silently around to the other side to face the entry to the large hall, straining her covered ears for any sound. Reaching up, she flicked the helmet from one side and cursed as a tendril of silver hair fell from the braid looping around her forehead. A rhythmic clicking came from the shadows on her left.

"Who is there?" she called, deepening her voice. It was unfortunate her hair had revealed her sex and she cursed again, pushing the curl back under her helmet.

A rhythmic clicking now came from her right and as she

glanced around a movement above caught her eye. Looking up, Sofia gasped as the ornate roof of the *porte-cochere* slid open and the bright lights of a small airship shone down, illuminating the floor around her. A rope ladder coiled down from the dark recess of the polygonal roof flanking the entrance and hit the ground beside her.

Sofia stepped back quickly as a figure clothed entirely in black, slid down toward her. Before she could run, the acrid smell of machine oil assailed her nostrils and a sudden pressure descended onto her left shoulder. Metallic talons pinched the top of her arm and as she attempted to pull away, her woollen cloak ripped exposing her bare white flesh.

"*Merde,*" she cursed looking up into the dead eyes of a machine man, twice her height. A human face on a metallic body. Another one approached from her right, the monotonous clicking of the brass joints getting louder as it came closer, metallic claws outstretched to grab her other shoulder.

Before she could pull back, a loud clang echoed as the magnetized talons touched her gun and she dropped it, knowing she was not strong enough to break the connection.

"*Vielen Dank, Mademoiselle.*" A flat monotone from the automaton.

Deep breaths. Don't panic. Think your way out of this.

Sofia twisted to escape the claws of the brass machine, and the lifeless faces of the two automatons glowed eerily in the dark above her. The black cloaked figure on the rope ladder was almost to the ground. She had mere seconds to escape, she knew now she was their quarry.

Frantically scrabbling in her pocket, she pulled a small knife from the depths and pushed the magnetic handle onto the centre of the chest plate of the automaton holding her shoulder in its sharp, cold grip. At the same time, she twisted to the right with a strength far beyond anything the automaton would have allowed for her slight frame. She broke free of the metallic clasp at the same moment the automaton on the right stretched its shiny claws out to grab her other arm. As the first machine man whirred to a standstill, rendered inactive by the magnetism of the small knife on its chest plate, Sofia ducked under the snapping talons of the second as its talons clicked in vain bare inches above her exposed shoulder.

Sofia ran for her life. Her cloak swirled around her legs, impeding her flight. Lifting her skirt, she ran for the shadows; her soft boots made no sound on the ornate terracotta floor. Realizing the floor would also mask the sound of anyone pursuing her, unless they were metallic, she kept to the shadows along the side of the station. Grateful she lived in a progressive city, she silently thanked the architects for the design of the building. One of the most modern in Europe, the departure lounge of West Wien *Bahnhof* ran the entire length of the eight hundred feet of the station. Numerous doors led down to the arrivals level, where a multitude of carriages and omnibuses could load passengers at the same time. She knew one of the exits along the departure level opened to a corridor leading to an enclosed garden and small restaurant overlooking the street below.

Heart pounding, Sofia glanced at each door trying to remember which one she had entered when the designer from Paris had met her, prior to his departure on the afternoon train just last week.

"*Merde*," she muttered under her breath again, they all looked the same.

Think.

She recalled they had come up the stairs and taken the first exit after they had turned into the departure lounge. Sofia slowed when a sharp stitch pulled in her side. Stepping behind the penultimate ornate pillar before the end of the building, she leaned back against the cold marble and caught her breath, sure any pursuer would hear her ragged breathing

Total silence surrounded her. The train and the few arrivals had left the station, and all was quiet. She craned her head forward and peered around the column. The mysterious black clad figure, face obscured by a helmet similar to the one she was wearing, was backlit by the light streaming from the dirigible. He was six columns behind her, trying each of the doors along the side as he searched for her exit point. As she watched, he paused and attempted to open the next one. The rattling of the brass knob as he pulled at it before he made his way along to the next door drifted down to where she was hiding. She stood, transfixed, as he tried three more, moving closer to her hiding place with each step. Standing absolutely still behind the column, with her breath held, Sofia was close enough to hear the grunt of satisfaction as the third door opened and the figure disappeared into a dark passageway.

Before he could reappear, Sofia hitched her skirt and ran for the last exit. The door loomed in front of her in the semi-darkness and she prayed silently that it was unlocked as she reached for the handle.

Her gloved hand slipped on the brass knob and she impatiently removed her glove and pushed it into the deep pocket of her cloak. Fingers shaking, she tried again, turning the large circular brass handle as firmly as she could, and sighed with relief as the cogs inside the lock clicked loudly and the door creaked open. Entering the narrow dark corridor, she turned and gently closed it, leaning against the solid timber as her eyes became accustomed to the dim light shining through the high windows of the restaurant at the far end. Stretching on her toes, she reached above the brass lock with trembling fingers and slowly slid the large bolt into place. Sliding down onto the cold floor, she exhaled with relief, and reached into her pocket for her glove.

Gottverdammt.

The pocket was empty; her glove must have fallen as she

opened the door. Pushing to her feet, Sofia turned around, torn between hiding here safely locked in, or opening the door and retrieving her black glove as she cursed herself for the vain SdV monogrammed on the inner flap of the leather. Foolish vanity could lead to her identification and if it were discovered that she, Sofia de Vargas was waiting in the station in the wee small hours, observing the delivery of her critical cargo, there would be many questions asked.

Merde, merde, merde. They were so close to an outcome.

Sofia clenched her bare fingers in the cold as her mind worked furiously. If she were caught by the mysterious man and his automaton henchmen, it would all be over anyway, so she was better to take the risk and claim she had dropped the glove on another occasion, if indeed it were even discovered. Deciding to settle in and wait them out, she pulled the folds of her thick woollen coat around her and leaned against the door once more. The cold air was creeping through the tear on the shoulder of her coat and she folded the material over for warmth. The restaurant was open to the elements on the northern wall and the cold wind whistled down the corridor. Her head and neck were warm, protected by the tight-fitting helmet, although her eyes were stinging as the cold settled around her. Her goggles were in the carriage with Henri, her manservant

Placing her bare hand over her face, she cursed the events of the night. Not only had she almost been caught, she had not achieved the goal for her foray out in the cold pre-dawn.

Henri would be concerned when she did not return to the carriage as expected after the train's arrival. She had not been able to raise him through the mouthpiece on her helmet, and was loath to try again, while ever the dark stranger was on the other side of the wall. It had been imperative that she know who was travelling on the train this morning with the latest delivery.

Her brother-in-law, Captain Zane Thoreau, Sheriff of

Cornwall and official keeper of the Queen's peace, had sent word her operation was under surveillance and had possibly been infiltrated but it was not known who was interested in their activities. Zane had sent her word a person well known to her— someone she would apparently least suspect, would accompany the latest cargo on the Paris train. A person who would be most interested to follow the cargo to its destination. No further clue to their identity was given and that was why she had come here tonight, and not sent one of her trusted servants. It had been emphasized the suspect would be clearly recognizable to her.

She had used the Paris train to move their products for over two years. Hidden amongst the fabrics and fashionable accoutrements for the salon of the highly respected Sofia de Vargas, it had been the perfect hiding place for the products destined for the laboratory in the lower level of Vienna University.

Society matrons and their daughters came from afar to visit her salon, to be dressed in the latest fashion as decreed by one of the most highly respected couturiers outside Paris. She even provided a dirigible service for the ladies of the colonies to visit Vienna and be outfitted in the latest European fashion. This had proven extremely valuable for importation over the preceding years.

Now thanks to the unexpected appearance of the stranger from the dirigible and his clockwork men this morning, she had achieved nothing and seen no one.

Were the two incidents related? Had it all been an elaborate trap? Had there indeed been anyone on the train? What was the stranger in the dirigible seeking? If—

Her reverie broke when the door pushed slowly against her back. The cogs of the knob rattled and clicked as someone attempted to push the door open behind her. Sofia held her breath, praying the bolt would hold as the door strained forward. The pressure on the door stopped and she let her breath out as the sound of footsteps faded.

* * * *

Some hours later, Sofia pulled her cloak up around her neck and dropped her chin into the folds of the soft vicuña wool as she stepped from the side entry of Westbahnof onto the footpath of Neubauguertel. The high glass windows of the apartment buildings reflected the mid-morning sunlight and she quickly rounded the corner into Mariahilfer Strasse. She had stayed locked in the station corridor until the morning light had pierced the darkness and waited another hour before carefully unbolting the door leading back to the departure lounge. It had been timely. She had passed a man laden with trays of food, obviously heading for the restaurant when she had descended the stairs to the street level. He had looked at her curiously and not greeted her as she still wore her helmet and Sofia had put her head down and scurried past him.

Stepping into Mariahilfer Strasse, she paused in the shadow of a doorway and quickly scanned the street around her. All appeared normal, the steam tram was making its way along the street past the small businesses and delivering fresh produce from the outlying farms, and the shopkeepers were putting their wares on tables in front of their shops in the warm spring sunshine. There was no sign of automatons nor black garbed figures, nor were there any small dirigibles flying low over the street. Sofia removed her cloak and helmet, twisting her hair into a loose knot as she stepped out into the bright morning sunshine.

"Guten Morgen, fräulein."

"Good morning, Hans." She returned the greeting of the baker as he opened the doors of his establishment and the smell of fresh baked pastries wafted out.

"You are early this morning, Sofia. I didn't realize you were about as I saw Henri with your carriage only a short while ago."

"Just out for a stroll in the lovely sunshine," Sofia replied,

106

pleased to hear Henri was still out in the carriage and obviously looking for her. As they chatted, the baker's wife came bustling through of the doorway and passed her a steaming *mélange*.

"*Danke*." Sofia gratefully sipped the steaming concoction of frothed milk and coffee and smiled as Hans pushed a small croissant, still warm from the oven, into her ungloved hand.

"Are you setting new fashion, Madame Couturier? You are only wearing one glove?" He smiled at her.

Sofia laughed. "I dropped one as I was walking, and I could not find it. Luckily it is monogrammed and hopefully will be returned to me if it is found."

Finishing her coffee, she bid them farewell and strolled along the street as though she had not a care in the world and was a highly respected couturier out taking a stroll before her morning appointments. Hooves rang out on the metallic tram track in the middle of the road only a few hundred yards from the turn to Lindengasse where her apartment was located. Placing her hand over her chest to still the pounding of her heart, she paused and turned slowly. For a brief moment, it had sounded like the clicking of the automaton's talons and she sighed with relief as Henri brought the horse and *barutsche* to a stop beside her. He climbed down and held her gloved hand assisting her into the open carriage, whispering close to her ear.

"Madame, I have been so worried. I have been searching for you since first light." Her trusted manservant glanced at her as he flicked the reins and the horse broke into a light trot.

"It was a trap…but I am all right," she reassured the elderly man as a look of concern crossed his face. "I am tired, but I have appointments all day. I must meet with Professor Schmidt and the others as soon as possible. I need to find out what has happened, and we must take extreme care."

"When shall we meet, Madame?"

"Organize a gathering for eleven this evening please,

Henri," she replied as the carriage pulled up in front of her salon. "At the university."

"Are you sure, Madame? Will that be safe?" She quelled him with a steady look as she stepped down from the carriage and her voice was terse.

"At the university," she repeated. "Have the carriage ready at eight. If the stable staff asks where I am going, I shall be attending a music recital at the *Musikverein* and you shall return the carriage in the morning.

* * * *

Sofia glanced into her salon as she made her way to her apartment above. Pulling the glove off and placing her cloak on the cloak stand in the foyer, she cursed once again at her carelessness in dropping the glove. As she moved through her apartment, her thoughts turned to the meeting tonight. It was most unusual for a woman to participate in any activities at the University; women were not allowed to enrol there and there were no female staff involved in any of the research. Sofia's involvement at the university had begun when she had read the research notes her father had bequeathed to her when Indigo had passed them on after her marriage to Captain Zane Thoreau ten years ago.

Sofia smiled as she remembered Indigo's wedding. It had scandalized society as she had been heavily pregnant with the twins, and Indigo in her usual brash manner had thumbed her nose at the society matrons who had expressed their displeasure. Nevertheless, curiosity won out and the ceremony and reception in the tropical biome was attended by all who were invited… with the exception of Duke Lorca.

Sofia had stayed in the manor with Mr. and Mrs. Grimoult to oversee the operations of the holiday complex while Zane and Indigo had travelled to Scotland for a brief honeymoon. She had enjoyed her time there and Sofia had spent the following year in the household assisting with the twins when they were born. Jago

108

and Jory had their mother's lust for life and created a multitude of work for the household.

She had been fascinated by Indigo's biomes. Word of the passionflower pharmacologicals and their healing properties had spread across Europe and the colonies.

Indigo had shared the research notes with her, and Sofia had been intrigued by their father's writing on the properties of the moon flower and his belief that human life could be extended if the liquid from this rare white flower from the alpine region of Austria could be extracted. For years, she had carried the idea with her and a chance meeting with Professor Schmidt, an old colleague of her father in Vienna three years later had resulted in her acceptance into the elite ranks of Vienna University. A small group of scientists allowed her to became a part of their secret society in exchange for Professor de Vargas notes and Sofia had eventually led the research and still held control

A recent missive to Indio had described how close they were to achieving their goal. Sofia now wondered if she had been foolish detailing their progress in writing and trusting the missive would travel safely from Vienna to Cornwall, although she had camouflaged the true content in sociable family news.

My dearest sister

I trust this finds you in good health and I trust that Captain Thoreau and your four sons are also well. It is hard to believe that Jago and Jory are attending boarding school. I certainly enjoy reading their adventures in the letters I have received from them. Are young Kit and Ruan still enjoying their nursery studies?

I shall try to visit you in late summer as the twins tell me that their scientific experiments at New Cross College will be on display. It is amusing that although they are attending a naval school, their interests lie in the botanical research of their grandfather! Jory tells me they are researching the effect of the full moon on their experiments and that they are close to a result.

I am sure the officers of the naval college are less than amused, unless they see a future for the boys in botanical exploration, following in the footsteps of our dear departed papa.

I recently had an enjoyable trip to the Alps, and I made some new contacts in society for the salon. Business is blooming as the boys would say...and I have many new matrons taking up the dirigible flight from the American colonies, although the new war over there is causing some uncertainty.

I look forward to visiting you, my dear sister, and shall come and stay in the late summer after I visit the twins at New Cross.

Kind regards to Captain Thoreau and Mr. and Mrs. Grimoult. (and of course the boys.)

Sofia knew Indigo would decipher the information from the letter that her recent trip to the Alps had sourced enough of the moon flower, and the full moon experimentation were bringing them close to a culmination of their research. They anticipated success by the end of summer.

The ringing of the bell in the salon brought her back to the present and Sofia quickly dressed and proceeded down to the salon to meet her first customer of the day.

Chapter 2

The full moon illuminated the University of Wien as they passed the Rathaus Park. Henri had opted for a closed carriage from the stable, still concerned by the events of the preceding night. He smiled at her as he looked down into the carriage. Sofia had come from the music recital and in an aside, Henri had commented on her alertness after she'd bid farewell to her acquaintances. He had turned the carriage toward the Landstrasse district in case anyone was taking notice of their direction

"Rest, madam, we are still early, and I will do a few circuits of the Ringstrasse in case we are under observation. I will be able to check if any vehicles or airships pay particular attention to us."

His mistress was now dozing with her head resting comfortably against the padded side of the velvet-lined carriage. He glanced down occasionally to check that she was comfortable. Only a couple of airships dotted the brightly lit sky as he guided the two horses around the road ringing the inner district and the Hapsburg palaces, constructed when Emperor Franz Josef had ordered the demolition of the city walls and moats four years ago.

By the time eleven o'clock approached, and they had completed their third circuit, the sky was clear, and Henri was content they had not been followed around the famous road.

Henri scanned the area alongside Rathaus Park as he pulled the horses to a gentle stop. He was reluctant to wake Sofia as she'd had no sleep the previous evening. She had worked with society matrons all day, before attending the musical soiree.

He shook his head, no matter how tired she was, his mistress was always kind and calm, and he held a deep affection for her. He glanced over at her, deep in sleep, her silver blonde hair fell in ringlets onto her bare shoulder and her pale skin was accentuated by the deep ruby of her velvet gown. Four small rubies were inserted in each ear, in a line following the curve of her ear.

Henri stepped down and entered the carriage and shook her gently, smiling as she stretched, and her pale blue eyes widened in surprise.

"Are we there already, Henri?" Sofia yawned.

"We have done three circuits of the Ringstrasse, madam. It is just before eleven." He stepped out and took her hand and they strolled together across the park, looking as though they were a father and daughter out for a late evening walk.

They entered a dark lane at the back of the university and Henri pulled her into a dark corner beside the building as he scanned the wide lawn lit brightly by the full moon, for any sign of activity or observers.

"All appears well, madam."

He led her across to the next building and they walked along a winding path to a small wooden door set into an ivy-covered brick wall.

Henri gave four short knocks, paused and then tapped two more short raps on the concealed door, constantly looking around as he checked there was no one following them.

The heavy wooden door groaned as it opened slowly, and they entered a dimly lit foyer.

"Welcome, madam, it is good to see you again. Good evening, Henri." Johann, one of the doctoral students, ushered them into a larger room. The light was brighter, and Henri looked around as he escorted Sofia to the table. Pulling out a chair, he glanced to the side of the room and Sofia nodded.

"Yes, please, Henri. I will need coffee to keep me alert. I fear this may be a long meeting." As Henri poured Sofia's coffee, he observed the others already seated at the long table.

Professor Ernst Schmidt who led the project at the university listened gravely as Sofia spoke to him in a quiet undertone. The two research assistants, Johann and Genevieve sat on the other side of the table, Henri placed a glass of coffee in front of Sofia and he sat at the table, ever alert, even though they were in a safe room.

****

Sofia finished her coffee and pushed the empty glass to the side of the table as she looked around the room. Candles in sconces provided a soft light and the rich aroma of the coffee took away the musty smell of parchment that usually overwhelmed the senses in this old meeting room in the basement of the university laboratory. She looked around at the four people in the room and smiled.

People she would trust with her life.

Professor Ernst Schmidt sat at the head of the table, muttering softly to himself in his native German as he flicked through a pile of papers. Ernst had worked with her father in London, prior to his death in 1840 and had sought her out when she had moved to Vienna. He and his brother, Henri, had become like surrogate fathers since the professor had continued her father's moonflower research. Ernst had published many papers on the science of the nature of matter and its transformations, but the moonflower research was known only to the select few inside this room.

She caught Henri's eye and he smiled back at her, although she could sense the tension in his body. He had been on edge since the incident at the station. Henri was the indispensable assistant in her household and salon activities, and Sofia allowed him to think he fulfilled the role of her bodyguard.

Johann, a brilliant young doctoral student from the university at Bologna, sat across the table from Sofia, impatiently clicking his pencil on the side of his glass, obviously eager to start the meeting. His assistant and the chief illustrator for the project, Genevieve, sat still and silent, taking in the scene around the table.

"I would like to thank you all for being here at this ungodly

113

hour. I am very grateful," said Sofia

"We didn't stay back, Sofia. We are so close to success, we have been working through the night for two weeks," replied Johann.

She frowned "It is imperative you take the utmost care. Any unusual interest in your work must be reported to Henri…immediately."

Sofia quickly filled them in on the events of the previous night at Westbahnhof.

"I am sure it is related to the shipment on the train." She shrugged. "Somehow, somewhere there is an awareness of what we are doing." The three scientists all tried to speak over each other, protesting.

"But—"

"We haven't—"

"There is no way—"

Sofia held up her hand. "I trust you all implicitly. However, it has happened, so there is no doubt. Somehow, word has spread of what we are close to…"

She paused. "I will not say immortality as that is tempting to the Fates. Let me say, we are close to discovering a life-giving elixir that may prolong human life."

Professor Schmidt nodded sagely." No, madam…we will not be presumptuous."

Sofia placed her hands on the table in front of her and turned to the professor. "Now I want a full report on what you are up to. Did the cargo come in from the station last night? Was it intact?"

"Yes, madam. All was well."

Sofia turned to Johann. "Henri tells me there has been a significant development in your research?"

Johann inclined his head and reached for the illustrations in front of Genevieve.

"Indigo's research has confirmed the stamen is vital in the healing properties of the passion flower, but our research indicates it is the petal of the night blooming moonflower that provides the catalyst for the elixir. If we are to successfully propagate the flower in a controlled environment, it must be planted at full moon and bathed in moonlight until the full moon wanes. Any plant germinated at other times of the cycle and harvested without the requisite moonlight has not had the life-giving properties once the elixir has been reduced in the laboratory."

Sofia was intrigued. "How did you establish that?"

Johann looked over at Genevieve and smiled." It was serendipity, madam."

Sofia turned to the young woman. "Serendipity?" she asked.

"I had an idea when I was illustrating the report on propagation for Professor Schmidt." The young woman blushed. "I was sketching and as I was drawing the petals, the shape of the petal reminded me of a new moon, and I got carried away and illustrated the botanical with the background of a night sky."

Johann interrupted and his words spilled out excitedly. "When I saw it, it gave me the idea of experimenting with different stages of light…you know how Indigo's passionflower uses luminiferous aether to stay vital, well… we put the moon flower through the monthly lunar cycle and transformation was almost instantaneous."

Professor Schmidt interrupted, his head bobbing in excitement. "And what we had spent years trying to create artificially by the transformation of the botanical matter, occurred naturally in one night under a full moon."

Sofia was delighted to hear of the progress made since her last visit.

"So, where are we up to… do you need more flowers? Do we need another trip to the Alps to harvest more seeds?"

"Yes, Sofia," replied Johann. "Now we know the moonlight is critical to the process, we can propagate each crop in the laboratory from the seeds."

"It will be the final trip," agreed the professor. "So one final trip to collect the plants in midsummer when the flowers turn to seed will be enough to continue our research."

Sofia smiled.

"I shall organize a trip in midsummer. I believe my twin nephews may like an expedition to the Alps. Having the boys with me will provide good cover."

The professor frowned. "Do you really believe, Sofia, there is a need for all this subterfuge? Do you really think the incident at the station was related to our research?"

Sofia shook her head slowly. "I honestly do not know. However, I am not prepared to take the risk. Although I do not believe it can be the fool Lorca who causes my sister so many problems in her ventures." She smiled grimly "Although since Captain Thoreau has become Sheriff and is a highly respected representative of the queen, Duke Lorca has pulled in his little head considerably."

Sofia walked over to the window and stared into the darkness for a few minutes before continuing. "There was something much more sinister behind the incident at the railway station. The dirigible and the automatons indicate this is a very well-funded operation.

Whilst you are waiting for the new seed, Johann—" Sofia turned to the young man "—I have a mission for you. I would like you and Genevieve to take a trip together and undertake some research on automatons and dirigibles for me."

She smiled as the blush spread up the young scientist's neck. She had long suspected he harboured a secret passion for his colleague who remained blissfully unaware of the esteem in which the young man held her.

"I will meet you in Cornwall at my sister's holiday biomes in late July when I return from the Alps and you can report your findings to me then. I am sure by combining two intellects such as yours, you will discover the source of this operation.

"Remember to take care and pretend you are simply on holiday. I will deposit funds into the Professor's account for you."

The professor turned to her, eyes twinkling. "When do you intend travelling to the Alps, madam?"

"I will collect the twins in their summer holidays and bring them back to Austria in middle of July. I shall have your seed for you by the end of the summer. In the meantime, if there is anything of concern or you make a breakthrough, send a message to Indigo that says..." Sofia put her finger to her cheek.

"Invite her to the opening of the new wing of the chemistry department mentioning that it is to be named after our father. An innocuous message, but if either of us receives such a missive, we shall know all is not well."

She crossed the room and placed her arms around the professor.

"Take care, Ernst. Do not work such long hours. We have waited many years for this moment, and we need to be assured all is safe before we continue.

Sofia turned to the young couple and smiled as Genevieve glared at her.

Hmmm…maybe she is not as unaware as I thought.

"Now, I want you to be extremely careful. I suspect there are forces at work here, which, if we let our guard down, may mean the end to our research. At the moment, they are unsure of the progress we have made. We need to challenge them and ensure that they do not discover our advances. We will send them off on a wild goose chase."

She bid them all farewell, feeling confident once again.

"Come, Henri… I really need some sleep. It has been a

very long day."

Chapter 3

The sun had taken on the dull burnished copper of coming dusk as Dougal, Earl of Rothmore rode away from Castle Dean, one mile northeast of Kilmarnock. Since Lady Lucy Cavendish-Bentinck, married Charles Ellis, the 6th Lord Howard de Walden and moved to his family estate in London, Castle Dean had been empty but was now maintained by a small resident chapter of the ancient Scottish Order of the Knights Templar.

Even though he was a peer of the Kingdom of Scotland, Dougal was a lowly steward in the order, having inherited the position on the death of his father, when he became Earl of Rothmore, before his fifteenth birthday. His castle was on Little Rothmore, some twenty miles west across the Firth of Clyde, and it was his duty to prepare the Great Hall for the meeting of the Council of the Great. An urgent missive had been received from the Grand Conclave of Knights in Edinburgh and there had been little time to prepare for the meeting.

The gelding was unused to a road wide enough for several horsemen to ride abreast, being used to the deer trails and the rugged terrain of the island. Dougal held the reins tightly as a carriage passed them on the outskirts of the small town that was Kilmarnock, reaching down to pat and reassure the skittish young horse.

"Just a few more minutes and I will water you at the brook while I collect some ale from the inn for this evening."

The more ale, the better, he mused. He was also a little curious as he had been instructed to collect a small vat of wine for the gathering tonight. It was the first time since he had inherited on the stewardship of the order that such preparations had been put in place for a meeting, and at such short notice.

Perhaps there may be a special guest tonight?

He knew the Council would be most unhappy with the news from Vienna and his failure to deal with the stranger at the station. After tethering his horse, he walked across to the inn and supped on bread and ale as he considered the best way to broach the unfortunate news.

Even though it was commonly believed the small chapter based in Kilmarnock was a division of the Freemasons, the Council of the Great was actually the governing body of the descendants of the Knights Templar who had taken refuge in Scotland in the fourteenth century. Dougal was not privy to the inner workings of the Council as he would not be fully inducted until ten years had passed. He was, however, aware of the deepest secret of the Council, as his father had shared the information on his deathbed, begging his son not to take up the hereditary position. Dougal kept the information close to his chest and knew his mission in Vienna was closely related to the ancient order's whole reason for being.

Tonight will be very interesting.

The members of an order, who embraced life and immortality, would not be pleased with the news he would impart tonight. He had been under instruction to kill the female observer at the station and bring the body to Kilmarnock for identification, so the suspicions of the Council could be confirmed. The whole trip had been the culmination of an elaborate set-up with false information spread through the Queen of England's network eventually filtering down to the Sheriff of Cornwall as intended.

Dougal reached into his pocket and fingered the monogrammed leather glove. He would wait to see the reaction of the Council before he confirmed, or indeed if he even revealed, the identity of the observer. The role of steward was not one to be involved in the taking of life, and he was concerned for the reasons this mission had been allocated to him. It may be that he had been chosen simply for his youth and strength or it was a test of his loyalty. For the time being, he would stay with the Council and seek his own understanding of the ventures of the white-haired woman. Tonight he would allay the fears of the Council.

* * * *

The sonorous beating of a drum heralded the entrance of the Holy Five, the leaders of the Kilmarnock chapter of the Council of the Great. A dozen or so white-cloaked men of varying ages sat on benches arranged in the center of the Great Hall. Dougal and the one other young member of the order had prepared the seating, lit the sconces and filled the jugs with ale.

The red wine was on the front table and covered by a white cloth. Dougal and his fellow usher stood flanking the entrance and when the drum stopped beating, each lifted their side of the heavily embossed red curtain as the Five walked slowly into the Hall.

After they had taken their seats at the table, Dougal and his fellow usher acted as cup bearers and filled their goblets with the ale, before lowering their heads and backing to join the other men seated on the benches.

As they sat, the leader of the Five stood and reached for a manuscript on the table. He unfurled it with great ceremony and his deep voice echoed across the large Hall as he began to greet them in French.

Dougal watched as the manuscript unfurled, taking care to keep his face solemn. He observed their Leader as he greeted the gathering. A tall man of indeterminate age gripped the manuscript with long, bony fingers. His skin had a faint tinge of yellow as though he had recently suffered an illness. Long white hair trailed past his shoulders and his matching beard fell almost to his waist. A white surcoat fell to the floor, and a large red cross on his chest was just visible behind his long white beard. Dougal smothered a smile; the archaic dress would draw attention to the Leader if he were to be observed outside the castle. His robes befitted a Knight from the twelfth century rather than the progressive times they

121

were now in. However, it was the eyes of the man that caught his attention. His cold, expressionless eyes seemed to look into your very soul.

Dougal shivered as the old man pinned him with his gaze—it was almost as though he could read his thoughts—before turning his attention to the parchment in front of him.

I certainly pray that he cannot.

"Good evening, my lords. I welcome you unreservedly." He held up the manuscript and briefly reverted to the language of the Knights Templar

"Je me félicite de cette charte"

I welcome this Charter, Dougal translated in his head, while some of the Scottish knights looked confused

"Tonight we are here for two purposes. I have recently been summoned to the Council of the Great in Edinburgh and have been advised our chapter has attained the forty first degree of perfection." Two of the old men on the front table gasped and the remainder of the Five looked at each other in confusion.
"Yes, my fellow knights, the Unutterable Degree."
Dougal turned his head and glanced at the men who were sitting in the front row with him. Expressions of confusion vied with fear and he caught the eye of the other young man, who raised his eyebrows at Dougal in question. Dougal shook his head imperceptibly and the young man raised his fingers a fraction to acknowledge the unspoken message.
The two older men at the front table stood and embraced their leader.
They sat and the Leader raised his hand.
"However, before the Unutterable Degree is conferred upon our small chapter, we have been given a mission. We must have unerring evidence the scientific quest for immortality in Vienna has been destroyed. The Order of the Lunar Temple has chosen our encampment for this mission."

His voice rose in anger.

"Our knights have taken centuries to achieve immortality, through spiritual growth and working upwards through the degrees of perfection."

He slammed his fist on to the table and the goblets rattled.

"Our spiritual perfection will not by threatened by the physical sciences." He stood at the front of the gathering, silently observing the men as he fingered his long beard. The small group of men of all ages focused on him, each with rapt attention.

"Earl Rothmore, I give you permission to rise and address the gathering of your findings in Vienna."

Dougal stood and made his way to the centre of the room where the Five looked solemnly across at him.

He was a big man and not easily intimidated, and as he caught the gaze of the leader of the Five, the determination in the eyes of the old man sent a shiver down his spine. A shiver that settled into a pit of cold in his stomach as heads turned to see the source of a metallic clicking across the paved floor near the side entry of the Great Hall.

The two automatons he had left at the border with the dirigible, moved awkwardly across the large open space toward the table in the center of the Hall, their brass extremities ringing sharply on the cobblestones and their brass joints clicking as their robotic movement pushed them forward.

He kept his face expressionless as they moved past him and stood on either side of the table. The gravity of the situation was illustrated by the presence of the automatons. Their presence flouted the edict of the Scottish parliament, that no mechanicals or paraphernalia of the new order enter the country. The roads to the border were always busy with carriages and cabs conveying Scottish passengers to the dirigible stations in many of the English border towns.

"My Lord?" The Leader's voice was impatient, and he

rustled the paper in his hands

Dougal slowly made his way to the front of the assembly and bowed reverently to the Five, before turning to the knights in front of him. His mouth was dry, and he cursed himself for not taking a sip of ale before he rose.

"My Great Leader, I have difficult news to impart. Our intelligence was correct; the shipment arrived in Vienna as expected." He closed his eyes briefly, as his mind worked furiously. He was going to have to be very accurate in his representation of events at the Westbahnhof as the automatons would have an analogue record of all that had occurred. He assumed they were fitted with miniature analytical engines, as wealth was no hindrance for this Council. He could only hope they were placed at such an angle, so they did not see the woman's hair fall from her helmet, nor record him retrieving the glove from the floor outside the last exit after she had escaped.

"The product was collected at the station by a courier and we were unable to follow it to its destination as we were otherwise occupied"— he turned and inclined his heads to the automatons— "attempting to catch the observer at the station. Our mechanical friends were unable to hold that person and even though I gave chase, he managed to elude us, making good use of the darkness of the early dawn."

Bowing, he deferred to the mechanical men flanking the Leader. "Perhaps they observed more than I was able to see when I gave chase?"

He swallowed nervously, to moisten his dry throat and waited for the automaton to correct his version of the night's events.

The one on the left turned to the leader and extended his mechanical arms. A low rumbling came from his chest and a short-clipped voice followed.

"Observe, if you please."

There was a series of gasps from the assembled man as the Leader reached over and turned the cog on the top of the automaton's chest and a small screen slid out slowly in front of the five men sitting at the table. Dougal's heart pounded as they watched the events at the station play out. Clenching his jaw, he kept his face impassive as he stared silently at the men in front of him. As light reflected from their faces, Dougal was able to keep up with the events that were being re-enacted on the square glass.

As the light shone from the dirigible, Dougal had looked down and seen the blonde tress fall from the observer's helmet at the same time the automatons had moved out of the shadows. He waited for the Leader to speak, but the Five watched silently.

Dear God, please let it be too dark to let them see me pick up the glove. His jaw ached from the effort of keeping his face emotionless.

The cogs whirred and with a loud click, the automaton closed his chest plate. The Leader of the Great Council stood and stepped to the centre of the platform. Dougal held his breath, his heart thudding slowly as he kept his gaze locked on their leader without breaking eye contact. The cold eyes of the old man stared at him for a full minute before the Leader turned away and addressed the men assembled.

"We need to select another to join the Earl of Rothmore. Is there one among you, eager to co-operate in the venture to achieve our goal?" He looked across the small gathering and his gaze rested on Edward, the young usher who had assisted Dougal to set up the Hall.

"I will, your Lordship." His voice was eager.

"It will no doubt be dangerous," replied the old man. He stroked his long white beard and considered the young man for several moments.

"Is there no one of greater years who wishes to join?" He paused and looked solemnly at the men.

To Dougal's surprise, none met his eye. No one else stepped forward.

The Leader held both arms out, pointing to the young usher and to Dougal.

"Come, my Lords." Turning, he reached for the jug of wine, poured earlier by Dougal from the vat he had collected from the Inn, and waited as the two young men made their way to the table. The Leader ushered them to the middle of the floor and stood between them, reaching up and placing a gnarled, veined hand on each of their shoulders.

"The Order of the Lunar Temple has decreed we have attained the forty first degree of perfection. Our chapter has been entrusted with an extremely significant mission. The most important task assigned to a Knight Templar for hundreds of years.'

He looked at Douglas and Edward, his eyes like flint.

"Your presence in this castle tonight is testament to your valour as a knight, either through deeds or through hereditary bloods. You will be initiated into the next chapter. Are you prepared to take on this task so that we can fulfil our quest and attain the Unutterable Degree?"

He paused and looked from one to the other. "Think long and hard…if you fail in this task, your mortal life will end."

Dougal stood straight, keeping his expression sombre as he nodded at the old man.

"You old fool," he thought. "My father left me a near impossible task, and you have handed hand me the means to achieve it ten years before I ever imagined it would be possible. He looked across at Edward. The blood had drained from the younger man's face and perspiration beaded his brow. As Dougal watched, Edward nodded to the Leader. The old man filled two goblets and spoke to the assembled gathering.

"Lift your goblets while we complete the libations."

He handed a goblet to each of the young men and then looked up to the high domed roof of the Great Hall as he chanted the toast.

"To King Solomon, our Ancient Grand Master."

"King Solomon," the men held their goblets high and repeated the words after him, before sipping the wine.

Again, Dougal wondered if this was all part of an elaborate trap as the acrid liquid hit his throat and his breath caught.

Or was it simply, poor quality wine from the Inn?

By the time they finished the fourth libation his eyes were streaming. The old man continued to look to the heavens as he started the final toast.

"Young Lords, the fifth libation is taken in a very solemn manner. It is emblematic of the bitter cup of death, of which some of us may sooner or late taste. "He paused and looked down at each of them. "However, if you succeed in this quest, each knight in this room tonight will gain immortal life. Repeat the Templar vow after me."

He reached out and took each of their right hands in his and linked them together as he led them through the vow. They repeated his words solemnly in front of the assembled men.

"If ever I wilfully violate this, my solemn vow, as a brother of the Knights Templar, may my skull be sawn asunder with a rough sword, my brains be consumed by the scorching sun. If ever I wilfully deviate from this my solemn obligation, may my light be put out from among men, as that of Judas Iscariot was for betraying our Lord and Master."

As the Leader moved onto the vows of poverty, chastity, obedience, and piety, Dougal fought a smile. He was acquainted with each knight in this room, either through business or society. He could confirm with little trouble not one of them was pious, chaste, poor or obedient. The most decent man in the room was young Edward standing beside him, taking this ridiculous vow.

Dougal closed his eyes.

I am following the good. I will not have to keep these vows.

Warmth stole over him as he thought of his father and the final words he'd spoken on his deathbed. He had promised his father he would end the reign of these men and their political and spiritual power, even if it took him his lifetime.

Now that he had been inducted into the inner circle, he would have no trouble embarking upon his own personal quest. He looked up and smiled as he stared deep into the eyes of the Leader

The old man smiled down at the two young men, although his expression remained cold. "So be it. After our ceremony has concluded, I will meet with you both in the Solar."

The Leader raised his hands and looked over the men sitting in the room. "Go in peace, my Lords."

* * * *

An hour later, the candles dimmed, and the knights left to make their way back to their respective homes. They shuffled out of the Great Hall of Castle Dean, their quiet footsteps muffled by the clicking of the mechanical men on the stairs above them. The Five resided in the castle as per their rank in the Council. Dougal and Edward stood quietly in the shadows, not speaking as they waited for permission to enter the Solar.

"Come," said the Leader. "Follow me."

They climbed a twisting staircase and stepped out into a large open room. The full moon was rising, and a shaft of silver moonlight illuminated the small room. A manservant scurried around and lit the brass sconces on the wall with a taper from the fireplace. The cheery fire crackled in the hearth and the atmosphere was much warmer and welcoming than the cavernous Great Hall below.

The candle light reflected on the large Gothic rose windows at the end of the Solar. Dougal glanced across and noted the two automatons flanking the window. Even though they had been under his control on the expedition to Vienna, he was still unnerved by their grotesque appearance, now enhanced by the flickering candlelight on their brass extremities. Edward's eyes were wide, his gaze fixed on the mechanical men.

Dougal smiled grimly to himself. Obviously, Edward was unfamiliar with the technology outside Scotland…it seemed he had not seen anything of this nature before. It was essential Dougal turn Edward to his way of thinking before he accompanied him on his quest. They had spoken briefly on a number of occasions about their allegiance to the Knights and Dougal had sensed Edward was a doubter as well. Hence his surprise when he had volunteered to join the quest earlier in the night.

They sat around a less formal table in the Solar and the leader called his manservant to bring refreshments. While they waited, the silence became uncomfortable, but Dougal was reluctant to break the quiet. Young Edward seemed nervous and drummed his boots on the wooden floor until the Leader looked across the table and stared him down.

It was not difficult for Dougal to guess the tenor of the Leader's thoughts for he made no effort to be amenable. Everything about him, from his posture to the set of his mouth, spoke of mistrust. Poor Edward appeared increasingly nervous as the minutes passed. The flames crackling in the fireplace was the only sound to be heard. The first words spoken by the Leader after they had partaken of refreshments in absolute silence confirmed Dougal's suspicion.

The Leader of the Five fixed Dougal with a steely glare.

"Your father was not devoted to our quest."

The safest response was to plead ignorance.

"My Lord, I had no knowledge of the quest until this evening. I have been inducted into the petitions of the lodge and am learning more about the charters each day," replied Dougal with his head bowed in an attempt to appear compliant. When he finished speaking, he lifted his gaze to meet the hawk-like stare of the older man.

The old man nodded, before turning to the younger man.

"Edward of Kilmarnock, I will allow you to accompany the earl as I know you to be loyal to our quest." Dougal almost choked on his ale; by implication the Leader was telling him that he was not fully trusted.

The old man stared into space and spoke in a deep sonorous tone. "Four hundred and two score years ago…"

For thirty minutes, he regaled them with the history of the Knights and their quest for immortality through deeds. He explained each of the forty-five charters in great detail and by the time he reached the description of the Unutterable Degree, Dougal's eyes were heavy, and he stifled a yawn.

Suddenly, the Leader brought his goblet to the table with a loud crash as his voice rose. "I will not let that woman in Vienna destroy the work of four centuries."

He turned to Dougal and his voice was hard and cold as he questioned him about the events in Vienna.

"Are you certain, you were not able to see who was awaiting the delivery at the station?"

Dougal held the dark gaze as he lied.

"No, my Lord. It was dark and the observer took flight as soon as they escaped the clutches of the automatons."

"Could it have been a woman?" the old man asked tersely.

"I do not think so, my Lord. "The strength required to pull away from the mechanicals would surpass that of a woman."

"So be it." The old man stood and pushed his chair behind him, and his manservant ran across the room to assist him but took a step back when the Leader shook his head. "Now, it has come to my attention that the research in Vienna is close to completion and that will threaten our entire existence.

The lieutenant sitting across the table from Dougal raised

his hand. "My Lord, may I speak?"

The Leader nodded.

"What about the sister in Cornwall, is she also a part of this research in Vienna? It is of concern as her husband is now in the employ of Queen Victoria."

A peculiar smile spread across the face of the Leader and Dougal shivered. Evil emanated from the old man as he smiled at the three men at the table

"He is no longer in the employ of Queen Victoria."

The lieutenant looked confused. "I beg to differ, my Lord. It is only three days ago since we fed the information about the cargo to Lord Lorca and ensured Captain Thoreau would receive it as Sheriff of Cornwall?"

"Oh…" replied their Leader. "Captain Thoreau is still the sheriff; however he is no longer in the employ of the Queen."

He looked across at them as a satisfied smile lifted his pallid lips and his dark eyes gleamed.

"You may not have heard the sad news from England. Queen Victoria died earlier to-day. I believe she was poisoned."

Once the shock of his announcement passed, Dougal's mind worked furiously.

You evil bastard…you are obviously behind it. You are a much greater player than I gave you credit for. Edward and I will have to be on our guard. I need to know more.

He bowed to the Leader.

"My Lord, may I seek further information? If I am to achieve our quest—" he turned to Edward and inclined his head, "—the Earl of Kilmarnock and I shall need to know more detail of the two sisters and how their work is threatening the Knights?"

For a moment, Dougal thought his question was to be ignored.

After a lengthy silence the old man spoke. "Very well."

He looked to his manservant and the man assisted him back

to his chair.

"Many years ago, one of Queen Victoria's leading botanical scientists was financed by the realm to undertake research around the globe to discover the healing properties of plants which would enhance the health of her majesty's subjects."

He paused and took a sip of his ale.

"Unfortunately, Professor de Vargas was a little too successful and discovered a plant high above the snows in the Austrian Alps with properties that—shall we say—conflicted with our spiritual goals."

He smiled coldly, his bloodless lips set in a thin line. "Professor de Vargas unfortunately met with an untimely end in the Amazon jungle about twenty years ago." He raised his brows and his smile grew. "I believe he was killed by bandits."

I'm sure there is more to it than that, Dougal thought.

"The professor had two daughters. Indigo de Vargas y Irausquínno, the elder daughter is married to the Sherriff of Cornwall, Captain Thoreau. She travelled with her father to the Amazon and after his death she continued his research into the passionflower. It is of no consequence and is used merely for its medicinal properties."

He frowned and looked from Dougal to Edward. "The second daughter by a later marriage, Sofia de Vargas, is a couturier of note in Vienna."

"Captain Thoreau and his wife have a holiday complex in Cornwall where research is also carried out, and they have four children. The cosmecuticals she plays around with are merely a product for vanity and pose no threat to us. We have a loyal, if foolish, member, Duke Lorca of Cornwall, who keeps us informed of the doings of Madam Thoreau." He paused and took a long draught from his goblet, before turning to the men listening to him. "She is of little concern to us. However, we have received intelligence that the de Vargas sister in Vienna is close to succeeding in the research she leads. Ten years ago, we were advised she had retrieved her father's notes and we have observed her activities closely since that time."

Dougal watched with fascination as two bright red spots flared on the papery cheeks of the Grand Master contrasting with his pale face and white robes. The older man placed his goblet on the table with a resounding thud.

"And you know what that will mean for us."

He turned to the automatons. "That fool, Lorca played right into our hands by sharing the information we fed him. The imbecile almost broke his skinny little legs in his enthusiasm to help our cause. He has a vendetta against Madam Thoreau and the Sheriff."

Dougal interrupted. "But with all respect, my Lord, there is no evidence it was Madam de Vargas at the station?"

The Leader glared back at Dougal and his voice shook as he replied.

"It was her at the station…it had to be. Now we just need you to destroy their laboratory and all research notes and kill Sofia de Vargas. It is but a simple task for you and the Earl of Kilmarnock which will prove your allegiance to the order and assist you to begin your spiritual growth."

The Earl of Kilmarnock raised his hand tentatively. In a trembling voice, he asked naively.

"My Lord… if…if we take the life of another…will that not condemn us to hell and end our spiritual growth?"

The Leader looked across at the red-faced young man and smiled. "Our spiritual growth culminates in immortality and if it is necessary to kill to preserve our order, it will move you through the petitions even more quickly, my son."

He stood and gestured to his manservant before turning back to the two young men.

"We will not allow non-believers access to our quest for

immortality. Dabbling in the physical sciences is sinful. It will end
our quest and it will end our lives." He moved across and stood
between Dougal and Edward. "Can I trust you, gentlemen, to
undertake this task?"

Dougal and Edward stood and bowed to their Leader.
They both replied. "Yes, my Lord."

Chapter 4

A soft tap at the door of her boudoir informed Sofia the first clients for the day had arrived and were waiting downstairs in her salon. She twisted the final silver ringlet with her hair steamer, and it fell gently to the shoulder of her tunic. Glancing in the mirror, she frowned at her reflection. Her silver white curls accentuated the pallor of her cheeks and she reached for her pot of rouge. She was a little heavier-handed than was her norm and applied more colour to her cheeks.

A week had passed since the incident at the railway station, the cargo being safely delivered to the flower stalls in the Naschmarkt as had been arranged. Johann had strolled past the markets situated on the roof of the Wienfluss and purchased his usual bouquet from the stallholder on his way to the University. The cargo for the laboratory was secreted in the bouquet amongst the white tulips, bellflowers, and snowdrops. Once the shipment had arrived at the laboratory, Sofia and the professor had spent the past few nights deliberating on her plan to visit the Alps.

Ernst had shaken his head. "It was only one instance, Sofia, and it was obviously a trap. However, I believe we should continue with the train and the flower market for the delivery of the flowers.

"No. I believe it is fraught with danger. We are too close to success to risk both losing the cargo and being discovered. It is time to sit quietly and bide our time."

"Johann and—"

Sofia cut him off. "Ernst, it is decided. I have deposited the funds for Johann and Genevieve to embark on their trip. I expect you will keep writing up your research. She looked at him intently. "It is imperative you take care of things at the University."

"And what about you?" he asked, his beetling eyebrows almost meeting as he frowned at her.

"What about me?" She laughed. "Madam Sofia de Vargas has a spring showing in her salon to organize. She has three dirigibles arriving from the colonies over the next week full of New York mamas and their eligible daughters to outfit for the upcoming season. I shall continue to be a doyenne of European society. When the show is finished, I will travel to Cornwall to visit my sister and collect my two scallywag nephews and take them on a wonderful holiday, skiing in the Austrian Alps.

As the Professor opened his mouth to argue, Sofia stood and raised her hand

"Enough, Ernst." She kept her voice firm. "We have worked for this outcome for almost ten years and we will wait until we are sure our research is not in jeopardy. One month of rest will not hurt."

The professor had been unhappy with her decree and she had not heard from him for several days.

Another soft tap on her door broke into Sofia's' reverie. "Enter."

Madam Lucienne de Voisy, the elegant salon manager stood in the doorway.

"Madame, the dirigible has docked, and the ladies have disembarked and are currently taking refreshment in the lounge. They will be ready for you in a few minutes."

"Thank you, Lucienne, I am coming now." Sofia stood and smoothed down her close-fitting silver tunic.

Following the taller woman into the narrow perambulator at the end of the hall, Sofia lightly touched the descent cog, and there was a quiet whoosh of steam as the machine slid noiselessly to the ground floor. As they descended, Sofia smiled at the memory of her introduction to the perambulator in Indigo's ancient manor in Cornwall. The workings of that machine were so archaic, it was necessary to wear earmuffs to block the noise of the hissing steam and the clunking cogs.

Stepping out of the perambulator, Sofia walked to the doorway of the Salon de Sofia and paused, taking in the scene before her. As always, she took a great deal of pleasure in looking around the business; she had established the salon from her humble beginnings as a seamstress when she had moved to Vienna, after attending Indigo's wedding in Cornwall just before her own twentieth birthday.

The greeting salon was simple and understated in its decor. Sofia's signature colour—silver—was evident in the furnishings and the walls were draped with soft grey silk. The morning sunlight streamed through the long narrow windows at the eastern end of the long room and refracted from the crystals hanging from the ceiling. The rainbows provided the only colour in the room. Two waiters with silver trays of champagne in crystal goblets circulated among the excited clients.

Watching the dozen or so women chatter and laugh as they indulged in elegant pastries washed down with the finest of French champagne, Sofia knew this group would be easy to work with.

I hope so. There is much to plan before the day is out.

She caught Lucienne's eye and the salon manager clapped her hands as Sofia stepped into the room.

"Attention, Mesdames and Mademoiselles." The women fell silent as Lucienne introduced Madam de Vargas, and Sofia smiled at them in welcome.

"Welcome to my salon. I trust you had a pleasant journey in my dirigible?" Sofia spread her arms wide in welcome. "As you can see, we have the latest in exquisite fabrics and accoutrements to prepare you for the upcoming season in New York."

Five assistants entered the room as she spoke, each carrying either a bolt of cloth or a box of adornments. Sofia reached for a bolt of silk, holding it high as it slipped sinuously to the ground, the sunlight catching the rainbow colours of the fabric. She smiled with satisfaction at the many *oohs* and *aahs* from the assembled women.

She had paid a small fortune for that bolt of fabric from Turkey, and it was the most expensive item in her salon. As she lightly clapped her hands, another six assistant couturiers dressed in silver tunics stepped from the cubicles on each side of the salon and Lucienne introduced each client to their own personal assistant. Sofia would spend time with each group to ensure they had the attention of the couturier herself to meet their needs.

Lucienne lightly touched Sofia's arm and drew her aside as the women sat with their advisers. "Sofia, are you able to have a personal appointment this afternoon? A messenger has arrived from the Earl of Rothmore. He is in Vienna with his wife and they depart tomorrow. He begs your forgiveness for the short notice and has asked for an appointment for late this afternoon."

"The Earl of Rothmore?" Sofia frowned and tried to remember the name. "Has his wife been here before?"

"His message seemed to indicate his wife has been here before. Perhaps before they married?" Lucienne replied.

"No matter." Sofia walked to the back of the room and slipped behind the velvet curtain, smiling to herself as she heard a young lady beseech her mother.

"Oh, Mama, I must have the rainbow silk."

Tapping the alphabet keys in front of the analytical engine, she searched for Rothmore in her customer list. Her memory was excellent, and she had no recall of that name and her records confirmed this.

"It is all right, Lucienne. I shall see the earl and his lady at four this afternoon."

"Very well, Madame. I shall send a messenger."

Sofia returned to her clients and was kept busy as many orders were placed. *Salon de Vargas* was becoming known across the globe and providing the dirigible service to the colonies had resulted in a tenfold increase in the number of clients who visited and spent their money each season. She smiled to herself. There would be no problem funding the upcoming trip to the Alps to collect the next shipment for the university.

* * * *

Dougal leaned forward in his seat and lifted the hood from his wife's head and shoulders. The hum of the dirigible covered the sound as the hood folded down from the side of the airship and he secured the straps to the hooks on the wall. He smiled at the automaton and patted her hand gently. "I will wake you when we arrive, my dear."

Dawn was breaking, and Edward pointed to the ground as fingers of sunlight dappled the treetops of the forest below. They had left the English Channel behind and were moving swiftly over the French countryside as they made good time to their destination.

"Have you had a reply from the messenger?" asked Edward.

"Yes," Dougal smiled. "Sweet Celestine and I have an appointment at four o'clock." Dougal pointed to the quiet woman staring vacantly at the side of the dirigible.

Edward reached over and flicked a lever on the control panel of the steam-powered air ship. "We had better make haste, then."

Dougal looked at the young man and decided to broach the subject that had been at the forefront of his mind since the meeting at Castle Dean. Their conversations to date had concerned their journey and collecting Dougal's 'wife'. Edward, surprisingly, was familiar with the steam propulsion system of this airship and explained to Dougal he had spent some time in France learning the intricacies of steam-powered travel.

"Edward, may we speak?" The younger man looked up eagerly.

"Don't worry, Dougal, we shall arrive in Vienna before noon."

139

Dougal waved his hand dismissively.

"Oh, I have no fear of that Dougal. I need to have a conversation with you regarding the purpose of our visit."

The young man's eyes widened, and Dougal watched with interest, as Edward swallowed nervously and his Adam's apple bobbed up and down. The younger man adjusted the large cog on the side of the control panel and secured it with a brass chain, before turning to Dougal.

"There. Our course is set."

Dougal leaned back in his set and steepled his fingers, looking at Edward and he realized the life of this eager young man was in his hands.

"Edward, tell me about your vows."

"Well… I understand that I have committed to this task and my vows will ensure my loyalty to you and the completion of the task," he replied. The young man's reply was cryptic, and Dougal sensed he was not being completely honest.

"And your thoughts on the termination of Madam de Vargas?" Edward held Dougal's gaze silently for a full minute, the only sound to be heard was the gentle whooshing of the steam from the cylinders and the soft rushing of the air past the side of the airship.

"May I be frank, Dougal?"

"You may."

"Your father was a very good friend to mine and they shared a common goal. I am unsure of your allegiance to your father's philosophies or if you were indeed aware of his goal before he died. At Castle Dean when our Leader asked for someone to join you in this task, I prayed to myself that you were privy to the thoughts of your father. That is why I volunteered and took the vows."

Douglas smiled. The expression in the young man's voice as he mentioned the vows left him in no doubt that they were of the same mind.

"Well then, Edward. We have an interesting task ahead."

He leaned back and closed his eyes.

"Wake me when we are over Vienna."

Chapter 5

At precisely four o'clock, a carriage drew to a halt in the Lindengasse across from the salon. Sofia sat on a velvet-lined love seat beneath the window sipping a cup of chamomile tea and glanced across at Lucienne who waited at the entrance to greet the Earl of Rothmore and his wife.

"Ah…merveilleux," Lucienne exclaimed.

"What is it?" asked Sofia.

"We have a very wealthy client by all appearances." The petite salon manager peered through the spy hole on the main door. "He drives one of those new horseless carriages. There are only a few in the city and they are costly."

Sofia's curiosity was aroused. She'd had no clients from Scotland before and would be interested to hear how a wealthy earl and his wife had come to hear of *Salon de Vargas*.

"*Ooh, la la*," chirped Lucienne. "And his wife is very drab. We will have some work to do here."

Sofia stood and patted her hand over her hair now coiled in braids around her forehead. A short rest after the departure of the ladies from the colonies had refreshed her and now she looked forward to meeting a new client…especially one with a wealthy husband. A substantial sale would be well received financially, with Johann and Genevieve's trip to England looming and her own trip to the Alps in the preparation stage.

The bell on the front door rang and Sofia stepped back into the shadows at the side of the room to observe her new customer. Lucienne ushered a short woman dressed from head to toe in black through the door and into the main salon. Her black dress was fashioned from Henrietta crepe, a bland fabric Sofia detested. A weeping veil of more black crepe covered her face and she wore no adornments. Her head was lowered, and she didn't speak.

Sofia's gaze moved to the man who had followed the drab woman into the salon. He was tall and broad…one of the tallest men she had ever seen, and he was clad in full Scottish regalia. The dull colours of his wife's attire accentuated the colours in his tartan kilt and cape. Bright magenta, umber brown and a deep sky-blue edged with a fine white line contrasted with her drab black dress. Thin brogues encased his feet, past a short colourful buskin tied above his calf with a striped pair of garters. Bare knees, a glimpse of muscular thighs, and a broad chest and shoulders flashed past her vision as she met his amused stare.

Deep blue eyes crinkled as the Earl of Rothmore smiled at her. "You will not have seen much Scottish dress in Wien, Madame?" His voice was deep and full of laughter, and Sofia had to listen carefully to understand the words beneath his strong Scottish accent. She walked across the room to him and nodded to Lucienne.

"Refreshments, please. I am sure our guests would like to partake of a cool drink?"

Lucienne went to the rear of the salon and pulled the bell rope to summon the maid.

"No, sir. I have not" Sofia extended her hand to the earl. "I apologise for staring but the magnificent colours in your kilt caught my attention."

"It is the Rothmore tartan, Madame. The blue is the glimmer of light on the sea around my island and the white is the sudden shaft of sunlight on the waves. The purple represents the heather."

"Fascinating and very beautiful," she replied looking down at the strong hand still grasping hers. "Please forgive my rudeness. I am Sofia de Vargas and I welcome you and your wife to my establishment."

He raised her hand to his mouth and gently kissed the edge of her wrist and Sofia looked at him curiously.

An unusual man, well-spoken and confident. Not what she had been expecting at all.

"A pleasure to meet you, Madame. This is my… er…Celestine. The small woman nodded and lowered her head before her husband led her to a seat in the corner. He tucked her shawl around her shoulders and patted her on the knee. "Are you comfortable, my dear?"

The woman nodded without speaking and the earl crossed the room back to Sofia. He took her arm and led her across to the window and lowered his head. Sofia shivered when his warm breath touched her ear. "My wife is most unwell and has been in a decline since the sudden death of Queen Victoria. She is English and mourns her monarch deeply. I thought a visit to your salon may help her recover." He took her hand again. "She hasn't spoken since the news of the Queen's death reached us."

Sofia looked down at her hand still in his grasp. He turned it over and looked at it with unusual interest before she pulled it back and spoke briskly.

"I am very sorry to hear of your wife's illness. The death of Queen Victoria was most unexpected. Now shall we begin?" She clapped her hands and two of her assistants came immediately into the salon. "Jeannie and Belle will take your wife's measurements and I will show her some fabrics." She looked up to find his gaze was fixed on her face. "Perhaps you would like to retire to the room we have set aside for gentlemen?"

"No," he replied. "I will choose the fabrics. My…wife is not in any state to make decisions."

"Very well." Sofia walked to the end of the long salon and gestured to him to follow.

Many bolts of fabric lay draped over the large tables at the back of the room and she watched with growing pleasure as he reached over to the Turkish silk.

Yes, that would be a very nice purchase.

"A wonderful fabric—suitable for an afternoon dress," she commented as the sinuous silk slipped between his fingers.

"Yes," he replied. "We will order one of these for each day in seven different colours."

Sofia nodded. "And what else do you require?"

"After we depart Wien, I am taking my wife into the Alps for a summer holiday, so some bright dresses and evening clothes will be required."

Sofia nodded. "The mountain air should help her recover. The Alps are wonderfully restorative."

"Can you recommend an establishment high in the mountains?" he asked.

Sofia looked up and warmth filled her as his intent gaze fixed on her lips. She stared at him and he lifted his eyes to meet hers. A feeling such as she had never experienced before pooled in her chest and the warmth travelled down to her stomach and her legs trembled.

He held her stare while she sought the words that would not come to her lips.

"Ah…ah…there is an excellent inn at Schladming. I have stayed there myself on many occasions and the service and the accommodation are first class. It has been there for many years." She gathered her thoughts together, despite the trembling of her limbs." I believe the poet Wordsworth stayed there and is oft quoted as lauding the wild spaces of the mountains as sublime and a countervailing force to the corrupting influences of civilization."

She turned away from him and reached for a bolt of serviceable fabric, cross with herself for her response to his touch and look. "Now, if you are walking in the Alps, your wife will need some warmer dresses as the cool afternoons can bring on a chill." She called for Lucienne before turning back to the earl and was dismayed to see his gaze still firmly fixed on her face. "Lucienne, would you please take the details for the—"

"Dougal," he interrupted. "Please call me Dougal."

"Very well. For Dougal." She knew her voice was clipped. She needed to get away from his intense blue gaze. It was strange but it was as though he could see her innermost thoughts, and no-one was allowed into her mind. Not even Ernst…the only person who she was open with was Indigo and they met very rarely.

She nodded at the earl and turned back to look at his wife who was being measured by the one of the assistants. Celestine did not move and stared into the distance as though she was uninterested.

"Very well…Dougal." Sofia held out her hand, determined not to let his touch affect her this time. "My staff will take care of your needs. It has been a pleasure meeting you and—" she turned to the woman standing immobile in the corner "—your wife." I hope the alpine air has the desired benefits for her health."

Dougal lowered his lips and kissed her hand once more and smiled down at her. "The pleasure has been mine…Madame."

She turned and left the salon without a backward glance although her legs were trembling, and her heart was pounding. When she reached the safety of the perambulator, she drew a deep shaking breath and closed her eyes.

Never before, had she been so enthralled by a man. And the earl had simply provoked those feelings with his intense blue stare and the touch of his hand on hers. Sofia raised her wrist and held it against her mouth, imagining she could still feel his lips pressing against her skin.

****

Dougal walked across to the window and stared out, deep in thought. He reached down and fingered the glove in the small leather bag on his hip.

She was the one.

Not only would her tiny hand be perfect fit for the small glove, but her height and the way she moved were identical to the cloaked figure in the station. And she had mentioned visiting the Alps.

He had no doubt it was her.

For the time being, Sofia de Vargas was safe. He and Edward had been given the task of disposing of her and if the Grand Master could be trusted, no one else would be pursuing her just yet.

He smiled grimly. Edward had shared his despair with the Charter of the lodge and his distrust of the Council of Five. They'd had a lengthy conversation before they had disembarked from the dirigible when it had touched down at the landing stage in the Prater, the former imperial hunting ground, one of the most modern landing areas on the continent.

Edward was still on board the small airship awaiting Dougal's instructions for their next move. It would be necessary to find lodgings in Vienna for a few days while he sought more information on Sofia's trip to the Alps. A plan was beginning to form in Dougal's mind. He would take the automaton back to the dirigible and then he and Edward would seek some lodgings.

He turned to the salon manager. "How long will it be before we can take delivery of my wife's garments?"

"Less than a week," she replied. "Madame de Vargas has a team of reliable seamstresses awaiting her direction."

"Very well." He walked over to the automaton who was sitting with her head bowed. "Come along, my dear, we shall go to our lodgings." Dougal place his hand under the elbow of his 'wife' and was dismayed to hear a whirring sound. To cover the malfunction, he bent and swept the automaton into his arms and walked quickly to the door.

"My wife is feeling poorly," he called over his shoulder. "I shall return with the details of our accommodation on the morrow."

The salon manager ran past him and opened the door to the street for him. "I hope your wife recovers quickly. Are you sure you would not rather she rest here until she recovers her breath?"

Dougal shook his head and stepped through the door and thanked the salon manager before striding across to his carriage. After he had lifted the whirring and clicking Celestine into the vehicle, he glanced up and smiled to himself. A shadowed figure stood at the window of the apartment looking down at him. He vowed to himself he would do everything in his power to see Sofia de Vargas remained safe. Her guarded reaction to him indicated she was well aware of the danger around her.

Climbing into the vehicle next to his 'wife', Dougal grimaced at the array of springs beginning to protrude from her body. Luckily, she had managed to stay intact while they were in the salon. He was sure the chapter could have afforded to fund their quest to a more satisfactory level and at least let them purchase an automaton that would last longer than one day. As it was, he and Edward had already put their own funds to the hire of the dirigible and the carriage. Shaking his head, he reached for the brass headset and placed it over his ears before flicking the power cog to start the carriage.

The drive to the Prater was slow as both air and ground traffic were heavy, and it was nearly dark by the time Dougal turned into the carriage bay closest to their airship. Edward sat on the steps of the dirigible awaiting his return and jumped to his feet as Dougal slid from the vehicle.

"Was it her? Did you find her?" His voice was full of excitement.

"Yes, I became acquainted with Madame de Vargas and I am sure she is the cloaked woman from the station last week," Dougal replied. He removed his gloves and ran a hand though his hair in frustration. "Are you talented with mechanicals?" he asked the younger man. "My wife appears to have lost some springs."

"I *canna* fix those creatures," said Edward. "They spook me almost as much as the Grand Master."

Dougal laughed. "Well, I seem to have become a widower very quickly. Anyway, not to matter. I have established contact with Madame de Vargas and we now have to find ourselves some lodgings for a few nights."

"Very well,' replied Edward. "But first a meal, I think?"

Dougal nodded. "I will just store poor Celestine safely in the airship and we will go and find a good *Kaffeehäuser*."

Chapter 6

There was a sharp snap as Sofia drew the cogs together on the front door of the salon. Lucienne had been the last to leave and had relayed her misgivings about the earl's wife as she had prepared to leave for the day.

"There is something very strange about that woman," she insisted. "She may as well have been comatose when Bella took her measurements. Bella was most upset. She said it was like touching a corpse. Her skin was cold, and she did not move." She shook her head at Sofia. "I fear if we have any more visits from her, the young ladies will be reluctant to attend to her."

"Yes, the earl and his lady wife were certainly not what I expected," Sofia agreed. "Anyway, it was a very good sale. I will reward Bella for her trouble this afternoon."

Sofia stood with her back against the door and surveyed the room. As usual, her staff had cleared everything away before they departed. The expensive bolts of fabric were locked in the storeroom and the room had been restored to its immaculate condition. She wandered through the salon and into the small office at the back of the lower level, running her fingers through the silk hanging in the doorway. Sitting at her rosewood writing table, she rested her chin in her hand and closed her eyes. She should contact Indigo and let her know she would be coming to Cornwall to collect the two boys for a visit to the Alps, but she was restless.

Impatiently she stood again and walked across to the cloakroom and pulled out her long silver coat. Tomorrow would be soon enough to send a missive to her sister. For the moment she needed a walk to clear her head. The Earl of Rothmore would not leave her thoughts and she must have clear head to plan her journey.

Sofia let herself out the door and stepped on to the footpath. All was quiet. The gas lights shone dimly in the early evening gloom and cast eerie shadows onto the deserted street. She shook herself, irritation settling in her chest. Since the attack at Westbahnof, she had avoided going anywhere alone, but tonight she was determined to overcome her trepidation. A visit to Café Schwarzenberg and Herr Hochleitner would help her regain her confidence. The Kaffeehäuser was on the Kartner Strasse on the other side of the Ringstrasse and a two mile walk from her salon and she set off, composing the message to Indigo in her head as she headed toward the palace on the Museumplatz.

If she left the Rothmore order under Lucienne's direction, she could leave for Cornwall within a couple of days. She had warned Indigo the visit was imminent so it should not be a problem to collect the boys. The last she'd heard Jago and Jory had been sent home from their boarding school because of their spirited behaviour. She smiled to herself; the chaos in her sister's household kept her in a constant state of amazement.

Sofia enjoyed her own quiet life alone in her apartment above the salon. Granted, it did become lonely at times, but she would not be able to function in the noisy chaos that was Indigo's manor house. The boys had all inherited their mother's strong will and were determined to demonstrate it at every opportunity. Unfortunately, none of the schools they had attended were predisposed to dealing with such boisterous young men.

The noise and chaos were kept in check to some extent by Mr. and Mrs. Grimoult, Indigo's trusted servants. Nevertheless, Sofia loved visiting, and it gave her respite from the constant worry of overseeing the moonflower research at the laboratory.

She paused as a carriage sped past her and blinked in confusion. As it had flashed past it had reminded her of the carriage the earl…Dougal…had entered earlier. Biting her lip, she determined to forget this man who had occupied her thoughts since the moment he had walked into the salon.

Even if she had been interested in a liaison, it was out of the question. He was a client—or rather his wife was— and that was the gist of the problem. He was married and therefore she would give him no more thought. Taking a deep breath, she thought of the forthcoming expedition, as the sweet fragrance of the spring flowers in the Burggarten drifted out to her. There was a gap in the wall and a viewing area for the public to see the private garden and Sofia stood with her hand on the cold fence rail. The night flowers were illuminated by the rising moon and she craned her neck to get a glimpse of the moonflower which she knew was growing amongst the ferny fronds behind the fountain. It was the only place she knew where the moonflower had been propagated successfully out of the Alpine region.

For a brief moment, she pondered the possibility of breaching the garden one night and collecting the specimens from there, but quickly realized there were few flowers in bloom. She stretched on her toes and froze as a cold metallic finger brushed her arm. Turning swiftly, she put her hand on her rapidly beating heart, and let a relieved breath out when she realized it was only a decorative piece of the fence rail.

Looking around at the mist settling in the spring evening, she tucked her head down and walked briskly toward the Café Schwarzenberg, crossing the great Ringstrasse boulevard which was in the midst of construction.

She pushed open the door and smiled at the seated cashier who was flirting coquettishly with a young man in a kilt. Sofia closed her eyes. The city is full of Scots today.

"Willkommen." The booming voice of Herr Hochleitner greeted her. "Madame de Vargas. It is such a pleasure. We have not seen you for a few weeks."

Sofia glanced across at the young man staring at her with his mouth open, before she reached across and took Herr Hochleitner's arm. "Yes, Hans. The salon has been busy, and I have come to say farewell before I depart for the Alps to take some mountain air."

She watched curiously as the young man scurried into the gambling room at the back of the coffee house. Herr Hochleitner smiled down at her affectionately before leading her to the special lady parlour.

"Now tell me what has your dear wife prepared today?" she asked as she slid into a single bench along the window.

"An egg in a glass, or a sweet perhaps?" he asked. "Maria has made some *Buchtein* this afternoon with jam from the spring plums in our garden."

"Then I must sample one," she replied. Settling back against the timber-lined wall, she positioned herself where she could observe the evening crowd who would soon be making their way to the opera. It was early and she was the first customer in the parlour. The gilt-edged mirrors reflected the candlelight coming from the many ornate chandeliers hanging low from the high ceiling. A low buzz of noise drifted from the smoky atmosphere of the gambling room across from her. She glanced across to the room; it was full of men, lounging around on the padded seats or leaning over the pool tables.

Sofia turned her attention to the street as a carriage hovered past outside the window. A footman ran forward and pulled down the steps and she smiled as she recognized an evening gown from her salon. Business had been brisk over the past few weeks as local society prepared for the spring launch of the musical season. The Vienna State Opera hall had recently been commissioned by the Viennese City Expansion Fund and would provide further opportunities for her salon once completed.

Sofia sighed. As soon as her staff had completed the

creation of the elixir from this expedition to the Alps, she was going to hand the research over to Ernst and Johann. It was time—

"A penny for your thoughts, Madame?"

The warm rolling words of a deep Scottish brogue interrupted her thoughts. She turned slowly from the window, knowing before she looked up the voice belonged to the Earl of Rothmore.

"Sir." She nodded to him. "It is a surprise to see you so soon."

"It is a pleasure to see you again too, Madame." The earl slid onto the bench beside her.

"You are unaware, sir, this is the ladies' parlour?" She was determined not to let the warmth of his thigh pressing against her leg affect her and she moved away. "Are you with your wife? I trust she has recovered?"

Dougal reached across and held her chin gently with his hand. "I know it is the ladies' room. However, when my manservant told me you had entered the establishment, I could not resist coming in to see you." The warmth from his strong fingers travelled down her neck and lodged in her chest, just above her fast beating heart.

"And your wife, sir?" she repeated.

He looked at her with a strange expression on his face and did not answer.

"I am not a courtesan, sir. I may be liberal and forward-minded, but I am not in the habit of partaking of a dalliance with a married man," she said firmly. "However flattered I am by your attention, it is unwelcome. I am about to partake of my meal. It has been a long day and I am tired." She turned and waited for him to leave but the grip on her chin tightened and the first prickle of unease flickered across her skin.

"Sofia?" His voice was soft. "May I call you Sofia?"

She did not reply and tried to inject displeasure into the

stare she directed at him. He let go of her face and trailed gentle fingers down her neck before placing his hands on the table.

"Sofia, I am an honest man and not used to deception." He held her gaze and continued. "I do not have a wife. The woman you met this afternoon is… my…" He paused and looked at her. "She is the wife of an acquaintance who knew I was travelling to Vienna."

Her first reaction was relief, but then discomfort covered her like the cold fingers of the mist outside as suspicion began to build in her mind.

"Why, then sir, did you pretend she was your wife?" Her voice was heavy with displeasure. He hesitated and she sensed he was being less than truthful with her.

"I did not want you to think I—"

"Why were you in my salon?" She cut off his words before he could complete the lie she knew was about to come from his lips.

"The truth?"

She nodded.

"I wanted to meet you and it seemed the only way to make your acquaintance. You do not mix widely in society."

"No, that's true," she replied. "However, sir, you have me intrigued. Why would you wish to meet me? So far from your earldom and your island…or is that all a fancy as well?"

Dougal straightened in the seat and smiled at her. "I apologise for the one and only untruth I told you today, Sofia. Yes, I am an earl. I have a castle on Little Rothmore, and I am travelling to the Alps to take the mountain air. I am with my manservant, Edward, and I will be leaving the…my acquaintance's wife in Vienna until her garments are ready."

"And her health?"

"Er…she is indisposed and is need of medical attention which has been arranged."

He turned his gaze to the window as he spoke and she knew once more, he was not telling the truth. Despite his lies, she was pleased he was sitting here with her. It was not often she had the company of intelligent men in a social setting. The time she spent in the laboratory with Ernst and Johann was fraught with tension, and Henri, her own manservant was more like a father to her.

"Would you like to join me for coffee?"

His features relaxed as a smile broke over his face and he reached across and picked up her hand. "I would be delighted, Madame."

Hans returned with her *Buchtein* and sweetened milky coffee. He assured Dougal it was acceptable for him to stay in the ladies' parlour until more customers arrived later in the evening. Sofia sipped on her coffee and observed the man sitting across from her.

His dark hair was pulled back and tied in a tail with a strip of leather and left his features clear for close inspection. Deep blue eyes of a clarity she had not seen before, were framed by dark curling lashes. Her gaze travelled down to his full lips and on closer inspection, discovered a narrow white scar ran from the side of his mouth to the centre of his cheek. His cheeks had the ruddy glow of a man who spent a lot of time outdoors and the hand that had held hers was work-roughened.

"Tell me about yourself, Dougal. Why are you in Vienna?"

"I had business to attend to and then I am taking a holiday in the mountains," he replied. "There is an Austrian cattle breed which survives in the rocky conditions and cold temperatures in the alpine pastures I wish to inspect.

"The rocky condition and bitter temperatures are the same as my island home." He laughed. "Very different to the sophistication of Vienna."

"I am well used to travelling in your country. My sister lives in Cornwall and I visit her." Sofia sighed. "Although not as frequently as I would like."

The sound of laughter drifted in from the foyer and Dougal stood and held his hand out to her.

"I shall depart the ladies' parlour," he said with a smile. "Perhaps you will allow me to escort you to your apartment?"

Sofia looked up at him, torn between her suspicions of him and her intuition he was a good man.

She shrugged. "Certainly, it is a lengthy walk, but a pleasant evening. I would appreciate the company."

Dougal insisted on paying the cashier for Sofia's coffee and after a quick word with his young manservant, led her out onto the street. Sofia shivered as the cold wind from the Alps met them. Dougal's warm fingers brushed her throat as he tucked her cloak more snugly about her shoulders and she shivered again, but not from the cold this time.

"If we walk close together, it will shield the wind from you," he said thoughtfully. "I am used to the cold. My castle is cold and draughty, and the wind blows from the sea in all directions.

They walked soft-footed in the stillness of the clear night and only her occasional direction to take a turn, here or there, broke their companionable silence. It seemed to be no time at all before they reached the Lindengasse and they stood together under the gas lamp outside the door of her salon.

Sofia gasped as a rhythmic clicking surrounded them and looked over her shoulder waiting for the metallic grasp of an automaton. Dougal pulled her close and his arms banded tight around her.

"What is it? What's wrong?"

She grasped his shirt and burrowed into his hard chest trying to control her shaking.

"Can you see it? Where is it?" She was barely able to get the words out as fear snaked up her spine. Lifting her head, she peeked around his solid bulk. A piece of metal had come loose from the gas lamp and the wind was blowing it against the lamppost. She drew a shaky breath and let go of his shirt.

His hold gentled and he reached up and tucked a stray strand of hair behind her ear. "Why so timid?" he asked gently.

Her heart was thudding in her chest and she leaned into him once more. It was safe…and warm…and comforting. She could get used to this very quickly.

Dougal lowered his head into her hair and breathed in the exotic fragrance. She was so small, he thought. Delicate shoulders barely reached the middle of his chest, her waist beneath the flowing cloak was tiny— he could almost have spanned it with his hands. Without giving it more thought, he gathered her even closer and a soft sigh settled in the air. She fitted against him so well, almost as though she had been tailor-made to fit into his body. He inhaled the fragrance of her hair once more as he stroked the tension from her shoulders. Guilt overcame him as he understood how much the chase at the station must have frightened her. But despite her fragile appearance, he knew she was brave and determined.

Would she be so brave if she knew she was beneath the watch of the Knights Templar?

An overwhelming desire to protect her consumed him and he vowed to himself he would protect her. Before he knew what he was doing, his mouth lowered to hers and it took his breath away. Her soft lips opened under his and her sweet breath mingled with his. His knees trembled and his mind cleared of any thought apart from the delight of her lips. She returned his kiss and the sensation ran through his blood.

"Dougal," she murmured his name against his mouth as she lifted her hands to caress his neck.

The soft gasp of his name brought him back to reality and he pulled back and blinked to clear his head.

Dear Lord, what was he doing?

He was here to protect her, not molest her. He could ill afford for her to get into his blood. Look how much one simple kiss had distracted him. He had a mission to accomplish although he had no idea what he was going to do about it.

"I'm sorry, Sofia." He lowered his hands and put his arms by his side, away from temptation. Her wide green eyes looked up at him and the flickering light from the lamplight reflected in the four small brass studs in her delicate ear lobe.

"Don't be," she replied softly. She turned to the door and ran her hand in front of a square brass plate. A sharp snap was followed by the slow opening of the door as the cogs freed the lock. She looked up into his face, which he knew was full of curiosity; he had never seen a door open with a simple touch of the hand. Most of the doorways in his castle did not even have a door to lock…and that would be problematic if the plan formulating in his head came to fruition.

"A recognition device embedded in the cogs," she explained with a laugh. He sensed she was trying to lower the emotional tension lodged between them like a solid door. At the moment, he had no wish to pass through that doorway, although if all went to plan…

He gathered his thoughts and harrumphed before taking his leave. Taking her small hand between his, he lowered his lips gently to the inside of her wrist and pleasure shot through his body as she shivered at his touch.

"May I call on you again before I depart for the Alps?" he asked.

Sofia nodded without speaking and stepped through the doorway. She turned and smiled up at him.

"Thank you for a pleasant evening, Dougal."

Before returning to their lodgings in Mariahilfer Strasse, Dougal called into the Café Schwarzenberg to collect Edward. The young man was still sitting in the entry flirting with the cashier.

"There is no doubt, Edward. We are a fine pair. Too long in the wilds of Scotland and the first pretty face brings us both to become a quivering mess." Edward followed Dougal to the street and flushed when Dougal slapped him jovially on the back.

"Enough of that. We have some serious planning to do." Dougal lowered his voice as they retraced almost the same route he had taken with Sofia, less than an hour ago. The streets were now busy with carriages, both horse-drawn and steam-powered as the city came alive after the end of the evening's music recitals.

They entered their lodgings at the end of the street and Dougal looked across at Westbahnof, just across the road from their building. Much had happened since he had chased Sofia along the departure platform, and he smiled grimly as the sight of the railway station reminded him of the journey ahead.

"Tomorrow we shall book out our tickets to Salzburg. I would not feel safe travelling through the Alps in our airship. And if the quality of the mechanicals in the ship is anything like those in dear Celestine, I would prefer to be on the ground."

"How we will travel from Salzburg to Schladming?" Edward asked.

"It all depends how quickly we want to get there and when we wish to arrive." Dougal laughed at the expression on the younger man's face as he tried to decipher the cryptic reply. He crossed the room to his travelling bag and removed a velvet pouch.

"It will all depend on how long Madame de Vargas takes to return from Cornwall with her nephews." If the interlude with Sofia in the Kaffeehäuse had not been pleasant enough, he had also gleaned information from her about her forthcoming trip to Schladming and the fact she would have her nephews with her.

He reached into the pouch and slowly withdrew an elaborate inclinometer from the bag.

"What is that?" Edward asked curiously.

"This, my dear man, is an Astrolaberors which will get us to our destination. As long as we can plot against the sunrise or sunset, it will allow us to navigate through time. We shall arrive at Schladming before we leave Salzburg if we so desire.

The young man's eyes were huge in his face. "So we dinna need the airship after all?"

"Yes, we needed to bring the automaton. However, now she is no longer functioning, we may send her back to England on the airship. We will use the Astrolaberors for our return journey when the time comes. An inclinator of this size can transport three people with little worry.

Dougal smiled as understanding dawned on Edward's face.

Chapter 7

Sofia passed the first two days of her journey in Paris taking delight in visiting three couturier houses. At the end of the second day, she was met by Mr. Grimoult, her sister Indigo's manservant, who conveyed her to Indigo's airship for the short journey across the English Channel to the manor house in Cornwall.

The old man held her arms and looked at her closely. "As usual you are working too hard. You have shadow under your eyes, Sofia."

"The season has been very busy and business from the colonies is growing," she replied with a smile. The Grimoults had looked out for both her and Indio after their father had been murdered in the Amazon jungle.

"And the other business?" he asked softly.

"There has been a problem," she answered. "I believe the information sent from Captain Thoreau was a set-up. We are obviously being watched so I have taken the utmost care. Ernst is working at the laboratory alone and we have stopped all shipments for the time being."

"And I am sure there is a reason for your holiday to Schladming with the boys…apart from being a loving aunt?"

Sofia reached down and handed her carpet bag to Mr. Grimoult. "Yes, we are going to have some walks in the alpine summer and who knows we may even come across some botanicals. It will be a good experience for the boys."

Mr. Grimoult rolled his eyes. "Those scallywags. Quite honestly, their behaviour has been appalling and they need to be taken in hand. Captain Thoreau and madam are both so strong-willed, they can never agree on a suitable consequence for the two lads and they are becoming wilder by the day." He put out his hand and assisted Sofia up the steps of the dirigible. "A week with the calm influence of their aunt will do them no end of good."

"I am looking forward to it." Sofia smiled. "As I am looking forward to reacquainting myself with my dear sister…and Captain Thoreau of course."

She settled into her seat and closed her eyes as Mr. Grimoult prepared the airship for ascent. Thoughts of Dougal flitted through her mind and she wondered if he would write to her as he had promised when he had come to bid her farewell two days ago. He had been quite withdrawn and although her heart had raced when he took her hand and kissed it farewell, she doubted she would hear from him again. Although it had been very kind of him to visit her, he had been distant. The mistruth he had told her about having being married to the strange woman they had fitted in the salon, had been peculiar and she could still see no reason for it.

A strange interlude, a pleasant kiss and she would not see him again.

There was much to do and much to plan and she would put the handsome earl out of her thoughts.

The journey was pleasant, and the sky was clear as they approached the manor house. The dirigible passed over Castle Lorcathian, the home of her sister's arch enemy, Duke Lorca. It would not be surprising to her if he had somehow been involved in the conveying in the recent misinformation conveyed to Captain Thoreau in his capacity as Sheriff of Cornwall.

Sofia stood and looked down at the sloping green grass at the cliff top. She smiled—Indigo's holiday biomes were in the distance and there was a welcoming party gathered on the lawn. Although perhaps gathered was not the correct term. The four boys raced around, and Indigo's voice floated up to her as she called the boys back from the edge of the cliff.

To no avail.

Sofia watched with mounting horror as a toy dirigible inflated at the edge of the cliff and Ruan, the youngest, egged on by his older brothers, grabbed the trailing ladder as it ascended. His little feet left the ground and his screams of delight reached their airship as he climbed higher and higher above the cliffs.

"You bring your brother down immediately, Jago Thoreau." Indigo's cross voice carried up to Sofia. "Right this instant."

Sofia craned forward and followed the direction in which Mr. Grimoult was pointing. Jago held some sort of device in his hand and was pointing it at the toy dirigible. As he lifted it, the small airship rose and when it was lowered, Ruan's feet almost touched the ground.

"Last chance, young man. Bring him down or you will not be going to Austria with your Aunt Sofia."

"Oh, Mama." The shrill young voices floated in the air as the small toy plummeted to the ground. "You spoil all our fun."

Mr. Grimoult chuckled. "Young Jago and Jory built that airship and the device which allows it to be controlled from the ground. They have inherited the scientific mind of their mother, their aunt and their grandfather. God rest his soul."

"And the other two boys?" Sofia asked.

"Kit and Ruan do play with their older brothers, but much to their father's delight they are far less adventurous and prefer their studies to creating chaos," he replied.

With a final whoosh of steam, Mr. Grimoult manouvered the airship onto the landing pad. When it was secured, Sofia descended the ladder to the ground and into her sister's waiting arms.

"Oh, look how elegant you are," Indigo exclaimed. "You make me look like a country matron."

Her husband, Zane stepped across and kissed Sofia on both cheeks. "You are a country matron, my dear." He laughed when

Indigo glared at him. The four boys lined up to receive a kiss from their aunt and managed to contain their excitement for a few moments. Indigo looped her arm through Sofia's. "Come, Mrs. Grimoult has prepared your favourite refreshments. We have much to discuss."

Much later that evening, Indigo, Zane and Sofia retired to the viewing room on the top level of the manor. Sofia placed her hands on top of the ear muffs as they rode up in the directional perambulator. The squeaks, grinds and the humming of the perambulator as it ascended were not masked by the ear muffs.

"God's truth, Indigo. You need to maintain your equipment. There is no need for that noise."

Indigo smirked as she gestured for her sister to enter the viewing room. At first, Sofia's attention was taken by the spectacular view through the glass walls of the circular room. The sun was setting over the Celtic Sea and the sky was shot with all hues of gold and purple. Indigo cleared her throat and her impatience was conveyed to her sister. Sofia turned and gasped as she surveyed the new equipment in the room.

"No wonder you cannot afford to replace your perambulator," she said as she walked around touching the analytical engines filling one entire wall.

"And look at this." Indigo's excitement was contagious, and Sofia smiled. "We now have a new communication device which allows us to speak to you anywhere in the world…and in any time." She handed her sister a small brass device. "If you place this within your clothing as you walk the Alps with the boys, you will be able to contact us at any time."

"Amazing," Sofia replied. "It may come in very useful. Where did you source that?"

Zane smiled. "Mr. Grimoult and I developed it. When we were in the Amazon, ten years ago, the chronometer which allowed us to stay in touch with the submarine gave me an idea. It has taken a long time; however, it is now refined and can be used with little trouble and with little knowledge. We have a device for you to travel with to—"

Indigo grabbed her arm and interrupted her husband. "We have had some worrying news and wish to stay in touch with you at all times when you are sourcing the moon flowers."

Sofia looked from her sister to her brother-in-law. "What sort of news?"

"It has come to our attention the information which we conveyed to you, about the passenger on the train coming into Westbahnof, was given to my man by a colleague of Duke Lorca. We traced the message and it emanated from Scotland. A small town called Kilmarnock."

Sofia narrowed her gaze. "Scotland, you say? How coincidental."

"And the worrying thing is, there is a chapter there in Castle Dean who have links to the Knights Templar," Zane continued. "So it is essential you take the utmost care in the Alps. You are being observed."

"Would you rather I travel alone?" Sofia asked. "And leave the boys here?"

"We have considered that, but it will be a good cover for you, and they are looking forward to it. As a precaution, Mr. Grimoult will travel with you." Indigo held her gaze. "I expect you will have more bother from the boy's hi-jinks than—"

"Sofia, what did you mean by the Scottish coincidence." Zane interrupted his wife, concern lacing his voice.

"No…it is nothing. I recently had a Scottish client in the salon. Not long after the incident at the station."

"And you don't think it was related?" Indigo moved across to the analytical engine."What was her name?"

Sofia shook her head. "No matter. It was purely coincidental. This was an earl from the Little Rothmore…and an acquaintance."

Indigo quickly tapped a few keys and pulled up a map. "Hmm. Little Rothmore is only thirty miles distant from Kilmarnock."

"No, Indigo. It was purely a coincidence."

"Sofia, you are way too trusting. There is no such thing as coincidence."

Sofia's temper began to rise, and warmth suffused her face. She knew her older sister had little time for her couturier business and undervalued her intelligence. She bit back the retort on her tongue and decided not to mention there was chance she may hear from Dougal again, or perhaps even cross paths with him in the Alps.

"Come, I am in need of an early night. I am quite exhausted from my time in Paris," she said, keeping her voice light. "You must tell me all about your holiday biomes and about any interesting guests you have had."

Indigo looked back at her and obviously thought it better not to pursue her questioning. Sofia groaned and reached for the ear muffs as they headed toward the perambulator.

Chapter 8

"Aunt Sofia!" The shrill, combined voices of her nephews rang out over the whistle of the steam train as it pulled into Salzburg station. "We're almost there. Is this the mountains? Where's the snow?"

Mr. Grimoult smiled at her and reached across to grab the shirts of the two boys who were leaning out the train window before they fell out.

"We have a short trip in a steam carriage and then we will be at the mountains," Sofia replied patiently. "Although we will not see much snow until we walk the alpine paths." She reached up and adjusted the light gold chain around her neck and tucked the black jewel inside her blouse. Zane had embedded the device onto the back of a black stone, and it resembled an elegant piece of jewellery rather than a chronometric communication device. She had already used it to transmit news of their safe arrival to Indigo.

"Come, we have arrived." With a flurry of leg and arms, Sofia managed to catch the hands of the two boys while Mr. Grimoult struggled along behind them with the luggage. She was enjoying the company of her two nephews and had delighted in their intelligent conversations with her on the train journey. They had a far deeper understanding of the world than she would have expected at their age.

The steam carriage Mr. Grimoult had booked to convey them to Schladming was waiting for them on the paved road outside the station. The boys laughed with delight as the driver took their luggage from Mr. Grimoult. The carriage was painted with cow bells and when it started, the musical sound of bells rang across the still morning air covering the hissing of the steam.

Sofia nodded with satisfaction; they certainly looked like a family on holiday and she was glad the boys were accompanying her.

The owners of the Schladming Inn welcomed Sofia with affection. She was a regular visitor and had been staying there for many years. It had been several months since her last visit and Herr Schwandt fussed around her.

"As you *haf* the children, we *haf* given you the large cabin." He assisted Mr. Grimoult with their bags and Sofia grabbed the collars of the two boys as they went flying down the path past her.

"Just one moment, you pair," she cautioned. "We need to have a little discussion."

She tucked her arms through theirs, one child on either side and walked up the grassy incline behind their cabin. As they crested the hill, a panoramic view met them. Snow-capped mountains rose from the low fields where cattle grazed and the ever-present tinkle of cow bells drifted across to them. In the distance, two small figures walked out of the narrow green valley that passed between the two highest peaks.

Sofia pointed to the edge of the fields where the cattle grazed, to a line of tall conifers edging the lower slopes of the mountain. "That is the limit of your explorations when you are by yourselves. You can roam the fields and explore the valley, but you are to go no higher than the tree line." She was met by a chorus of protest. "When Mr. Grimoult or I are with you, we will climb into the snow."

Jory and Jago agreed, albeit reluctantly, and headed to the small shed at the front of the inn where Herr Schwandt had invited them to see the woodcarver at work. Sofia stood and breathed in the alpine air. It was a pleasure to be away from the noise and grime of the city and she decided to rest for a couple of days before they trekked to the snow level. The two hikers moved closer and crossed the grass fields below her. They paused to examine the cattle before disappearing into the trees at the bottom of the hill.

Sofia's heart thudded in her chest.

It couldn't be.

Both men wore kilts, although they were too far away for her to see the tartan. She closed her eyes and swallowed. In one breath she hoped it was Dougal…yet in the next, she knew if it was him, it was too much of a coincidence and he couldn't be trusted.

Sofia opened her eyes and sighed as the Earl of Rothmore and his manservant broke from the tree line and walked up the grassy hill toward her. Feelings warred within her and she didn't know if it was joy…or sadness…or fear.

Chapter 9

When Dougal stepped from the trees and looked at the lone figure on the top of the hill, excitement filled his chest.

She was here.

Sofia stood at the top of the hill above them. Her bright scarlet dress contrasted with the soft blue of the sky and her hair was bound in coils on either side of her face. She raised a hand and waved, and he knew in that moment, he would do anything to protect her. He had not been able to get her from his thoughts since he had left her in Vienna a week ago and had given much consideration to the method of ensuring her safety. Together with Edward, he had hatched a plan and they had been in the mountains taking readings for the inclinator journey. It had to be three days hence and after noon for the co-ordinates to be suitable for their destination.

As he watched, two young boys joined her at the top of the hill, and she reached down and put her arms around each of their shoulders before pointing down the hill.

Damnation, who the dickens was that?

He groaned and turned to Edward. "I believe we may have an impediment…or two to our plan."

Edward nodded. "I see."

They reached the top of the hill to the excited voices of the two young boys and Dougal smiled at Sofia. "I was hoping the Madame de Vargas, Herr Schwandt mentioned, was you, Sofia." He bent over, took her hand and kissed it gently, pleased to see the flush in her cheeks.

"A wonderful coincidence, Dougal." She smiled at him, but her voice was cold.

An astute woman.

"And who have we here?" He turned to the two boys.

"I'm Jory Thoreau." The one on the left one spoke first, followed quickly by the identical boy on the right.

"And I'm Jago."

"Boys," Sofia said. "This is the Earl of Rothmore, an acquaintance of mine." She inclined her head to Edward. "How do you do, I am Sofia de Vargas."

The young man blushed and stumbled over his reply. "Ah…Edward of Kilmarnock."

Sofia's eyes narrowed and Dougal sensed her withdrawal.

She gathered up the twins and pulled her light cloak across her shoulders. "Come young men, it is almost time for dinner." Holding her hand out to him, she held his gaze for a moment before speaking. "No doubt we shall see you there, Dougal?"

Warmth shot up his arm and he ignored it as he replied. "It will be my pleasure, Sofia."

Dougal asked Herr Schwandt to set a table for five. He would invite Sofia and the two young lads to join he and Edward for dinner. The elderly innkeeper shook his head. "*Nein, we will haf sechs.* There is her man as well."

Dougal's chest tightened and he frowned at the old man. "Her man?"

"Her servant."

The relief was profound. When this whole quest was done with, and he and Edward had hastened the demise of the ancient order in Kilmarnock, he had every intention of courting Sofia. The instant he had seen her, when he had entered her salon with that damned automaton, she had bewitched him. He was not looking forward to the events of the next few days, but they must carry out their plan. Her life depended on it. However, now they had the complication of the boys and her manservant to contend with.

At least the boys would not be left alone when they took Sofia with them.

* * * *

The firelight reflected in the crystal wine glasses on the table and brought out the deep warm hues of the timber-lined dining room. Dougal sat back in his chair and sighed, replete from the sumptuous meal provided by Frau Schwandt. Jory and Jago had been escorted to their beds by Mr. Grimoult when they had begun to nod over their dinner. The old retainer had kept them all entertained with tales from his navy days with the boys' father—Sofia's brother-in-law. Edward had followed them yawning and now Dougal and Sofia were alone in the dining room; their group were the only guests at the inn tonight.

A bright shard of light reflected from the unusual jewel sitting between her breasts and he leaned forward. "May I?"

He reached over and lifted it and turned it to the light. It was obsidian with intricate gold and silver wire holding it to the chain. He had not seen anything like it before. "It is most unusual. Was it handcrafted for you?"

Sofia nodded and tucked back into her bodice as soon as he let it go. A high flush on her delicate cheekbones indicated she was not as immune to him as she was pretending to be. She held his gaze.

"The boys' father, Zane, tinkers with jewellery making," she replied. "Speaking of whom, it is time I went to check on the boys."

She stood and brushed against his shoulder as she moved around the table, and he smelled the sweet fragrance of her skin. His arm seemed to lift of its own accord to circle her tiny waist and pull her closer to him, but she moved away from him and crossed to the doorway. Sofia looked at him, her features warring between a frown and confusion—and if he was correct—desire.

"Ah," she breathed. "Dougal, you are not good for my composure." Her chest rose and fell quickly, and he smiled to himself as she fought the attraction between them. He stood slowly

173

and crossed the room to her. He took her hands between his and lifted them to his lips.

'Will you walk in the moonlight with me, Sofia?"

She nodded without speaking and he sensed she had come to a decision. Together, they strolled through the garden to the hill where they had spoken earlier in the evening. He kept a firm grip on her hand until they paused at the top of the hill.

She sighed and turned to him, placing her hands on his chest. "Dougal, will you answer one question for me?" He held her gaze and nodded. "Why are you here? I am asking you to speak the truth. Are you following me?"

He looked down at her and rested his brow on the top of her head and gently pressed a finger to her throat, touching the pulse beating madly in the alabaster skin. Tonight she wore her hair loose for the first time and he had imagined running his fingers through it all night. Now he grasped it gently and tipped her head back looking down into her eyes. "That is a strange question, Sofia. Why would I be following you?"

She shivered and he drew her closer. "Do you believe in coincidences?" she asked. Pulling away from him, her eyes flared. "You were less than truthful with me in Vienna and now I want to know the truth."

"No, Sofia, I am not following you. I am here to partake of some mountain air and look at the cattle breed I spoke of that night in the *kaffeehäuser*. If you remember back, it was you…you, yourself… who recommend this inn to me."

Her shoulders slumped and she pulled away from him. "I am sorry, Dougal. There is much in my life that makes it impossible for me to trust. I am not good for you and this… attraction between us can only lead to trouble." Her eyes shone in the moonlight as tears threatened to spill. "I cannot speak of what is between us, but it cannot continue." He moved closer to her and he lifted his hand letting his fingers wipe the single tear on her

cheek." Her sad eyes tugged at his heart and he vowed once more
to protect this woman, not only from the evil men who were
plotting her demise, but from the sadness consuming her. A
missive from the Grand Master had been waiting for him at their
lodgings in Salzburg with a warning that the demise of the target
must be sooner rather than later; he had deliberately not told the
leader of their final destination so the automatons could not be sent
to follow.

"We can be friends, Sofia? We will enjoy our time on the
mountain with Edward and your little family. It can be a time full
of laughter and joy and we will ignore those things worrying you."

She smiled up at him and peace stole over him despite the
contents of the missive he'd received. He would trust in good
triumphing over evil. All would be well.

Chapter 10

Two days passed and Edward and Dougal had hiked to the upper reaches of the mountain to look at the cattle each day. Sofia had her hands full looking after the boys and keeping them safe and thanked Mr. Grimoult many times each day for assisting her.

"You are a pair of young devils." She laughed as she removed a live frog from her pocket. "To-day, when we hike with Edward and Dougal, you must do as we say at all times. Is that clear?"

Jory and Jago giggled and nodded. Sofia knew how much they were looking forward to going up into the snow. She glanced across at Mr. Grimoult and he nodded.

"I am ready to go as well, Sofia. We are going to pick some flowers to take back for Indigo." He turned to the twins. "Will you strong young men assist me to collect some botanicals for your mother's laboratory?"

They both groaned. "More smelly flowers for our mother to boil in her biome. We won't see her for a week." When Mr. Grimoult raised his bushy eyebrows at them, they agreed, albeit with moans of displeasure. Sofia smiled at him across the boys' heads. He was setting up a good cover for her.

The party set off after lunch. They had set aside time for the boys to play in the snow and Sofia planned to gather her moonflowers while they played under Mr. Grimoult's watchful eye. She would trust her life to him, as well as the boys. He and his wife had been faithful retainers to her own father many years ago and had lived with Indigo in Cornwall since their father had been murdered.

The cover was good; Sofia had told Dougal about the biome complex and Indigo's work with pharmaceuticals and cosmecuticals. Herr Schwandt had advised them not to go too high as the clouds were building to the west and could bode a change in the weather. The excited chatter of the boys kept them entertained and the walk had passed quickly. Sofia's legs ached and her calf muscles protested as she climbed the final steep section of the path.

Ahead Dougal and Edward led the way and she smiled as the cold wind plastered Dougal's kilt to his brawny thighs. He certainly looked at home in the outdoors, although he had been withdrawn and quiet since they had commenced the outing.

For the first time since she had left Vienna, Sofia was certain she would succeed. Mr. Grimoult carried the containers for the moonflowers in his rucksack and Dougal and Edward had shown little interest in their talk of moonflowers. It was strange they were both preoccupied today. She had attempted to start a conversation with Dougal on two occasions and he had answered in monosyllables and kept walking.

Now she hurried to catch up to Dougal. "Do you think the weather will hold out long enough for us to stay for a while?"

He stopped and shaded his eyes with his hand, looking up to the peak.

"Aye, it will be fine." He turned away from her and she shrugged and kept walking along behind him. A sharp squeal came from Jago and she turned swiftly to him, but he was only expressing his delight at the snow ahead of them. Both boys raced past her and dived into the snow drift. Sofia shook her head— they did not see much snow in the Cornish winter, but they were still children and she took pleasure in their play. She smiled and spoke to Mr. Grimoult as he caught up to her, puffing and red-faced as a snowball came whistling toward them. She ducked and shook her finger at her nephews, laughing as Edward formed a snowball and caught Jory unexpectedly in the shoulder with a perfect shot. The boys squealed and giggled as Edward returned snowball for snowball, despite being outnumbered by the twins,

"You watch the boys and I will climb a bit higher. If there are any moonflowers up there, I will call you. We should be close by now, surely."

The old man nodded and sat on a large rock with his back against the sheer rock wall which edged the mountain pass they had reached. Sofia looked down past him to the edge of the rock face. Her stomach dropped and her legs trembled as she looked over the sheer precipice. The inn and the forest were like toy buildings far below them. They had climbed higher than she thought.

"Make sure the boys stay well away from the edge," she instructed.

"I will guard them with my life." Mr. Grimoult smiled at her. "Now go and search for your flowers, Madame."

The twins were engrossed in building an igloo by the time she reached them and satisfied they were safe, she climbed further up the narrow track. Edward had left the boys to catch up to Dougal and they had both surged ahead, obviously following the cowbells which tinkled down from higher up the path.

A few hundred yards ahead, a clump of green foliage peeked out of the sheer rock and Sofia smiled. The patches of white scattered amongst the green appeared to be the elusive moonflower. Dougal and Edward had disappeared, and she surveyed the path ahead of her. An outcrop of fallen rocks covered in snow blocked her way and she looked around for an alternate route. An eerie quiet had fallen over the mountain and she shivered. The cries of the boys had stopped, and the cow bells were silent. For a moment she debated going back for Mr. Grimoult and the rucksack. She shook her head; it would be better if she made sure it was the moonflower before she went down. A cloud passed over the sun and she looked up, the high clouds were scudding; they would have to return to the inn before the weather changed.

To her right, there was a gap in the rock face and Sofia

stepped toward it and clung to the sharp rock with her fingers as she tried to see if there was a path around the rock fall. She squeezed through a narrow slit between two rocks and gasped as a deep precipice yawned in front of her. Clutching her chest, she stepped back slowly and hit a solid warm wall. She turned and Dougal's chest filled her vision. She looked up at him, the words dying on her lips. Edward stood close to him with a strange brass contraption in his hands. Dougal grasped her arm with steely fingers and held her gaze silently. Her head spun and fear crawled into her stomach. She backed away from them and gasped as her foot flailed in the air searching for a foothold.

Dougal reached back and held onto Edward's arm. She searched their unsmiling faces trying to understand what was happening.

"I'm sorry, Sofia. It is the only way."

Dougal pushed her and Sofia screamed as she plummeted to the rocks below.

Chapter 11

Dougal bowed his head and listened to the sonorous beating of the drum heralding the entrance of the Holy Five. Four of them moved to the table and sat, but the Grand Master remained standing. The white-cloaked men seated on the benches in the Great Hall looked up expectantly as their Leader summonsed Dougal and Edward were to the front of the gathering

A huge smile broke the usually solemn features of the old man and he bid them kneel in front of him. Reaching out he placed a hand on each of their heads and gave thanks for their loyalty.

"You may stand." He pointed to the raised dais in the centre of the room. Dougal and Edward climbed up the two steps. The gathering stood and a rousing cheer echoed through the hall as the Leader led the men in praise.

"Earl of Rothmore and Edward of Kilmarnock, you have proven your loyalty to the Knights. You shall be rewarded in this life and the next."

Dougal glanced across at Edward. The young man stared ahead; his face devoid of any expression and Dougal directed his own gaze back to the Leader.

Tonight, the Grand Master did not commence with the libations but moved straight to the vows of poverty, chastity, obedience, and piety. Dougal allowed a smile to creep onto his face. The collective relief of the knights at the shortened ceremony was almost palpable and he knew his quest to end this chapter would be made easier by the motivations of the men gathered in this room

The motivations of these knights were known to him and none were for any spiritual reason. Greed motivated each one of them and not one could lay claim to a pious life. Soon, he and

Edward would embark on their plan to end the corruption of this order. He had promised his father he would end the reign of these men and their political and spiritual power, and the decline had finally begun.

Unknown to them.

The death of Sofia would ensure the induction of both he and Edward into the inner circle and they would be privy to information which he could use against the Grand Master. The trip to Austria would be rewarded greatly.

The chanting ceased and the sonorous voice interrupted his thoughts. "I will meet with you and Edward of Kilmarnock in the Solar."

* * * *

Indigo pulled the black veil over her face and wiped her eyes. The boys were playing in the garden, but their usual exuberant cries and whoops had been missing since the twins had returned from the Alps. Jory and Jago still had trouble sleeping, and she and Zane had taken turns sitting up with them at night.

Mr. Grimoult was inconsolable and had been unable to carry out his usual duties, He had aged ten years in the month since she and Zane had been called urgently to Austria after Sofia's murder.

They had just returned from a memorial service for Sofia in London. The staff from Salon de Vargas had travelled over by dirigible and Lucienne had sobbed in Indigo's arms.

"I knew there was something strange about that man. His wife was like a dead woman, but Sofia was so taken by him." Lucienne's voice trembled

None of the staff from the university in Vienna had attended. Indigo had beseeched them to stay away in case of more danger and they had been unable to contact two of the researchers who were on some mysterious journey. She did not want to put the boys at further risk. Until it was discovered who was behind

Sofia's murder, they would take the utmost care and she had personally supplied funds to place a guard on the laboratory in Vienna.

Sofia's body had not been retrieved. Even though it was summer in the Alps, there were so many crevasses and fissures, the search teams had been unable to find any sign of her. They knew she had fallen…or been pushed, as her silver cloak was caught on a protruding rock half way down the sheer rock face. The two Scottish men had disappeared, and Indigo still held onto a slim hope her sister had been kidnapped. But Mr. Grimoult was adamant he had heard her scream as she had fallen and had seen the rocks tumbling down after her.

But Indigo refused to accept her sister's death. A month had passed, and she sat by the chronometric receiver at all hours of the day and night, hoping and praying Sofia would send her a message. Finally, Zane had come to get her one morning and she had looked up into his sad eyes and broken down. She had finally accepted there was no hope and organized the memorial service. She had the boys to think of, her biomes to run and Mr. Grimoult to console.

Sofia was gone.

But she planned one trip once the boys had settled.

She and Zane would travel to the Isle of Little Rothmore.

* * * * *

A chill wind blew in from the sea and the fire sputtered in the hearth of the huge fireplace. Any heat disappeared up the cavernous chimney or up into the high roof of the large room. The solid wooden door was bolted from the outside and only a glimpse of grey sky was visible through the high narrow gap at the top of the stone wall.

She knew the wind was from the sea. It was salt-tanged and occasionally a sour whiff of sour kelp would float through the room. The keening of seabirds kept her awake at night and when the wind was quiet, the soughing of the sea sweeping across pebbles slipped into her consciousness. Two days ago, she had woken up to fingers of mist seeping in through the high windows. She was not in the Alps, that much she knew. But wherever it was, it was a bleak godforsaken place.

Sofia leaned against the cold stone wall and stood on her toes. If she stretched high enough, she could see the green leaves of a large tree fluttering in the wind through a small gap in the stone. It was the only thing moving in her lonely prison.

The fluttering of leaves and the glowing charcoal on the fire.

Tiredness overwhelmed her. She pulled her cloak around her throat and touched her bare neck. The communication device Indigo had given her had not been around her neck when she had woken up three long days ago. Even if she'd had the device it would have been useless because she couldn't have called for rescue; she had no idea where she was. Her thoughts were confused and ran into each other.

Woken up in a bed alone. Cold. With no idea of where she was.

She stood with her cheek pressed against the cold stone wall. She did not know where Dougal was. Nor did she really care.

He could rot in hell.

The last time she had seen him was the moment he had pushed her over the precipice. All she could remember was a kaleidoscope of images, places and people flashing past her eyes as she fell.

Like one of her nephews' toys.

To certain death, she had thought as she screamed.

Now she was alone in this cold, cavernous room. She hadn't seen nor spoken to another soul for three full days and nights. For a time, she had imagined she was dead. Clothed in a long white nightgown, her hair was loose, and her feet were bare.

So if it wasn't heaven or hell, someone had ministered to her since she had been brought to this unknown place. If she could get out of here and find Dougal, she would kill him without a second thought.

Her throat ached with unshed tears as she imagined the grief Indigo and her family were going through. Oh, God, she prayed the twins had not seen her fall nor heard her screams. She rubbed her eyes with the heels of her hands but refused to let the tears fall. Dropping her arms to her side, she crossed the room and climbed into the bed and turned her face into the feather pillow

Drifting in and out of sleep for another night, the room darkened and lightened with the passing of the hours, and Sofia finally awoke to a freshly stoked fire and food on a tray next to the bed.

She could not live like this. It was the path to madness.

If someone didn't come soon…

There was a loud clang as the bolt lifted on the door and it creaked open. A small woman is a maid's uniform and a cap covering her hair scurried in, her eyes downcast. She went over to the fire and put a large log on top of the lowering flames, before turning her attention to the bedside table and reaching for the tray.

Sofia had not touched the food. The woman raised her eyes and said in a soft voice with a strong Scottish burr in her words.

"You *moost* eat, ma'am."

"Where am I?" Sofia demanded. "What is this place?"

The woman bowed her head and backed out of the room, clutching the tray. The door slammed shut behind her and the bolt dropped on the other side. Sofia climbed up into the bed and pulled the soft woollen blanket over her head and cursed the man who had taken her away from all she knew.

* * * *

The sun shone from a palette of gold and pink as it rose into the summer sky and Dougal, Earl of Rothmore rode away from Castle Dean, turning his mount eagerly toward the coast road. He had left Edward at his manor at Kilmarnock where he had passed the night before calling into Castle Dean for a private meeting with the Leader of the Council of Five.

A financial reward in gold had been offered to them however Dougal had assured the Council the spiritual recompense of recognition by the knights was sufficient payment for their quest.

He and Edward had discussed their plans late into the night and were satisfied; they would be able to move against the Council within months. Edward would continue to meet with the local knights to gain their allegiance, under cover of his official position on the civil parish board of the Kilmarnock parish. In the meantime, Dougal was anxious to return to his castle on the island to check on the well-being of Sofia.

He would not use the Astrolaberors until he reached the coast for fear of being observed and would travel on horseback until he reached the small, flat boat he had stored in a cave in a small bay across from his island. It was only two miles across at the closest point but once he pushed the boat offshore and was sure he was not under observation he would to use the device to reach his island and Sofia.

As he rode, his thoughts turned to Sofia. A pang of regret lodged in his chest for the way they had staged her murder on the mountain. He knew there would be much grief and his heart ached for her family, particularly the boys who had been present. It was only a matter of time before he and Edward would be summonsed to an investigation.

Edward had reassured him over a gillie of whisky in the wee hours. "'Twas the only way, Dougal. If there had been any doubt, the Council would have sent their henchmen to dispose of her and Madame de Vargas would be deceased by now." The young man raised his glass. "Patience. That is what you told me when we first travelled to Vienna. Although—" the young man looked at him "— I suspect you may be thinking with your heart and not your intellect. A bit of fondness for the lassie?"

Dougal had ignored Edward's comment. "I know, we must be patient, but I fear the grief caused by this event, may override any rational thinking before all can be explained. However, an investigation into our involvement will be the final evidence for the Council." He swigged his whisky and it burned all the way down his throat. "I am not looking forward to meeting with Sofia on Rothmore on the morrow."

Now Dougal turned his mount onto the narrow coastal road and focused his thoughts on the meeting to come. He reached into his pocket and rubbed his fingers on the shiny black stone he had removed from around Sofia's neck. She had lain in the huge bed, deeply asleep and breathing softly. A soft murmur had left her lips when his fingers brushed her neck as he'd released the clasp and placed the black jewel in a pouch against his heart, wanting to keep her close.

His instructions to Mary, his young, loyal housekeeper had been clear. Under no circumstances was Sofia to leave her room until he returned. He frowned, imagining how cross Sofia would be after three days locked away in that cavernous room. At least it had a privy. He would let her show her displeasure before he told her why they had to stage her murder.

But he could not tell Sofia everything…not yet.

Mary had at first been resistant to his direction. "I see a *puir* woman in that room who *dinna kens* her place in this house an you expect me to keep her locked in there? She's just as deservin' of some respect and you're a *fule*, man…"

Eventually he had convinced her it was a matter of life and death and Mary had agreed to his request.

His horse whinnied and Dougal looked around, but it was only the proximity of the water exciting his mount who knew there was hay for him in the small enclosure on the coast. Dougal pulled on the reigns as they crested the last hill and smiled. His island, Little Rothmore, sat a short distance across the firth, jewel-like on the sea before him. Smoke puffed lazily from the kitchen chimney and the larger chimney on the eastern side where Sofia was …resting. He would not use the term imprisoned, even in his own thoughts. She was a guest and would be a guest on his island until he and Edward achieved their quest.

After tethering his mount and ensuring it had enough hay, Dougal reached into his small knapsack and removed the Astrolaberors. He clambered down the cliff; the small stones skittered beneath his feet and disturbed the nesting seabirds. They rose into the air squawking around him. He stopped halfway down and settled to wait until the sun was at its zenith; the co-ordinates were set for midday. The wait would also ensure he had not been followed and he looked back at the cliff top to watch for any sign of a follower.

* * * *

Sofia woke slowly as voices drifted into her consciousness. *It was Dougal.*

She would recognise the voice of the man who had haunted her dreams for the past three days, whether awake or asleep. Climbing down from the high bed, she shivered as her bare feet touched the cold stone and she reached for her cloak, before walking over to the door once more. She had pushed it and pulled at the solid oak door for the past day.

Finally deciding to wait and overpower the maid when she next came to replenish the food, she had waited in vain because the woman had not returned again. Hysteria had clawed at her throat in the dark of the night as she imagined the worst; being abandoned in this godforsaken place until she starved to death. There was no way out. She had felt her way around every inch of the sold walls pulling at every protruding piece of stone. Crawled across the floor

187

and lifted every woven rug, looking for a trap door…to no avail.

"Mary, hand the tray to me and I will take it in." Dougal's voice was close.

Sofia could not understand the words of the woman who seemed to be arguing with him, but eventually her voice faded away with her footsteps. She stepped back to the side, looking wildly around the room. There was nothing she could use as a weapon. The logs on the fire had burned to ash and there was nothing small enough to pick up to fling at the murderous bastard when he came into the room.

She pressed her back against the wall waiting for him. The bolt creaked and the massive door opened slowly. The shadow of a large body darkened the floor in the doorway. Dougal stepped into the room and Sofia shrieked and jumped onto his back, reaching around for his eyes and gouging with her fingertips. The tray he was carrying crashed to the ground and he reached up behind him and grabbed her arms.

"*Mord bastard.*" She screeched like a banshee trying to beat at him with hands that were now held securely in his grasp. "You murdering bastard, let me go."

"Calm down," he said quietly. "It is all fine, now."

"It is not," she sobbed with frustration as he turned her around and pinned her to the wall.

"Mary," he called. "Bolt the door."

Sofia screamed and lunged at him fastening her teeth onto his ear and biting as hard as she could.

"You little hellion," he yelled, releasing one hand and grabbing her chin roughly. "You've drawn blood." He pushed her away before turning her and putting her over his shoulder.

"And I'll draw more before I'm finished with you," she panted. "You...you…festering, ignoble cur."
Dougal lifted her and carried her across the room.

* * * *

The Earl of Rothmore fought a smile as the flailing fists pounded his back and a string of curses more suited to the gutter assailed his ears. The blows barely registered on his flesh underneath the thick vest he wore over his linen shirt, but her curses grew louder as he moved across toward the large bed in the centre of the room

"When you are quite finished, Sofia. I will put you down."

"I will kill you, Dougal. I swear by all that—"

"Enough, woman," he roared. "If you will hold your tongue for one minute, I will put you down and we can have a civilized conversation."

"Pah!"

He dumped her unceremoniously on the bed and took a step back as Sofia sat up and glared at him. She leaned back, her arms supported her on the woollen blankets and her chest heaved with each breath. Her face was pale except for twin spots of red, high on her cheeks.

Glaring at him, she opened her mouth to speak and he held his hand high.

"No." Dougal tried to keep his voice soft. Despite her anger, his body was responding to her. She dropped her gaze and grabbed at the white chemise, pulling it together over her alabaster skin.

He grunted and walked across to the fire which had almost burned out. Crouching down, he looked around for something to poke at the ashes but there was nothing.

"Yes, Dougal. I have watched the fire burn away. I have not eaten, nor drunk of the wine your whore has brought me. There is nothing here."

A reluctant smile twitched at his lips at the thought of his loyal housekeeper being referred to as his whore.

"Come, now, Sofia. That is very harsh," he said. "Did you not hear Mary expressing her displeasure with me outside the door?"

"I am not interested in anything but getting out of this godforsaken hole." She turned to him, her eyes bright with unshed tears. "Where am I? I presume by the insufferable cold and the keening of the wind I am in Scotland?"

He nodded wearily. "Aye, we are on Rothmore."

She kept her gaze fixed on his face. "Why? Why am I here?"

Dougal crossed the floor and stood by the bed reaching his hands out. "Come. We will eat and I have a long story to tell you."

Sofia pushed herself to the edge of the bed. A flash of a long slender calf caught his eye as her foot reached the floor. He turned and picked up her cloak and handed it to her, before striding across to the door.

"Unbolt the door, please Mary." He swung open the door when the bolt was lifted from the other side and waited for Sofia to follow. She stood slowly and a soft cry escaped her lips as she crumpled to the cold, hard floor.

The housekeeper pushed past him. "The wee lass has eaten nought since you brought her here," she admonished him. She crouched next to Sofia and picked up her lifeless hand and rubbed it. "*Och, mon.* She is as cold as ice. It's a wonder you haven't killed her."

Dougal scooped his hands beneath Sofia and picked her up from the floor. He stood cradling her as her head nestled into his chest and her eyes fluttered open. She weighed nothing and he held her close to him as he strode to the door and pushed it open with his shoulder. "We'll go to the kitchens. That is where the best fire is. She needs warming."

Mary hurried ahead of him and he walked to the end of the long corridor and stepped quickly down the dozen stone steps carved in the rock on the eastern wall. It was the quickest way to the kitchen. Sofia's head bumped gently against his chest and he tightened his grip as she reached her hand up to his neck.

Her cold fingers spread against his skin and he looked warily down at her, waiting for her to scratch or pinch him, but her hand curled gently around the hair hanging past his shirt collar. Her wide-eyed gaze held his and the confusion on her face broke his heart.

"Not long, now," he murmured. "I will have you warm and fed soon."

He could not believe she had not eaten since he had left her two days before and cursed himself. He should have taken more care to ensure her physical well-being. No point saving her from the machinations of the Council, if she starved to death in his care.

They crossed the long hall and the two servants carrying in firewood looked at him curiously.

"Build up the fires in the kitchen, please," he instructed. They scurried to do his bidding and he strode to the end of the room and reached the arched entrance leading to the kitchens. The aroma of fresh baked bread preceded the warmth emanating from the first room where the loaves of fresh baked bread were laid out along the wooden benches along the side of the wall.

"Where is your perambulator?" Sofia muttered and he laughed drily.

The next room, although serving as of one of the kitchens, had a long bench in front of the fire. A large milk can filled with water stood in the huge fireplace and gave out almost as much warmth as the fire itself. Mary hurried in with an armful of homespun woollen shawls and spread them on the bench, but Dougal ignored them. He sat at the end of the bench closest to the fire and cradled Sofia into the warmth of his body. Mary looked at him without speaking and picked up a shawl wrapping it gently around Sofia who now lay quiescent in his arms. It appeared her rage had burned out and her energy was depleted. He looked down as she shivered and watched her warily as her gaze took in the room around her.

"What is this place?" she asked quietly.

"It is my home," he replied.

"Why am I here?' Her voice quavered and he could sense the fear behind her words.

"Don't worry. You are safe here," he reassured her.

"You tried to kill me."

He reached down and picked up one of her hands between his and rubbed it gently. Her eyes fluttered closed and she sighed.

"No, I saved your life. You were in grave danger…and you still are," he replied

She didn't answer and as her breathing evened out, Dougal wondered if she had even heard his reply. Mary came back in from the main kitchen with a jug of warmed wine and a plate of bread cakes and placed it on a low table between them and the fireplace. For a few moments, the only sound was the crackling of the flames in the fireplace, until a log popped and dropped into the fire. Sofia opened her eyes and pushed her hands against his chest

Dougal slid across the bench and made room for her between his body and the end of the bench against the wall. She looked up at him and tucked her bare feet beneath her. He lifted the shawl and draped it across her shoulders.

"What do you mean grave danger?" Her words were softly spoken but measured and calm.

He reached for the jug and poured the wine into the pottery cups Mary had placed on the tray. He held Sofia's gaze with his as he passed her the hot drink. She wrapped her fingers around the warm cup and smiled.

"Not a poisoned chalice, Dougal?" A nervous pulse flickered in the side of her neck and he realized she was attempting to stay calm.

He leaned forward and put his head in his hands. "Edward of Kilmarnock and I, were entrusted with the task of killing you."

He didn't look at her as he spoke, but she sat up straight beside him. I am a righteous man and I am on a journey to fulfil my father's wish to end the corruption that is rife in our country." He determined to tell her the whole story and she would understand why she had to stay in the castle on his island.

"Your research in the laboratory in Vienna has come to the attention of this evil group and you have threatened what they believe is their God-given right to immortality."

Her eyes were shadowed but fixed on his mouth as he spoke. He had her attention. But she didn't speak.

"I was sent to Vienna to observe you." He reached into his pocket and removed the monogrammed glove he had carried for weeks since she had dropped it at Westbahnhof. "You eluded me at the train station, but I could confirm to my masters it was you."

Her gaze was icy as he continued and she moved away from him, wrapping a second shawl around her shoulders.

"Edward and I were sent to kill you after we had confirmed in Vienna at your salon, it was definitely you we sought."

"So why am I alive?" she asked. "Why am I here?"

"We had no intention of killing you, but we had to make it look as though you were dead." He reached out for her hand, but she snatched it away. "Your sister and your nephews, your manservant, your staff. They all believe you are dead."

Despite the warmth of the fire and the warm wine he had sipped, the look on her face chilled him to the bone,

"I demand you take me to my sister's manor in Cornwall immediately." Her tone was imperious, and he could see the shrewd couturier who commanded such respect in the world of fashion. The Knights did not know the strength of this woman working against them.

Regret filled his chest and he shook his head, denying her request. "I am sorry, Sofia. For your own safety, you must stay here until Edward sends a message to say it is all clear."

"Stay here? Stay where? In this draughty pile of stones?" She stood and walked across to the fire, the deep scarlet shawls accentuating the pallor of her skin. "You will take me immediately to my sister's. If there is danger, I will hide there." Her voice dropped as she gestured to the walls around them. "You really expect me to live in this…this… it is really little better than a hovel.

Anger burned up from his stomach and Dougal clenched his jaw, highly offended. It might not be silk-lined and have the latest in gadgets like her salon in Vienna, but this castle was his home and it had been in his family for hundreds of years. He stood and drew himself to his full height. "You will stay here until I say it is safe."

She laughed. "Make me."

"Oh, I will Sofia. Have no doubt of that," he replied. The anger burned in his throat and he fought the attraction he had for this woman. It was not the time to follow the urges of his body, even if his heart was in agreement for the first time in his life. That may come later, after he and Edward were sure the Knights were no longer a risk. Once the order was gone, he would reconsider his feelings for Sofia.

But not before then.

"You will stay here. I will get you some clothes from Mary and I will show you your room. There is no need to lock you away…as there is nowhere for you to go." He left her sitting alone in front of the fire.

Chapter 12

Sofia kneeled in the kitchen garden and tugged at the weeds between the cobblestones. The Irish wolfhound who had been her constant companion for the past three months snored quietly beside her. Bored with gazing at the sea between the small Isle of Rothmore and the Scottish mainland, she now sought menial tasks to fill her days. Mary gave her chores in the kitchen and the garden.

The cold had chapped her once flawless hands and now green streaks from the moist plants she pulled from the cracks in the stones, coloured her fingers. Tucked behind a high stone wall, this small courtyard where Mary grew her kitchen herbs was protected from the chill wind which seemed to blow constantly from the sea. Sofia pushed herself to her feet and wandered across to the bench next to the gate in the wall.

She sighed as the dog followed her and flopped at her feet. It was almost as though he had been set to guard her.

Not that there was anywhere for her to go.

In the months she had been Dougal's prisoner she had walked around the small island every day. No one visited the island and the servants lived in the castle and did not speak to her. She had searched for a boat to no avail. Dougal disappeared for days on end and even when he was in the castle, she had not been able to find his boat.

They dined together each night and after the first few meals in stony silence, they had both thawed slightly and were able to converse without argument as they ate the food Mary prepared for them each night.

She now knew the Knights were fully aware of her laboratory in Vienna and she had expressed her concern for the

Professor to Dougal. He had assured her everything was in place to ensure the safety of her staff…and her family.

It had taken many days, but she had finally come to an understanding of the danger surrounding her quest and how close she had come to death. However, Dougal would still not explain how they had travelled to the Isle of Rothmore despite her insistent questioning. Although they spoke each evening, he remained aloof and withdrawn and had not laid a hand on her. She had been moved to a small room in the top of the castle where sunlight streamed in during the day, but she was bored.

No news of the outside world; she was keen to hear of the ramifications to the government and the business regulations since the assassination of Queen Victoria. Sofia had questioned Dougal at length, but he was not forthcoming. He treated her as a person who had no cause to be interested in the politics of the day

As a woman.

She clenched her fists; there had been enough of that in Vienna with the refusal to let women into the university. She would not be beholden to the whims of this man…no matter how much he felt the need to protect her.

If it is the last thing I do, I will get off this island.

Voices drifted over the wall and she rose and moved to the gate. Dougal stood with Edward of Kilmarnock on the grassy rise leading to the beach and she quickly crossed to them with hope in her heart.

Perhaps if Edward was here, all was well and she could leave.

Dougal watched her without expression as she opened the small wooden gate and held it back for the wolfhound to follow her.

"Edward." She nodded to the young man and smiled to herself as his face flushed a deep red.

"Sofia," he mumbled. "It is …er…it is good to see you

looking so well."

"And alive," she replied sharply. "Do you have news?"

Dougal shook his head at the younger man and Sofia drew a deep breath.

"Do not treat me like a simpleton." Her voice rose. "If there is news to be had, I want to know. Anything to get off this godforsaken island and leave this pile of stones behind me,

"When it is safe, I will tell you and you can go back to your fancy life in Europe." Dougal's voice was short, and a pang of regret lodged in her chest as the harsh words about his home left her lips. It surprised her but she had actually come to tolerate being on the island and living in his castle.

Time to think and time to enjoy every day.

It reminded her of the years she spent in the wilds of Cornwall with Indigo when the twins were born. Her time in Vienna was not her own and she had pondered on the reasons for the moonflower quest.

Were they interfering with nature? Should they continue their research or now let it go?

Now that lives were in jeopardy, it was time to rethink their plans, their ambitions, and their quest. Almost as though he had read her thoughts, Dougal continued in a softer tone.

"Sofia." She looked up into his face and was surprised to see sympathy on his face.

"What? What has happened? Is my family safe?"

Dougal took her hand. "There has been an…incident. In Vienna."

She looked from Dougal to Edward. "Tell me."

"I have been to Vienna carrying out a task for the Earl of Rothmore." Edward spoke slowly. "I have spoken with your Professor and with your manservant Henri."

He looked at her intently and Dougal held her hand tightly. "The laboratory has been burned to the ground and all of the work destroyed."

"The work? Does anything remain?" she asked urgently. Confused thoughts filled her mind. Just as she was wondering about the reason for their quest…to receive this news.

"The research notes, the elixir…all burned." Edward's voice was solemn.

"The staff?" She looked to Edward as she thought of the professor and how much time he spent at the university.

"All safe," replied Edward. "The professor is down in Cornwall with Captain Thoreau and your sister. I delivered him there myself. Henri is keeping watch at your salon where business continues as usual. The other staff are still on their holiday."

She turned to Dougal as despair filled her chest. It seemed as though she was no longer needed anywhere. "Please, can I leave here now? Can I go to my sister?"

He looked at her for a long moment before speaking.

"No, I am sorry. It is still not safe. It is essential they believe you are dead. There are too many spies in Cornwall. The influence and the money of the Knights have corrupted many across the country."

Sofia stamped her foot in anger and the wolfhound gave a low growl. "When? How much longer?"

Edward turned away as Dougal reached for her and held her close as wrapping his strong arms around her.

"Sofia, I beg of you to be patient. Edward and I are very close to achieving our goal. You have to trust. It is much more than your research and your life that is at stake." She let her cheek rest on his shoulder and his warmth comforted her which surprised her. He was her captor, he had staged her death and would not let her free, but the simple touch of his skin on hers was enough to make her want to stay in his arms forever.

She pulled away reluctantly. "So what now?"

"We continue as we were. You will stay here, and Edward

and I will continue to work against the Council."

Sofia looked up and caught such a look of naked longing on Dougal's face, she shivered, and goose bumps skittered down her arms. She shook herself angrily.

It is the cold wind that makes me shiver, not this man. She turned her back to the two men and snapped her fingers at the wolfhound. "Come Zeus, we will go to the kitchen where it is warm, and we can have a sensible conversation with Mary."

* * * *

"Come, Edward, we too shall go in from this cold and partake of some wine." Dougal spoke to the young man as they watched Sofia cross the courtyard. Despite the homespun wool dress, she still carried herself like a lady of quality and her beauty shone through the plain garb. Her hair had lightened from spending so much time outside. He knew she roamed the coast each day searching for a way to escape and he fully understood her desire.

Dougal looked up at his castle, an awesome grey stone silhouette against the darkening September sky. It was time to finish what they had to do and end the Council's influence forever. The next few days were critical; Edward had gathered support from the local knights, and they were about to make their move.

Although Dougal was longing to stay in his castle without the constant trips to the mainland, it would be a lonely place once Sofia returned to Vienna. He turned abruptly and went to call his hound, before he remembered the dog's allegiance was now with Sofia. He smiled grimly; she had bewitched the whole castle, servants and animals alike. Edward opened the gate and they crossed the courtyard to the castle where they would make the final plans to remove the Council.

199

Chapter 13

Mary and Sofia had prepared a special meal in honour of Edward's visit and Sofia and the two men of them sat at the large trestle table on the dais to partake of the meal as Mary served and cleared the courses.

Edward belched and then blushed his usual bright red. "Oh… please forgive me, Madame."

Sofia laughed at his embarrassment. "I will take it as a compliment, Edward. Mary has taught me much about preparing meals."

Dougal sat back and watched the candlelight play on her face. Shimmering silver light shot from her hair which was bound tightly in braids around her high forehead. Her deep brown eyes looked back at him unwaveringly and it was almost as though it could read her thoughts.

"I am going to turn in for the night," Edward said. "If I may be excused?"

"Certainly," Dougal replied. "You will need a clear head for tomorrow."

Edward bid Sofia goodnight and wandered out through the kitchen. The crackling of the flames in the huge fireplace filled the silence in the cavernous room. There had been a shift between them since he had held Sofia this afternoon in the courtyard and even with Edward between them at the table, the tension filled the room.

No doubt the reason for his hasty exit.

He sat back and sipped his wine, conscious of Sofia's

unwavering stare fixed on him.

"Dougal, would you walk with me?" she asked suddenly.

"Can I trust you not to assault me and try to escape?" He smiled trying to lighten the tense atmosphere between them.

"I think you can trust me," she replied. "I have come to trust you over the course of these weeks."

He stood and came around the table to her and held his arm out to her. "We shall walk on the ramparts. It is a clear night." He looked down at her as she stood and took his arm. There was something about the tilt of her head, the sudden smile that took Dougal by surprise. All antagonism had left her, and he sensed her confidence in him was growing.

"You do know it is almost over?" he asked in a low voice. Sofia's eyes narrowed as she took his arm and rose to her feet.

"I believe so," she replied.

"You will be free to go."

They walked silently across the large room and into the corridor at the base of the steps leading to the ramparts.

Sofia chuckled softly and the happy sound filled Dougal's chest with warmth.

"I have become accustomed to walking up stairs and not having the convenience of my automated devices in Vienna."

"I do not think we will ever have them in Scotland," replied Dougal. "Even with the death of Queen Victoria and the change in government, the Scottish parliament remains adamant we will not turn to what they call the 'newfangled' contraptions."

"Not so 'newfangled' in England." Sofia smiled up at him and his heart kicked up a notch as she leaned into him. "One day, I shall take you to visit my sister and you will be quite happy to do without them. The English models are so archaic it is necessary to wear ear muffs to ride in their perambulators."

"Their dirigibles are comfortable," he replied and then he chuckled. "But the poor automaton I took as my wife when I visited your salon in Vienna ended up a pile of springs in the airship. Poor Edward was quite distraught."

Their silence was companionable as they climbed the stairs, each lost in their own thoughts. Dougal pushed open the heavy door at the top of the stairs and they stepped onto the rampart that circled the entire castle.

Sofia's quick gasp filled him with pride in his home. The full moon was rising across the firth and a silver path of moonlight lay on the still sea. The wind had dropped at dusk and the sea was like a rippling sheet of silver cloth, a long slow and heavy swell rising and falling with the tide. Despite the lack of wind, there was a chill in the air and Dougal pulled Sofia close to him.

Sofia was taut with apprehension; for many weeks she had searched ceaselessly with one goal in mind—to escape this island. Now the time to leave was coming close, she was filled with regret and longing for this man holding her. He was a good and righteous man and she would miss him. She very much wanted to believe that he would miss her as well. Just a few months ago, she would have been appalled by the need consuming her. It was time to leave and return to her old life, before she changed her mind.

But they had one last night.

Dougal watched he without speaking, his eyes grave and wary. She lifted her hand and placed it against the rough stubble on his cheek. He held her gaze and turned his lips into her palm. Warmth shot through her skin and she pressed against his hard body. With a muffled groan he dropped his head and captured her lips with his. The need that rose in her was ripe and so huge it overwhelmed her. She wanted no more than to fall into it and wished suddenly they could just be two people who could stand and kiss in the moonlight while the shadows grew long and deep.

"Just one night," she murmured against his lips.

"Need me as I need you, Sofia." His breath was warm as it mingled with hers.

She couldn't deny him as he deepened the kiss and she closed her eyes losing herself in her feelings as the moment spun around them. He pulled back and looked at her for a long moment.

"Come to bed with me," he said softly as the shadows played across his face. Turning to the stairs, she held her hand out for him to follow and led him to the small solar where she had spent the past six weeks.

He sat upon the soft feather bed and she placed her fingers on his lips.

"No words," she murmured stepping back into the moonlight. The rough wool dress fell to the floor and she reached up and unbound her braids. Her hair fell to her waist as she turned to him. His breath was warm on her skin and she pulled his head closer and rested her forehead on his hair as his tongue flicked at the tips of her breasts.

He pulled her to the bed and quickly shed his breeches and shirt. He rolled on top of her, capturing her mouth with his and she clung tightly to his bare shoulders, kneading her fingers into the tight muscles of his broad back. His skin was wondrously smooth and hot, and she opened to him.

* * * *

Dawn light spilled across the bed thought the open casements. Sofia lay on her back staring up at the timber beams high above them. Next to her, Dougal breathed slow and even. A night of passion lay behind them and she stretched remembering the feel of him against her and inside her. She caught her breath on a muffled sob and a solitary tear ran down her cheek as she looked at him trying to imprint his face on her mind.

He lay sprawled on his back, only partially covered with the sheet and his chest rose and fell with each breath as he slept. It would be dangerous, he had spoken of what would come today and she was fearful. A small white scar, just faintly visible sat above his top lip. Her eyes lingered on his strong face and she traced the raised skin with a light touch.

This life was not for her and she could take no joy in the feelings she had for this man. She had to return to Vienna and continue in her quest, despite her doubts; there was a laboratory to rebuild and staff to care for. It was time to return to her own life and she would get there however she could. The bed moved beside her, and she smiled as Dougal's hand tangled in her hair and pulled her down to him.

Chapter 14

The next time Sofia woke the room was full of flickering sunlight and Dougal was gone. He had kissed her farewell and promised to return within two days, and she'd drifted back to sleep. Dressing with nervous haste, she reached for a warmer dress as the scurrying of the clouds across the sun warned of a chill wind. Today, she vowed she would find a way off the island and be gone when Dougal returned.

After she had breakfasted with Mary, she headed out for a walk. Breasting the slope of the hill furthest from the castle, she paused as a small flock of bleating ewes crossed beneath her. Shading her eyes with her hand, she looked down at the small shingly beach below. The tide was low and the entrance to a cave was exposed. A cairn of rocks was piled at the entrance and it appeared there had been a rock fall which explained why she had not noticed it before. Setting off down the cliff path, small pebbles slipped underfoot and rolled down the path ahead of her, disturbing the birds nesting in the cliff. They rose high above her squawking and complaining as she disturbed their morning slumber.

Reaching the bottom of the path, she held her dress above her ankles and jumped the last few feet onto the wet sand. A small cave had been exposed by the rock fall and Sofia stepped inside and waited for her eyes to become accustomed to the dark. Rotting wooden boxes and small kegs covered in glistening seaweed littered the floor. The cave was under the high tide mark and water had filled it just a few short hours ago. She shivered—it would be very easy to get caught here by the waves. Hesitantly she stepped further into the cave and to her delight, her gaze fixed on a small wooden boat. Hurrying over, she ran her hands along the sides—it was intact, and the oars were still fixed in the rowlocks. If she could drag it to the water, it was but a short distance to the mainland, even less with the tide out.

She recognized the old boat for what is was and for a fleeting moment wondered if Dougal was involved in smuggling. Many stories of smuggling on the Cornish coast had graced the dinner table when she'd lived with Indigo and Zane. Now in, she knew he despaired in his role of sheriff of ever defeating the smugglers

Sofia had no money and no other clothes and there were none of her possessions to retrieve. For a brief moment, she considered bidding Mary farewell, but she shook her head. The wind would come up even more as the day got later and it would be too rough to row the short mile to the mainland. She would worry about what she would do once she got there. Of immediate concern was the manner in which she would pull the boat out of the cave and down to the sea. The shoreline was pitted with rock pools and the beach was a mix of shingle and sand.

Sofia stepped from the cave and searched the shore line for the clearest route to the water. She raised her hand and shaded her eyes from the morning sun glinting off the narrow channel of water between the small island and the mainland. The beach circled around the bay in a deep horseshoe shape and piles of fallen rocks covered the sand. The shingle at the south end of the beach was clearer and Sofia tied her skirt up into a loose knot and set to work. It took than a half hour later of tugging and pushing before she grunted with satisfaction when the bow of the small boat reached the low tide mark. She took off her shoes and put them in the boat as small waves washed around her bare feet. Allowing the boat to float for a few minutes in the chilly water, she checked it was intact and free of leaks before she gave it one huge shove and clambered into it. Using one oar, she pushed at the shingly bottom and the boat scraped and floated in the deeper water. The wash of the outgoing tide pulled it into the channel and Sofia dipped both oars into the firth and started to row.

A shrill cry from the shore caught her attention and she

turned her head swiftly, half expecting to see Mary on the beach calling her back She breathed a sigh of relief as the kittiwakes circled above the cliff returning to their nests on the side of the cliff.

It took only ten minutes of gentle rowing before she reached the mainland and euphoria swept over her. Putting one oar aside she pushed to the right to turn the boat to the rocky shoreline, but the euphoria disappeared as a rogue wave caught the boat and spun it around. Sofia fought to control the direction of the boat as the current picked it up and carried it toward the rocks ahead. The front of the small boat slammed into the jagged edge of a large black rock close to the shore.

Sofia screamed as the boat tipped to the side and she slid into the icy water. She grabbed the rock with both hands and scrabbled to find a foothold in the shingle in the knee- deep water. Once her feet were firmly in the shingle, she turned and held the boat steady beside her. Pulling it behind her, she made her way to the shore as she looked back at the Isle of Rothmore and a pang of regret settled in her chest.

A cloud passed over the sun and the castle where she'd spent the last few weeks stood dark and shadowed. A sense of foreboding overwhelmed her and she prayed Dougal and Edward were safe.

After safely stowing the boat behind a large rock above the high-water mark, she squeezed the water from her skirts and put on her shoes. For a few moments she sat in the sun trying to get warm, but when her body began to shake from the cold, she decided movement would warm her more quickly. She climbed to the top of the low cliff cresting the edge of the beach and looked to the east.

* * * *

Dougal placed the Astrolaberors safely in its bag and stowed it in the bag slung around his neck. They had arrived on the edge of the small town of Kilmarnock in the year of 1861 and were expected at Castle Dean at sunrise. Now he stood at the window of the small inn staring out into the rain-drenched dark. A sudden squall had swept in from the sea as they had arrived, and most were still abed. Not only was the weather keeping them inside; the innkeeper informed Dougal word of the uprising had run through the town like wildfire and the townspeople would turn a blind eye

They had tolerated the Knights Templar in Castle Dean for many years and would be pleased to see the Castle empty, he said. If all went to plan, the uprising of the local knights would forever banish the Council of Five and disband the order. Dougal fingered the sharp dirk tucked into the waistband of this kilt hoping fervently the rising would not result in bloodshed. But he knew the Council would resist.

With all their might.

His thoughts turned to Sofia. Using the Astrolaberors to navigate through time had never bothered him before, but today uneasiness settled in his bones; leaving her in a previous time worried him. He shook it off— it was the anticipation of the quest *they were about to complete after the passion of the night he had spent with her causing this feeling of impending doom.*

Nothing to do with Sofia.

He ran his fingers over the black jewel he carried next to his heart. Edward followed Dougal from the inn, and they walked through the woods toward Castle Dean. The woods were alive with the morning rustling of wildlife and the trills of birds anticipating the sunrise.

The sudden scream was shrill and disturbed the peace of the woods. Edward ran ahead of Dougal heading for the Castle, drawing their knives as they ran. Jumping the small stone wall which formed the western boundary of the grounds, they encountered a group of men milling around the side of the castle.

Dougal recognized each of them as local knights. A cheer

went up as they saw Edward and they ran forward and lifted him onto their shoulders. Dougal hung back in the shadows of the castle wall and waited.

"They are gone, my Lord." One of the older knights, a wealthy landowner from Cumnock known to Dougal, slapped Edward enthusiastically on the back.

"The castle is deserted, and the servant advises they have sought retreat in St Mary's Chapel Lodge in Edinburgh. They left in the middle of the night."

The men cheered as Edward turned to Dougal with a huge grin in his face.

"Aye, breakfast, man, and then you can go home to your woman." Edward laughed and winked at Dougal.

* * * *

Sofia kept to the edge of the road from Troon. Her feet were cold, and her wet skirts flapped about her ankles. If any traffic passed by, she would shelter in the forest and remain unseen. Until she was sure Dougal and Edward had disposed of those threatening her in Kilmarnock, she would look out for her safety. The further she walked from the coast, the deeper the sadness settled in her chest. The physical ache of yearning for Dougal had grown as her journey continued and she chastised herself. It was one she would have to live with. He had no place in her life and she certainly couldn't live in that cold lump of stone. *Once she was back in her own world, she would forget all about* him.

She would.

Trying to control the shaking on her limbs from the cold devouring her body, she concentrated on her immediate problem. Her main worry was to find a way to get home...or first to Indigo in Cornwall. She would beg lodgings here for a day or two and get a message to Indigo to send Mr. Grimoult to collect her in the airship.

If only, she had the necklace. It would be so easy.

The distress Indigo must have endured for the past six weeks was unthinkable. Sofia put her sister's grief from her mind; there was nothing to be gained by dwelling on it.

As long as the boys were safe.

Dougal had assured her repeatedly they had come to no harm and Mr. Grimoult would have seen them safely back to their parents. Once she was home, she would make amends, but never would she trust herself to look after the children again.

Not until they were grown up anyway.

Distant voices and clanging from a blacksmith's forge brought a smile to her face. Not only did Dougal reside in a cold and draughty lump of stone, he lived in a country where technology was not welcomed. Queen Victoria's reign had seen the resurgence of technology in England, Wales and Cornwall but the stodgy Scottish parliament refused to accept any of the steam-powered machinery seen as essential in the rest of the country.

Sofia crept along quietly, not wanting to draw undue attention to herself until absolutely necessary. The watery sun was high in the sky; she had been on the road for a considerable time and her wet feet and skirts were made worse by the chill wind blowing at her back. A small bridge crossed the river that wound its way from Kilmarnock to the Firth—the path through the forest had taken her close to the water as she had walked, and she had stopped to take a drink. Now she walked cautiously across the bridge and her attention was caught by the noise of a small fair ahead. Her stomach growled as the aroma of roasting chestnuts assailed her nostrils.

No matter, she had no coin.

Sofia stood shivering behind a large oak tree and observed the crowd milling on the green to ensure all was safe. Patting her braided hear and straightening her wet skirts as best she could, she joined the throng

Wandering past the vendors selling a variety of foods and wares, she observed the odd dress of the women. Compared to the fashion of Vienna and the continent, their dress was very old fashioned and plain. Excited chatter surrounded her as she pushed unnoticed through the crowd.

"Her majesty has arrived in Edinburgh!" The shrill voice of a stout woman called across the crowd. "They say the crowds in Edinburgh are huge and most of the town duly turned out to greet her and Prince Albert."

Sofia turned slowly.

Who was she talking about? Queen Victoria has been dead for three months. She shook her head in confusion?

What new Queen was this?

Perhaps the Princess Royal had taken over the throne on the death of Victoria, her mother, but Sofia knew that to be high unlikely as Princess Victoria had married Prince Frederick William of Prussia three years ago. Sofia and Indigo had followed their love match with interest as the royal couple had first met at the Great Exhibition at Crystal Palace in 1851 and Indigo swore to this day, the Princess Royal had purchased some of her cosmecuticals.

Sofia pushed through the crowd holding her wet skirts high to avoid the mud trampled on each side of the path.

"May I trouble you, madam?" she asked quietly with her head bowed. "Who is visiting Edinburgh?"

"Why the Queen and her Prince of course." The woman looked at her with interest. "It has been the talk of the country since the trip was planned. They disembarked at Leith only yesterday."

Sofia raised her head slowly. "Her Royal Highness, the Princess Frederick?"

The woman was no longer listening. The crowds parted and a hush fell over the assembly as a group of six men walked through the fair. Sofia shrank into the crowd and hurried to step behind a tented stall.

Merde.

The men wore the cross of the Knights Templar on their tunic.

They were still here, so it seemed Dougal and Edward had been unsuccessful.

Oh, God. Let them be unhurt.

The stout woman followed her behind the tent and held out a bag of chestnuts.

"You are a trifle pale, my sweet. Would you like to try one of my chestnuts?" She gestured to the tent. "I have the best stall at the market."

"Please tell me, is it the Princess Royal in Edinburgh?"

The woman walked over to where Sofia was leaning against the stone wall at the edge of the grassed area and reached out to Sofia's forehead. "Have you had a wee bit too much sun, lovey?" Her voice was concerned. "Although it's nought been a hot day? And you are shivering."

"Please?" Sofia's voice was rising, and heads turned. "Who is in Edinburgh?" The foreboding in her chest was making in difficult to breathe.

"It is our Queen Victoria and her beloved Prince Albert, of course," replied the woman. "They are touring Scotland."

"But… but she's dead?" Sofia's voice rose even further. "She was poisoned in May."

"Methinks you are not feeling too bonny, lassie." The woman came closer and put her large hand beneath Sofia's elbow. "Come and sit in my tent for a rest and I will get you some ale."

Sofia's head was spinning, and she was no longer listening to the kind woman.

What was happening to her?

Where was she— or of greater importance—when was she?

She reached out and grasped the woman's arm and spoke

urgently. "What is the date…please?"

"It is the first of September," was the slow reply.

"In what year?"

"Why in the year of our Lord, eighteen forty-two."

The last thought in Sofia's mind before the world went black was that if it was eighteen forty-two, she was only ten years old

Not only had the murdering bastard faked her death, he had taken her back in time.

****

Dougal shared a meal with Edward and the knights despite his anxiety to return to the island …and Sofia. The Council had moved to the sanctuary of Edinburgh and the danger was gone…for the present. It was time to tell Sofia of the details of her kidnap and the use of the Astrolaberors to navigate her to the past. It was imperative she understood; it had been the only way he could ensure her absolute safety, but he had a feeling it would take some sweet talk to convince her of this.

He set forth in the midmorning and guided his horse westward to the coast under a watery sun. Thoughts flitted through his mind as the horse followed the deserted path and a warmth filled him as he thought back to the night they had shared.

She must understand.

Over the months she had been in the castle, his admiration had grown for this woman. Slight of stature, but strong in spirit.

He smiled and reached up to touch the black jewel at his breast.

She would understand.

His fingers touched the jewel and with his free hand he pulled on the reins. The horse whinnied in protest at the sudden jerk. Dougal slid to the ground and pulled the black stone from the pouch slung around his neck. It was burning hot…and making a sound. Curiously, he turned it over and around and narrowed his eyes as he noticed a small hand on the back of the stone moving from side to side. He hadn't noticed it before. Shaking it from side to side, the hand continued to move, and the humming sound became louder.

It was not a necklace; it was some sort of device. He had removed it from Sofia's neck when she first slept in his castle, before she awoke from the effects of the Astrolaberors travel. The stone vibrated in his hand and he looked at it for a long moment, before remounting and heading for the coast road.

Another question for Sofia...

Chapter 15

Indigo de Vargas y Irausquínno and her husband the Sherriff of Cornwall stepped from the dirigible in a field just south of Carlisle. Indigo had wanted to ignore the Scottish regulations which prohibited the flying of the steam-powered airships across the border however had listened to the calm words of her husband and they now awaited the arrival of the carriage that would deliver them to Kilmarnock. 'T is best if we draw no attention to ourselves until we arrive at the castle of the Earl of Rothmore."

Indigo looked at her husband with affection as he spoke. Always the calm and considered partner in their joint decision making, he had rescued her from many a scrape since their marriage ten years before. Now in his position as Sheriff of Cornwall, he was privy to information from the parliament and had recently received word of some nefarious activities in Kilmarnock related to the Earl of Rothmore. They had decided it was time to travel north from Cornwall.

Indigo blinked away the tears threatening to fall. It was three months since Sofia's death in the Alps and the grief was permanently lodged in her chest. She had fought to hide her despair for the sake of the four boys and Mr. Grimoult who blamed himself for the tragic death of Sofia.

Jory and Jago were still quiet but were beginning to lose a little of the raw grief they had carried when they returned from the Alps. As much as she had wanted to travel immediately to Scotland and confront the Earl of Rothmore on his isolated island, Zane had convinced her she was needed by their boys.

Also, Sofia's assistants from Vienna, Johann and Genevieve had arrived unannounced at their manor two weeks ago unaware of Sofia's death. They explained Sofia had sent them on a quest to investigate the strange happenings in Vienna and had been inconsolable when Zane had told them of her death and the fire in the laboratory in Vienna.

The information Johann and Genevieve had gathered and the intelligence that had come to Zane in his position as Sheriff continued to point to Scotland and the town of Kilmarnock.

"We will draw no attention to ourselves until I meet this man." Indigo said as they waited for the carriage in the early morning chill. "I will kill him with my bare hands."

A brisk wind blew across the bare fields and a smell of snow drifted down from the hills.

"Slow and easy, my dear." Zane reached over and tucked her coat high around her neck. "We will talk to the earl before we make any decisions. I don't like the feel of this whole investigation. Duke Lorca is involved, and you know he cannot be trusted. It does not sit comfortably with me"

"Better than most," she said with a cynical laugh. "But, Zane, I will see this man pay for the murder of my sister."

"Yes, my dear. When we establish he is involved in her death. Too much information has just appeared without explanation. I remain to be convinced of his responsibility."

"He pushed her over the Alps." Indigo's voice rose and Zane put his finger over her lips as heads turned. There were other passengers waiting for the carriage which would go onto Edinburgh after Kilmarnock.

"Come." He took her hand and led her away from the small group. "Now that we are closer to Scotland, we shall try the device one more time."

When news had first reached them of Sofia's demise, Indigo had refused to believe her sister was dead. At all hours of the day and night for the first month, she had tried to raise her through the communication device Zane had given Sofia to wear around her neck.

A slim hope was lodged deep in her heart, but she knew if Sofia was alive, she would have contacted her long before this.

"Very well." She sighed. "We may as well fill in the time we must spend waiting for this…this archaic transport."

They turned their back to the group and Zane pulled back the frilled white cuff of his sleeve and opened the top of the chronometer on his wrist. He flicked one of the small cogs on the edge and a faint humming began. A smile spread across his face as Indigo stared up at him.

"We have located the device, my dear."

"Where…how far… can you raise her?" The excitement built in Indigo's chest and her words ran into each other. She grabbed Zane's arm and dropped her gaze to the device which was hummed as the cogs spun furiously.

"I can plot the co-ordinates if you give me one moment." He shook her hand off his arm impatiently. "Keep calm and do not raise your hopes. It may be that whoever took her life removed the device and has it on their person." He frowned as he tapped away with one finger on the side of the device." Although it is strange that we did not pick up the signal before. The only way the signal may be obscured if it is in the proximity of a time slip device."

Zane tapped away for a few more minutes and Indigo paced the road, the stony ground crunching beneath her feet. Finally, he beckoned her across.

"Approximately fifty-five degrees north and five degrees west," he said the satisfaction evident in his voice. Indigo looked up at him at him and for the first time in three months she could see Zane had allowed a glimmer of hope into his thoughts. "The device is close by to us. By my calculations—and I sent a message to Mr. Grimoult and he has confirmed it on your analytical engine— the device is currently moving west past Dundonald Castle."

"And where is Dundonald Castle?" she asked impatiently.

"It is situated on a hill overlooking the village of Dundonald, between Kilmarnock and Troon not far from here." Zane looked at her. "It is heading at a slow rate directly for the Isle of Rothmore."

"We are soon to have answers." Indigo dared not let hope enter her mind again. She could not stand to be disappointed and she steeled her resolve as the clatter of horse's hooves approached.

"Come. The carriage is here."

* * * *

Dougal decided to cross to the island before using the Astrolaberors to return to the time where Sofia waited. The co-ordinates were set for midday and there was two hours to wait, so he tethered the horse in its enclosure and made his way down to the shoreline and entered the small cave where his boat was hidden.

As he pulled it onto the shingle, the drumming of hoofbeats from the road above the cliff top reached him and he secured the boat behind a rock arch. Stepping into the shadows at the base of the cliff, he waited for the horse to reach the top of the cliff.

Perhaps Edward had more news about the disappearance of the Council to Edinburgh, but he doubted it. It was most unusual for anyone to come to this part of the coast unless they had reason to visit his castle.

Voices drifted down to him.

"A boat—there is a boat on the sand," a deep voice called out. "Look down beneath that arch." There was a softer reply which sounded like a younger man's voice, but the wind carried the words away.

Dougal pressed his back into the cliff and removed the dirk from his waistband as a premonition of doom enveloped him.

Something was wrong.

Walking quietly, he edged along the base of the cliff toward the cave as small stones rolled down the cliff path ahead of the two people talking. He had only heard the hooves of one horse, so was certain there were only two.

The voices continued to drift to him, and snatches of words drifted down.

"…row across."

And the reply. "…safe water?"

Dougal reached the entrance of the cave and slipped behind the large rock on the northern side just as the sound of feet landing on the shingle carried across to him.

"Are you sure it will get us to the island?" It was a woman's voice

Carefully peering around the rock, his cautious gaze locked on a man and a woman standing next to his boat.

His mind worked furiously. If he let them take it, he would have to wait till midday anyway to get back to the island using the Astrolaberors, but he preferred to cross now. If they took his boat, he would have to wait.

He tucked his dirk out of sight and stepped from the cave. One man and one woman were nothing to do with the Knights and he was curious as to their intent.

"Good morning," he called and sauntered across the sand toward them. "Are ye lost?"

Coal-black eyes fixed on him and he recoiled at the sheer hatred on the woman's face. Dark curls tumbled onto her shoulders and her face was pale, devoid of any colour.

The man placed his hand on her arm to hold the woman back as she began to step toward him.

"Are you going to the island?" the man enquired. The Cornish lilt to his voice hit Dougal immediately. He now knew he looked into the face of Indigo de Vargas, Sofia's sister.

By all that was holy, he didn't need this yet. Not until he had been to get Sofia.

He stepped forward and bowed as the stare of the woman

he had heard so much about, remained fixed on him. "I am Dougal, Earl of Rothmore."

The Sherriff of Cornwall held tightly onto his wife and looked at Dougal. "You have much to explain, sir."

He inclined his head. "Yes, there is much to explain. We will travel to the island together." Dougal reached his hand out to Indigo. "Madam, it gives me great joy to be able to tell you…finally…your sister is alive and well in my castle." He gestured to the boat. "I will row you across the firth and explain all to you."

Sheeting rain began to fall as Dougal rowed them the short distance to the island. Indigo sat in the middle of the small boat and her husband held his cloak over her in an attempt to protect her from the rain. Small waves splashed against the side of the boat as a brisk wind began to blow and the short journey was fraught with tension. As they followed him from the rocky beach to the courtyard, not a word was spoken. Dougal was concerned for Sofia's sister. Despite the joy in her expression, her face was still colourless, and she gripped her husband's arm.

Mary stood at the open door and looked at them curiously.

"We have guests," he said to the middle-aged housekeeper. "Can you heat some broth, please?"

Indigo finally spoke. "We want no hospitality. Take me to my sister." She glared up at him and took a menacing step toward him. "Immediately."

"We shall have to wait until midday before I can get your sister," he replied. "She is safe where she is. Do not fear." He inclined his head toward the kitchen and Mary left the room. "Come and sit, there is much I have to tell you."

* * * *

Indigo shook her head in disbelief. "Are you sure this is not a fabrication you have invented to cover the murder of my sister?"

Dougal had explained the disbanding of the Knights

Templar and the danger to Sofia and her enterprise in Vienna. "Why can you not take me to her now? Why do I have to wait?"

Dougal looked at her steadily and despite her mistrust, she tried to believe the words this man was saying. He appeared to be telling the truth and she desperately wanted to believe him, but until she saw Sofia with her own eyes she would not believe.

Zane had explained how they had located Dougal through the jewelled communication device and Indigo's heart had raced when the earl reached into his shirt and removed it from around his neck. They had partaken of the broth and moved to the end of the dining hall closer to the fire. Indigo looked around and wondered how anyone could live in such a cavernous and cold abode.

If indeed, Sofia had spent the past three months here as the earl insisted she had, the austere surroundings and the cold would have made her stay unbearable. Indigo's anxiety increased as the time passed. She reached out and held Zane's wrist and looked at his chronometer. "It is ten minutes to midday. I demand you take me to my sister."

The earl looked at her for a long moment before speaking. "If all I have heard of you and your adventures is true, you will have little trouble accepting what I am about to show you." He reached into his shirt and removed a small velvet pouch before kneeling on the cold stone floor and placing the pouch on the floor beside him. "I can go alone to get your sister, or you can travel with me?'

Indigo gasped as he removed a small brass device from the pouch and placed it gently on the flagstones. "It is an Astrolaberors. I haven't seen one since the Great Exhibition."

Realization dawned slowly. She turned to the earl and glared at him.

"Where or when…have you hidden Sofia?"

"She is in the castle with Mary, but nineteen years past," Dougal replied. "The device is capable of transporting three people only, so one person can accompany me to get her or we will be too many for the return journey.”

Indigo turned to Zane. “I shall go.”

He nodded at her and she reached her hand up to stroke her husband’s brow. “I know time travel does not bode well for your equilibrium, my dearest.”

Indigo trusted the earl; she had seen the expression on his face when he spoke of Sofia and his concern for her. The Astrolaberors device was much more accurate than the time mechanism she used in her submarine and she had little fear of time travel, having travelled with her father and then her husband to a century in the future.

“Come then.” She reached up and kissed her husband. “We shall return shortly. I am sure.”

* * * *

Dougal closed his eyes and held Indigo’s hand in his. He nodded at the Sheriff. “Make yourself comfortable before the fire. “I shall take good care of your wife and we shall return within the hour.”

He pressed the switch on the device, and it emitted a low hum; they were sucked into the vortex of time itself. No matter how many times he travelled, the wonder of it awed him and he looked down at Indigo as she let out a delighted scream. Her face was full of happiness and the anticipation of seeing her sister shone from her expression.

The fire was burning low in the same hearth when they arrived, and the day was cold and bleak. Indigo smiled up at him. “The Scottish weather is certainly predictable.”

She looked around with interest. “How far back have we travelled? The room looks exactly the same.”

“Nineteen years,” he replied. “I chose that time as I knew the castle was empty. My parents died when I was a lad and I had moved to Edinburgh. Mary had come to the castle from the

222

mainland to be my housekeeper and I knew Sofia would be well cared for when I travelled with Edward of Kilmarnock."

He dropped Indigo's hand. "Wait here. I will find Mary and see where Sofia is." He smiled at Indigo; she was so very different to Sofia in colouring, size and sheer presence.

"Mary?" He called the housekeeper as he walked toward the kitchen, but there was no answer. Unease coiled in his stomach as he stepped into the cold kitchen. The huge range was cold and there were no loaves of bread cooling on the big table in the centre of the room. Two plates of congealed food sat untouched on the smaller table. Dougal ran to the courtyard and called for Zeus.

"What's the matter?" He jumped as Indigo pushed past him. "What's wrong?"

"I'm not sure," he replied slowly. "Something is not right."

A shrill cry drifted across from the fields to the south and he ran to the gate where had stood with Edward and Sofia only yesterday. Mary ran up from the shoreline with Zeus close at her heels.

"Oh, Dougal," she cried before placing her hands over her face.

"What's the matter?" he asked urgently. "Did someone come from the mainland?"

"No," Mary replied, shaking her head from side to side. "The lassie has gone."

"Gone how? Did someone come for her?" A vision of the Knights Templar kidnapping Sofia lodged in his mind and he shook the thought away angrily. "Tell, me girl."

"She has taken the boat and rowed across the firth," Mary replied, worry etched on her brow. "But I do not know when. I went to call her for the midday meal, and I could not find her. I went to the shore and the boat in the cave was gone." She burst into tears. "I could do nought as there was no other boat."

Relief coursed through him. It was simply a matter of

following her and bringing her back—she would not have got far in the few hours since she left.

"How will we follow her if there is no other boat?" Indigo asked.

Dougal groaned as realization hit him. There was no other boat on the island and the Astrolaberors could not convey them in the present time. The co-ordinates had been locked into the device for the two time periods and if he changed them, they would not be able to return to the present, where Zane waited for them. He paced the courtyard trying to think of another way to follow Sofia and Indigo strode beside him pulling at his sleeve.

He pulled his arm away angrily. "For God's sake, woman, let me think."

She stood and stared at him for a moment before turning on her heel and walking toward the shore.

Dougal watched her go as helplessness filled him. "Don't leave my sight," he called after her.

One woman lost is enough.

****

They returned alone.

After an hour of frustration, Dougal had realized there was no way to follow Sofia and he made the decision to take Indigo back to Zane. On the morrow, he would return to search for Sofia, but would change the co-ordinates to arrive at Kilmarnock and work his way back to the coast looking for her. He just hoped and prayed she would not travel far and would stay safe.

Surely when she realized she was in different time, she would go back to the castle, to seek a safe haven where she knew he would return for her?

He had promised her—two days.

He glanced up at Indigo, tired of being the recipient of her cold glare over the dinner Mary had quickly prepared for them. Indigo dropped her knife on the wooden table and opened her mouth to speak. Zane reached over and placed his hand on her arm, and she closed her mouth. He had heard enough from this woman.

How could two sisters be so different?

It was hard to believe she had produced the two fine young boys he had met in the Alps. Dougal stood abruptly and left them in the dining hall without a word, before making his way up to the solar where Sofia had spent the past three months.

He was probably being unfair to Indigo but was too concerned about Sofia's well-being to give it much thought. After all, she had come here still believing her sister was dead and then the disappointment of the travel back to the castle to find Sofia missing must have been overwhelming for her. Yet, even the soft reasoning of her husband had not stilled her shrewish tongue.

He did not need that tonight.

He stood by the bed and closed his eyes remembering the response of Sofia in this bed only two nights ago. It seemed like a lifetime since she had lain bathed in moonlight and joyfully responded to him. For the life of him, he could not understand why she had left knowing her sojourn on the island would soon end.

Chapter 16

Dougal held his cloak above his head and entered the Red Lion Inn in Kilmarnock. Despite being early afternoon, it was dark, and the town was deserted. Shaking the rain from his cloak, he made his way across to the innkeeper. Dougal's purpose was twofold—as well as seeking shelter from the torrential rain, he sought information on the whereabouts of Sofia. The innkeeper pushed a tankard of ale across the wooden bench, obviously taking pity on his wet and bedraggled appearance.

"A filthy day, sir."

"Aye, that it is," replied Dougal.

"You have missed the fair. Although just as well, it was on yesterday and not today."

"Fair?"

"To celebrate the visit of the Queen and her Prince. 'Twas a big celebration in here last evening." The innkeeper laughed. "There are still many sore heads abed."

"Ah…" Dougal nodded and took a swig of his ale. "I am looking for my …er …an acquaintance of my…er…wife," he lied. "A small woman with unusual silver hair. She would have enjoyed the fair if she had been in Kilmarnock yesterday?"

"Aye," the innkeeper agreed. "She did. She was visiting with Dame Molly."

Dougal closed his eyes as relief filled his chest. At least he knew Sofia had got safely across the firth. Thoughts of her drowning had haunted him all night.

"Dame Molly?" he enquired. "Would she be staying with her?"

"Perhaps." The innkeeper turned away, seeming disinclined to volunteer any more information.

"Ah…where would I find Dame Molly?" Dougal persisted. "It is all right. I am the Earl of Rothmore, and I seek to ensure the woman's safety."

The innkeeper looked at him for a long moment before answering.

"She lives in yonder wood." He inclined his head to the right and Dougal assumed he meant toward the wood further to the east.

Leaving some coin on the bench to pay for the ale and show his gratitude for the information, he pushed open the door and stepped out into the cold rain. He followed the path deep into the woods, keeping under the trees to avoid the torrential rain. Wet leaves lined the path and he slipped in the soft mud. Gradually, an aroma of wood smoke and damp peat drifted across to him and he paused. A small cottage lay at the end of the path and candlelight flickered through the windows in the mid-afternoon gloom. A brawny man stood in a wood shed to the side of the small dwelling and lifted a hand in greeting.

"A foul afternoon to be about, man," he said. "Can I help ye?"

"I am seeking Dame Molly," replied Dougal.

The man nodded. "There has been a steady stream of customers today." He stepped out of the shed and moved across to the cottage beckoning Dougal to follow him. "For a child?" he asked.

Dougal looked at him confused. "I am seeking a young woman who was with Dame Molly at the fair yesterday?"

"Aye. "The man nodded. "I thought you were after the infusion of the leaves for the cough. The chestnut leaves," he continued as Dougal looked at him, unsure what he was speaking of."

The man opened the door and leaned inside.

"Molly, there is a man here asking after the young lady."

Dougal looked up in anticipation as relief coursed through him, but it was an elderly, stout woman who came through the door.

"She has gone." The woman directed her words at her husband before turning to Dougal. "I did not wish her to leave as she was ill."

"Where? Where has she gone?" he asked urgently.

"She said she had to get back to the shore to wait for her man to take her home. I worry that she is delirious, but she would not stay. She had some strange ideas about the Queen being dead."

Dougal groaned and reached into his cloak for some coin. "Thank you for taking care of her. How long ago did she leave?"

"Mid-morning," the woman replied. "She accepted a dose of the infusion for her cough and I dried her clothes overnight in front of the fire. She told me she fell in the firth."

Dougal closed his eyes and cursed inwardly. If he had gone to the shore instead of Kilmarnock, he would have found her. He thanked the woman again and hurried back the way he came.

It took him a long half hour to locate the blacksmith in Kilmarnock where he was able to procure a horse. By the time he had covered the muddy road to the shore, it was almost dark. The sky was clearing from the west and a spectacular sunset shot gold and pink hues through the sky above the firth. Dougal jumped off the horse and hit it on the rump sending it back the way they had come. If he needed to travel again, he would risk using the Astrolaberors. His heart thudded in slow painful beats and he stretched his fingers to relieve the cramps from holding the reigns. He stood at the top of the cliff and shaded his eyes from the bright light in the west as the sun dropped below the edge of the cloud. A path of golden light shimmered across the firth silhouetting his castle in the background.

Scanning the shoreline, there was nothing to be seen and he cursed. A deserted shoreline and some lumps of kelp between the rocks. He strode along the cliff top, searching for the way down to the shore; it had obviously moved over the intervening years.

Finally, a break in the gorse directed him to the path. Screaming sea birds rose in the still afternoon air as he disturbed their slumber. A sudden flash of silver from below caught his attention. A slight figured moved in the fading light and stopped beneath a rock arch near the water. Dougal paused for a moment and stared.

It was Sofia.

He began to run, stones slipping beneath his feet and tumbling down the cliff. Jumping down the last four feet into the sand, he regained his balance and ran across the beach to the rock arch where a small boat was secured

The golden light framed Sofia's head within the arch and he could not see her shadowed face until he was one step away from her. He reached out to her and she turned away, pulling the cloak around her slight shoulders. But before she turned away, he saw the coldness of her expression. A racking cough escaped her lips and she leaned on the rock for support.

Dougal put his arm around her shoulders, and she looked up at him, her eyes devoid of any recognition. He cursed himself. It was not anger on her face, it was delirium; if any harm came to her, it would be due to his actions.

He had to get her to the warmth of the castle.

Scooping his arms beneath her, he carried her into the warmth of the small cave in the cliff face and quickly returned to the beach to check the boat.

Thank God, it was intact.

He dragged it into the water and secured the oars in the rowlocks and returned for Sofia. Pulling off his cloak, he ran quickly back to the cave. He crossed the small space to where she leaned against the rock wall. She lifted her head slowly; her face was pale and her eyes were wide.

"Dougal?" she whispered. "Oh, Dougal. You came back."

He placed his cloak around her shoulders and buried his face in her hair. It was damp and tangled and smelled of damp peat. Gently he placed her in the boat, cursing softly at the burning heat of her skin as he pushed out from the shore. He settled in behind her and leaned her back against his chest as he rowed across the narrow channel to the Isle of Rothmore.

Mary was waiting on the shore on the island.

"I heard the birds and when I looked, I saw ye carry her into the boat." Her voice was anxious. "*Ach, puir wee lassie*, is she hurt?"

"She has taken a chill from the icy waters of the firth," he replied. "Is the fire going in her room?"

"Yes, I *dinna* let it die. I knew you would find her."

Dougal paced all night as Mary ministered to Sofia. He allowed himself one visit into the solar and when he finally saw she was asleep and breathing normally, he stayed away. On the morrow, at midday, he would take her back to the present and to her sister.

Whatever happened then would be out of his control.

He closed his eyes.

Chapter 17

Sofia woke alone the next morning and looked around.

Had it been a dream, the row across the firth and the sojourn with Dame Molly?

Back in the solar at the castle once more and she had no recollection of getting there. Putting her hand to her head, she struggled to sit up, before reaching for the tankard on the small table beside the large four-poster bed.

Closing her eyes, she sighed as the cool liquid eased her burning throat. She thought back to yesterday. A recollection of a conversation tugged at her thoughts and drops of water fell on the bed linen as she began to shake.

The old woman had said eighteen forty-two.

Indigo and their father had travelled through time to the Amazon on several occasions to source the passion flowers for their research. But never had she needed to travel to another time.

But obviously Dougal had seen the need and it kept her safe from those who sought to harm her.

Warmth shot through her body and she wondered how long before he came to her. He was in the castle and she assumed it was he who had found her on the beach. The last thing she recalled was making her way down to the cliff and waiting in the cave. She had known he would come looking for her there.

Whatever, he had done. He was a good and righteous man and had saved her life.

She was beholden to him.

No matter how he had gone about it. He had saved her from the Knights.

The door creaked and Sofia looked up anticipation shooting through her chest. But it was only Mary.

"Ach, lassie," she crooned in her musical voice. "You're

awake and a fine colour ye are." She put her hand out to Sofia's forehead and clicked her tongue with satisfaction. "And as cool as the waters of the firth."

"Where is the Earl," asked Sofia.

"Pacing in the halls of the castle." Mary chuckled. "I told him it was only a wee chill, but he had ye dead and buried."

"Can you tell him I wish to see him, please?"

Mary smiled and patted her hand before leaving the room. "I think he will be delighted to see you, Ma'am."

A few minutes later the door opened, and Sofia turned from the window. She had left the bed and stood looking out over the firth as she pondered the events of the past few months. The morning sun was bright, and the brisk wind had whipped up small waves on the grey water. Gulls and kittiwakes circled ahead, occasionally dipping into the water to catch a fish in their beaks.

Peaceful. Very different to the busy streets of Vienna.

Now Dougal stood in the doorway looking at her, his brow wrinkled in a frown.

"Come in," she said softly.

He crossed the room to her, and she sat in the small alcove in the window and patted the seat next to her. Dougal hesitated, before sitting beside her; the space was small, and his arm and his leg pressed against hers.

"So, Dougal," Sofia began. She turned to him and grasped his strong jaw in her hand. "What you did was very brave. Once my anger passed, I realized you truly saved my life." She sensed his body relax next to her and he exhaled.

"For a time, I was angry that you made it look as though I were dead. Angry you made such a decision and did not tell me." She waited for him to respond.

Finally he took her hand from his chin and held it tight in his grasp. "I pondered on the matter for many nights, my love." Warmth shot through her as the endearment came from his lips.

"To hide you nineteen years in the past, using the Astrolaberors was the only way I could be sure the Knights would not find you. Even though they resided at Kilmarnock and were beholden by the restrictions of Scottish law, their influence spread far and wide and they had access to much technology." He lifted her hand to his lips. "You do recall how they sent me to Vienna with the automatons? The airship supplied to me that night was sleek and fast."

Sofia pulled her hands away from his and stood staring out at the lock. "I am beginning to understand. But I need to be sure of just one thing. Have the Knights gone? Did you and Edward succeed in your quest?"

She turned back to him and held his gaze as deep blue eyes looked deep into hers.

"Aye, the cowardly curs have run and sought refuge in Edinburgh. We shall see no more of them in Kilmarnock."

"But what of Vienna?" she asked. "Will they send others to try to stop my research?"

Dougal pushed himself up from the seat and looked long and hard at her before replying. "There is no Vienna research left. The laboratory was destroyed by fire."

She gasped and grabbed for his hands. "What of Ernst? Is anyone hurt?"

He wound his fingers through her before lifting her hand and placing it against his cheek. "All is well. No one is hurt and the professor is in Cornwall at your sister's manor. As are Johann and Genevieve."

She sagged with relief. "But Dougal, I do not understand. How have you come by such information? How is it you know my people?"

A low chuckle came from his lips and the laughter lines fanned out around his eyes.

"Not only do I know that, I have two visitors for you when we return."

"Return?"

"To my castle."

"But we are in your…oh…I see." She shook her head. The remnants of her fever clouded her brain and it was too confusing to think of traveling between times and still be in the same castle.

"We must leave at midday or we shall have to wait for another day." He smiled down at her. "Could you stand to stay in this…ah…let me remember… 'draughty pile of stones' for one more night? It is just as cold and draughty in 1861 as it is now in 1842. Are you ready to return? To come back with me to our present?" he asked.

Sofia shook her head.

Was it the experience of travelling back in time, or was it her fever? Or more likely it was her love for this man creating the whirling confusion in her mind.

She looked up at Dougal. He had placed his arms around her when she had been lost in thought. Now his lips were lightly parted, and a nervous pulse fluttered in his neck. The warmth of his body against her raised goose bumps on her skin and her heart began to race. She closed her eyes and nervous thrills ran to her fingertips.

It was definitely the man beside her.

Raising her lips to his neck, she murmured against the pulse point. "Wherever you go, I will follow."

Epilogue

Jory and Jago, Ruan and Kit ran across to the lawn to the landing pad, whooping and cheering. "Here they come."

Sofia looked down from the airship as their excited cries floated up to them. Indigo and Zane followed at a more leisurely pace along the path, although Sofia could see the excitement in her sister's step.

Dougal stood beside her and chuckled. "Who is the little lady running behind the children?"

A stout woman wearing an apron waddled after the boys, her little legs working furiously to catch them.

"That, my dear is Mrs. Grimoult." Sofia looked across at Mary, who passed the tiny white bundle in her arms to Dougal. The baby began to whimper, and Sofia looked up at her husband of one year and smiled.

"I think the heir apparent to the Earldom of Rothmore is keen to meet his cousins," she said softly.

Mr. Grimoult turned the airship and it descended to the ground with one final hiss of steam. Sofia hurried out into Indigo's waiting arms; she had not seen her sister since her last visit to *Salon de Vargas* before she had handed it over to Vivienne.

"Now show me my nephew." Indigo gave her a final squeeze and stepped back. Dougal gently placed the baby in her arms.

Dougal and Indigo had yet to make their peace. Sofia had begged Indigo to be forgiving before she had married Dougal last spring in the Belvedere Gardens in Vienna. "He saved my life."

Indigo had snorted. "There were other ways to protect you than imprisoning you in that ancient castle and leaving us to think you were dead for three months."

Now Sofia smiled as Zane pushed his wife toward her new

brother-in-law.

Indigo looked first at her younger sister and then down at the baby in her arms, before raising her eyes to meet Dougal's. "I am sorry, Dougal. For those weeks I had thought my dear sister had been taken from me…as our father was." She brushed crossly at the tears welling in her eyes. "Thank you for bringing her safely home…and welcome to our home…brother."

Sofia's heart filled with love for her husband and family as Dougal reached over and kissed Indigo on the cheek. "Indigo," she said. "I have some news for you."

"You are not going back to Scotland?" Indigo said hopefully. She had made her opinion of Dougal's ancestral home very clear.

"Yes, we are." Sofia held her hand out to her husband, the Earl of Rothmore. "But we will have company. Johann and Genevieve are moving to our island after their spring wedding."

The look on Indigo's face was one of astonishment. Sofia and Dougal laughed so loudly, the boys stopped their play and came running over to see what they were missing out on.

"What on earth will they do living on that isolated pile of rocks?" asked Indigo.

"Well." Sofia smiled and turned to her sister. "They shall be working in the new laboratory Dougal has constructed in the dungeon of our castle. Cool and dark, just like an alpine crevasse where the moonflowers thrive."

"So you are not giving up the quest after all, despite the fear of the Knights Templar?"

"I have no fear," Sofia replied. She stepped back and observed the people standing around her on the lawn. A much-loved husband and son. A loyal sister and her husband. Her four rambunctious nephews. Mr. and Mrs. Grimoult, their surrogate grandparents.

All would be well.

Not only would her moonflowers grow but her love for Dougal and the beginning of their next generation of scientists would thrive in the crisp highland air. The littlest scientist reached up and tugged on her loose braid. She smiled down at him.

The future was bright.

OTHER BOOKS from ANNIE

Whitsunday Dawn
Undara
Osprey Reef
East of Alice

Porter Sisters Series

Kakadu Sunset
Daintree
Diamond Sky
Hidden Valley
Larapinta
Kakadu Dawn

Pentecost Island Series
Pippa
Eliza
Nell
Tamsin
Evie
Cherry
Odessa
Sienna
Tess
Isla

The Augathella Girls Series
Outback Roads
Outback Sky
Outback Escape
Outback Wind

Outback Dawn
Outback Moonlight
Outback Dust
Outback Hope
An Augathella Surprise
An Augathella Baby
An Augathella Spring

Sunshine Coast Series
Waiting for Ana
The Trouble with Jack
Healing His Heart
Sunshine Coast Boxed Set

The Richards Brothers Series
The Trouble with Paradise
Marry in Haste
Outback Sunrise
Richards Brothers Boxed Set

Bondi Beach Love Series
Beach House
Beach Music
Beach Walk
Beach Dreams
The House on the Hill

Second Chance Bay Series
Her Outback Playboy
Her Outback Protector
Her Outback Haven
Her Outback Paradise
The McDougalls of Second Chance Bay Boxed Set

Love Across Time Series
Come Back to Me
Follow Me
Finding Home

The Threads that Bind
Love Across Time 1-4 Boxed Set

Bindarra Creek
Worth the Wait
Full Circle
Secrets of River Cottage
A Clever Christmas
A Place to Belong

Four Seasons Short and Sweet
Ten Days in Paradise
Follow the Sun

Others
Deadly Secrets
Adventures in Time
Silver Valley Witch
The Emerald Necklace
Christmas with the Boss
Her Christmas Star
An Aussie Christmas Duo (two Christmas novellas)
One Summer in Tuscany

About the Author

2023: Winner of the long contemporary RUBY award for *Larapinta*

Finalist for the NZ KORU award 2018 and 2020.

Winner ...Best Established Author of the Year 2017 AUSROM

Long listed for the Sisters in Crime Davitt Awards 2016, 2017, 2018, 2019

Finalist in Book of the Year, Long Romance, RWA Ruby Awards 2016 *Kakadu Sunset*

Winner ...Best Established Author of the Year 2015 AUSROM

Winner ...Author of the Year 2014 AUSROM
Best Established Author, Ausrom Readers' Choice 2017
Book of the Year (Whitsunday Dawn) Ausrom Readers' Choice Awards 2018

About the Author

Annie Seaton lives near the beach on the east coast of Australia, fulfilling her lifelong dream of being an author. After majoring in history at university, her career and further study spanned the education sector with the completion of a master's degree in education, and working as an academic research librarian, a high school principal and a university tutor until she took up her full-time writing career. Each winter, Annie and her husband leave the beach to roam the remote areas of Australia for story ideas and research.

Annie's Porter Sisters series is published in print, and she has recently signed another book contract with Harper Collins in the Harlequin Mira imprint. *Whitsunday Dawn* is the first of followed by *Undara* in 2019, *Osprey Reef* in 2020 and *East of Alice* in 2021. Her single title books have created a new genre: eco-adventure romance.

Annie also has many sweet romances published digitally across several genres. You can find them in a convenient slideshow on her website: http://www.annieseaton.net